EVERY LAST ONE

THE RISE OF SYLVIA BOONE

J. B. VELASQUEZ

WILD RUMPUS PRESS

For Sofia and Greyson

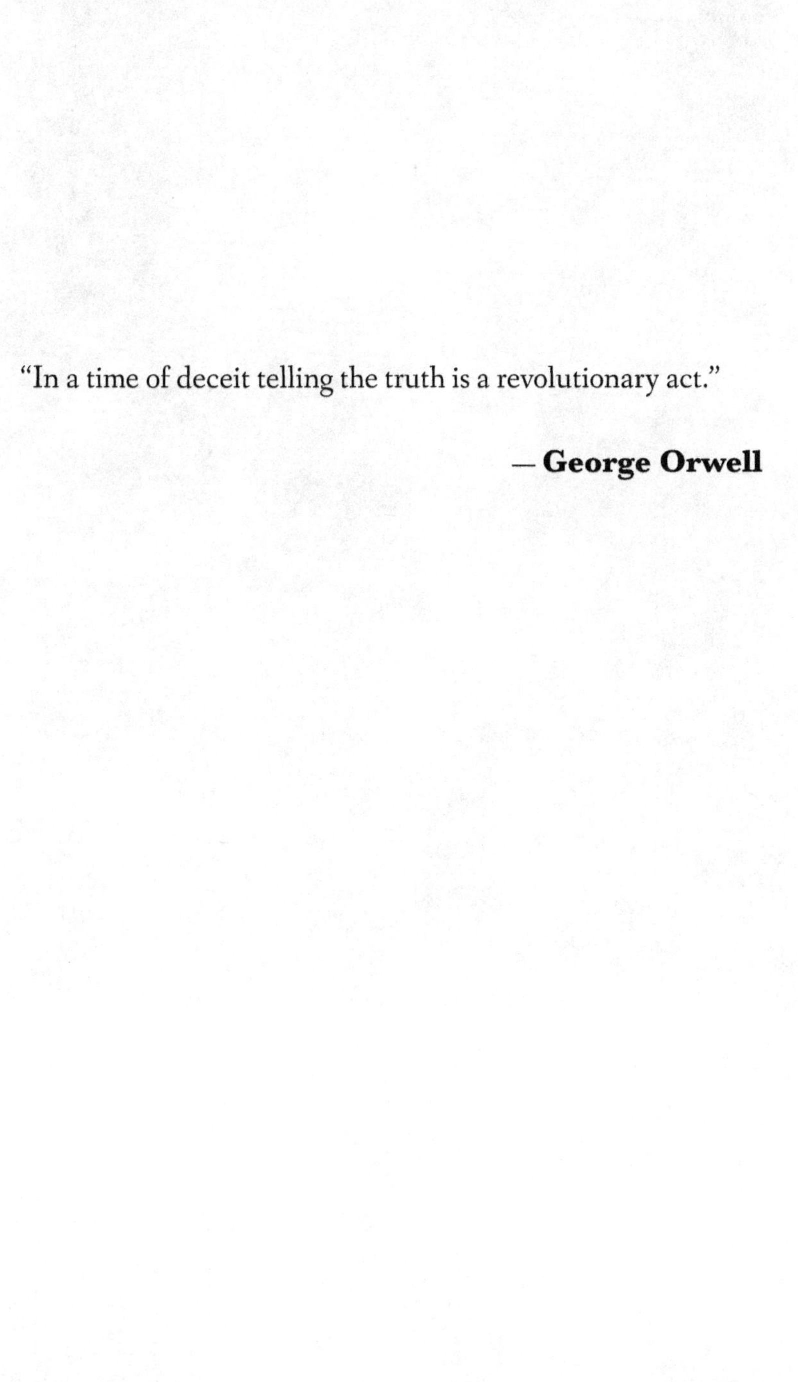

"In a time of deceit telling the truth is a revolutionary act."

— **George Orwell**

CHAPTER 1

H2O-NO: SYLVIA

SYLVIA PULLED a pillow over her head to drown out the sounds of people shouting outside her fourth-story window. This wasn't new. Winnipeg had been under a great deal of turmoil in the years since the Canadian government had fallen and the corporate regime took over. *What is it this time?* She rolled onto her side and looked at the clock—5:52 a.m. No chance she would fall back asleep now. Of course, this had to happen on her day off, the one day she got to sleep in.

She let out a deep sigh, dragged herself out of bed, and shuffled into the bathroom. She stepped into the shower and closed her eyes awaiting the pre-warmed cascade to dispense from the shower head, but nothing came out. She checked the digital control panel: Connect Water Source. *What the hell?* She stepped out and placed her hands under the sink's automatic faucet. Nothing. A notification appeared again, this time against the surface of her mirror: Connect Water Source. *Dammit!* Now she was going to have to put in a work order, and when they don't respond after a week, she'll have to put in a second one. In the meantime, she figured she'd have to stay at her dad's place, which had older yet more reliable plumbing, ironically.

Three gunshots rang out in rapid succession followed by screams. An involuntary yelp escaped her mouth as her shoulders tensed around her neck. When the initial jolt subsided, she scuttled to the window and pulled the blinds apart just enough to peer through. She searched for a gunman, but everyone seemed to be hurried and frantic. It could have been any of them. Pedestrians dashed around on the sidewalks below her downtown apartment, some carrying cases of bottled water over their shoulders.

Sylvia placed her holospecs over her eyes. "Show me the news," she commanded as she dressed. The augmented reality-enabled smartglasses displayed the following news headlines onto her visual field: *Water Crisis in Winnipeg, No Water for Winnipeg,* and *H2O-NO!* She highlighted the final headline by focusing her eyes on it and blinked twice to open the link. A 3-D holographic reporter appeared on a busy street corner not far from her building.

If you're joining us now, we're in downtown Winnipeg where looters are overtaking local establishments in search of the last remaining drops of water. This, of course, in response to a cyber attack on the city's water supply, which occurred early this morning around 2:00 a.m. Luckily, authorities were able to catch the breach soon after it was executed and immediately shut down water pumps through the city. We're not certain who is responsible for this cyber-attack but authorities are working to identify any suspects. Utility services are working to recalibrate the chemical balance in the water supply and get it back into homes and businesses as soon as possible. Authorities are urging residents to please stay home and ration available water responsibly. Stay tuned as we continue to report on this devastating event.

This wasn't the first time Sylvia had experienced cyber-terrorism. It was the basis for the Tech Wars that started in 2049, before she was born, and had never officially ended. This was the first time they'd attacked the water supply, but she'd been through several power outages, satellite disruptions, privacy and data theft—it happened so often that it had become a defining societal encumbrance for her generation. She just wished it had happened after her morning shower. She knew this meant she'd have to put in overtime this week.

Her holospecs produced a gentle vibration and the caller ID appearing in the top right corner of her visual field alerted her to an incoming call. She moved the cursor with her gaze and blinked twice on the caller ID: *Dad.* A full-color, 3D hologram of his head and shoulders projected onto her visual field.

"Hey, Dad. Is everything okay?" Sylvia asked with concern in her voice.

"I'm fine. Just watching the news. You're right smack dab in the middle of all this," he said in a raspy belabored voice from a chronic respiratory illness. "Do you have enough water there?"

"I don't know, probably not. I'll check the corner store here in a bit."

"I don't think that's a good idea, Syl. Looters probably got to it by now." He paused to take a breath. "Why don't you just come stay with me until all this blows over? At least I have the rain barrels."

"That's true. I probably need to head to the station first

though. I'm sure they're going to need all the help they can get." She let out a groan. "This city is falling apart."

"It's been falling apart for years. It'll still be a shithole tomorrow. It wouldn't kill you to call in for once."

"I'll come by later, I promise."

"Be careful out there, bug."

"Bye, Dad. End call." The hologram disappeared.

Sylvia threw a few changes of clothes and some personal items into her pack so she could go straight to her dad's house after checking in at the station. She figured she'd stay the weekend at least. Hopefully, they'd have this water crisis resolved by then.

Sylvia opened her refrigerator to take inventory of her water reserve. She sighed as she scanned her meager food supply: two beers, a bottle of BBQ sauce, and a pizza box with a single week-old slice of Hawaiian pizza. Her freezer contained a bag of whole coffee beans and a mostly empty pint of dairy-free cherry vanilla ice cream. An industrial sized container of protein powder sat atop her fridge. What good was that going to do her without water?

She drained the remaining water in the lines from the refrigerator's in- door water dispenser. She emptied all the ice from the ice maker to allow it to melt in an aluminum mixing bowl. Her coffee maker contained another liter in its reservoir. Altogether, she ended up with roughly six liters of filtered water. Sylvia shook her head in resignation as she pondered how she was supposed to ration such a minimal supply indefinitely.

Sylvia dipped her toothbrush into the pitcher of water to brush her teeth. She tried to expel as much frothy toothpaste from her mouth after she brushed so she wouldn't have to use precious water to rinse, then wiped her mouth and swallowed what remained with a frown. She needed to pee but quickly realized that once she flushed, there would be no more water left in the tank. It occurred to her she might have to use the remaining tank water to sponge bathe eventually. She would have to hold it until she got to the station.

Even though her dad warned her about going to the store, she felt a nagging sense of ethical responsibility to be somewhat present in her immediate community—even if it was her day off. She threw on a baseball cap, clipped her badge to her waistband, and shoved a fully charged bolt gun into her shoulder holster. When she stepped out onto the sidewalk outside her building, a distracted man bumped her shoulder as he rushed past. "Hey! Watch it!" Sylvia hissed.

She walked to the general store two blocks away, hands plunged deep into the pockets of her army green field jacket. Desperation pulled on the faces of passersby as they scuttled along dirty sidewalks, looking back over hunched shoulders with wild eyes and slack jaws. Broken glass crunched under her boots as she approached the aging storefront. The security alarm blared in futility. People ran out of the store with whatever they could carry. Before she could apprehend any looters, a grim scene caught her eye.

Inside, the store clerk slumped over the counter, bleeding onto the floor. Another man slipped on the clerk's blood and fell onto his back. "Hey!" Sylvia shouted. "Get out of here!" She addressed the rest of the looters holding up her badge. "CPG! Everybody out!" she shouted. "You!" Sylvia singled out a man with a box of canned beans under his arm. She unholstered her bolt pistol. "Leave that! Leave it! Get out!" *Unbelievable!*

Once the store was empty, she checked the man's pulse. Dead.

She tapped the side of her holospecs. "Get me dispatch," she commanded. An ellipsis appeared in her field of vision and the female voice calmly announced: *Calling dispatch.*

"Third precinct, go," came the voice after picking up.

"I got a one-three-one at the corner of Carlton and St. Mary. I repeat, one-three- one at the Becker's Mini Mart on the corner of Carlton and St. Mary."

"We have a unit in the area. They're on the way."

She hopped over the counter to disconnect the alarm, keeping her pistol out to deter further plunder. "We're closed!" she yelled at the next man who stumbled in, who upon seeing the barrel of her pistol pointed at him, turned as if on a swivel and stumbled back out. *Could this day get any worse?* Sylvia yanked the wires from a control panel under the register and the alarm stopped, yet continued echoing in her head. She looked around at the ransacked shelving. The coolers had been completely emptied of every available beverage. A siren chirped from outside.

Sylvia, who was out of uniform, holstered her sidearm, stood where she could be plainly visible, and held out her badge. Cops in this town were known to shoot first and ask questions later. When the two officers entered the store, one fat and unshaven, the other skinny and acne-laden, Sylvia announced herself. "Corporal Sylvia Boone, 9th Precinct."

The fat officer, more put out than alarmed, took a half-hearted glance around the shop giving the dead body no more attention than the overturned shelves. "What do we got here?"

"I just found him like this while the place was getting

stripped. That was at 7:22 a.m. He was shot at close range . . . nine mil, looks like."

The officer continued looking around the store. "You check those ice bins?"

"What?" Sylvia was genuinely confused.

"The ice bins, for the fountain drinks. Did the looters get all the ice?"

Sylvia's mouth was stuck in a half-opened position. "Ahh . . . No, I didn't check."

He ordered the younger officer to check the ice bins. Sylvia's eyes widened in disbelief. She looked back at the deceased man whose blood was still dripping from his fingertips onto the floor. The skinny officer climbed up onto the counter at the fountain station and opened the lid.

"Bingo! What do I put it in?"

"Find a bucket or something," the first officer said. "Check the back room."

The skinny officer jumped off the counter and entered a small storage room. He emerged with a yellow mop bucket, hopped back up on the counter, and began scooping ice into the bucket. After filling the bucket there was still more ice left.

"Isn't there another bucket back there?" asked the fat officer.

"No, I checked," the skinny officer confirmed.

The first officer snapped his fingers. "I know. Put the rest in a body bag. They don't leak."

"But we only have the one," the skinny officer replied.

"Not anymore." The fat officer flung the last remaining body bag toward the skinny officer who dutifully began scooping ice into it.

"Wait!" Sylvia protested. Were they blind? "There's an *actual* dead body here."

"We have to wait for the coroner anyway," the fat officer said. "They'll have more."

"Well, aren't you going to ID him?" Sylvia asked.

"Hey! Don't tell me how to do my job," the officer snapped. "We've been at this since 3 a.m. There's a dead body on every goddamned corner! You want any of this ice or not? If not, you can go. We'll take it from here."

Sylvia shook her head. She walked toward the doors and then turned around again. "You're going to notify his family, right?"

The officers looked at one another and laughed. "Yeah, sure thing, lady. Hey, try not to find any more cadavers on your way home." The half-witted laughter continued as she walked out.

Assholes! She despised cops like this for having the audacity to call themselves civil servants. The majority of officers from other precincts were nothing more than street thugs in uniform. The Canadian People's Guard were less concerned with justice than they were with compliance and civil obedience. *People's 'guard,' my ass.* Her dad was right. She shouldn't have gone to the store.

After leaving the ransacked market, Sylvia plodded back to her apartment to pack a bag. She figured she'd be staying with her dad for the next few days. At least he had a decent supply of water. But first, she thought she'd check in at the station to see if they needed another pair of hands.

When the elevator door opened on the fourth floor, she saw a five-gallon jug of water sitting on her welcome mat with a red bow and a card. She checked her security feed from her holospecs and rewound the footage to see a uniformed CPG officer, careful to hide his face. He placed the jug on the mat, knocked on the door, and skulked away. Chills cascaded through her body. *What do they want?*

Sylvia opened the door and dragged the heavy jug by its spout into the apartment. She opened the small envelope and pulled out a folded piece of cream- colored stationery. A photo slipped out onto the floor and rested against her boot.

It was a photo of her father's house and the bottom right corner had been burned. It was a recent photo because the sycamore tree in the front yard had been struck by lightning less than a week ago in a thunderstorm and one of its limbs was resting diagonally on the lawn. She hadn't gotten around to removing it. She turned the photo over. On the back were written two words in black sharpie: *Walk Away.*

CHAPTER 2

A WINDOW OF OPPORTUNITY: CLEMENS

LAST NIGHT, Sergeant Clemens, mid-fifties and carrying the weight of his high-stress job in the bags under his eyes, sat on the couch watching a talent competition with his wife and teenage son. His holospecs vibrated on the coffee table. He picked them up and placed them over his eyes. Unknown caller ID.

"Hello?" Clemens answered warily.

"You are wading into dangerous waters, Sergeant," said the caller who had disguised his voice as some kind of diabolical robot.

He handed his son the bowl of popcorn and excused himself to the kitchen. "Who is this?"

"These trafficking investigations have gone far enough, Sergeant. Drop it or your family will pay a steep price. Am I making myself clear?"

"Yes." His voice barely escaped his throat.

"Delete the files." The call ended abruptly followed by an incoming message. He focused his eyes on the holographic file and blinked twice to open it. A video played— drone footage of his wife washing dishes in their kitchen. His stomach dropped. The video ended with a look of shock on Esther's face when she noticed the drone hovering outside her kitchen window. She had told him about the drone when he got home from work that day, but assumed it was just some kids messing around. Clemens walked back toward the family room and watched the two most important people in his life playfully tossing popcorn into each other's mouths.

"Honey, I need to have a word." His voice trembled.

Esther was smiling at first but when she saw the grave expression on his face, quickly nodded and joined him in the kitchen. "What is it?"

"You know that drone you saw earlier?"

"Yeah."

"It wasn't kids. Someone sent me this video." He handed her his holospecs and she put them on. Her eyes widened when she saw herself.

"I think it's from within our ranks," he said.

"Why? Why would they send you this?"

"It's a long story. Basically, we're finding some evidence against some of the higher ups. We know the Minister of Order and some of the other councilmen are involved in a global sex trafficking operation. Now *they* know that *we* know."

"Oh, dear!" She covered her mouth.

"Honey, listen. I think we have to get out of here." He'd discussed this plan to escape the city and migrate north into the wilderness with her several times in the last few years. It was on most everyone's mind at one time or another. Things had been getting steadily worse over the last few years. He didn't need to rehash his bullet points. "For all the reasons

I've given before obviously, but this is different. I think we could be in some serious trouble here."

"You're serious." Her eyes searched into his.

"I am. I think we're in danger if we stay here much longer. All of us."

Esther shook her head. "Well, what do they want?"

"They want me to drop the investigation."

"Well, that's easy enough," Esther said, as if she didn't know her own husband of thirty years.

"Honey, you know I can't do that. What's the point of being a cop if I can't enforce the law? No. I don't want to be a part of this anymore. I'm done."

Esther nodded. "Okay. I trust you."

"What are you guys talking about?" James asked as he entered the kitchen. "What's going on?"

"Son, we need to talk," Clemens said. "Sit down."

"Wait. This isn't about moving again, is it?" James asked, looking back and forth at both parents with a look of desperation. "No way!"

"Son, things are different now. It's not safe here anymore," Clemens explained.

"But I just made the team this season! We start practice next week."

"I'm sorry, Jimmy," his mother said. "Your father is right."

"Screw this!" James shouted and stomped toward his room.

"Jimmy!" Clemens called sternly. Esther put her hand on his shoulder, reminding him that this was one of those times you just have to give him a little space. Clemens knew this was a big ask. He pinched the bridge of his nose between his thumb and forefinger.

She rubbed his back. "Give him some time. Let him sleep on it," she suggested. "He'll come around."

"I think we should probably get a team together," he said. "Safety in numbers."

"Didn't you say Miguel was ready whenever you are?"

"Yeah. I think some of the other guys might be on board, too. I know I'm not the only one sick of all this bullshit."

"Come on," Esther said, tugging gently at his elbow. "Let's get some rest. We'll figure all this out in the morning."

"I'll be in there soon." He was already making plans in his head.

"Don't stay up too late." Esther kissed his cheek and retired to the bedroom.

Clemens went into his home office, its walls covered with framed military aircraft photos, plaques, and other certificates of recognition. A shadow box with a folded Canadian flag was illuminated on the built-in shelves. Next to that, sat another smaller shadow box displaying the rare Cross of Valour, which was the last medal of its kind to be awarded before the Canadian government finally collapsed in 2070. Other mementos from his accomplished life of fifty-seven years lined the shelves, including military history books, aircraft models, and a signed hockey puck from Winnipeg's own, two-time Stanley Cup champion, Merrick Gibson.

He pulled up holographic maps at his desk which he had previously marked up with known militia-patrolled areas. These plans were a year in the making. He knew they'd have to go on foot. All vehicles, which had been electric and self-driving now for decades, had to be registered with the CPG, which meant their computers were synced with the CPG's network to make sure citizens remained within a specified boundary. Leaving this boundary was subject to heavy fines, or worse. Often it was much worse.

He reviewed the route that would take them north along the Red River. He figured if they ran out of bottled water they could filter the fresh water from the river. He'd charted several possible safe houses along the route. They would have to travel a great distance before settling somewhere remote, preferably somewhere with solar and running water with the potential to farm. Although he'd never planted anything in his life, he had a keen interest in the ancient practice, had read books about it, and believed it was still possible, given the right elements and tools. It was well after midnight when he finally got into bed.

The next morning Clemens woke to his wife shouting from the bathroom. He climbed out of bed and met her in the bathroom where she was waving her hands under the sink faucet to demonstrate the lack of running water. His initial thoughts were that there had been a malfunction in the motion sensors, which was a fairly common occurrence with these standard residential systems.

"What's up with the water?" James said emerging from his own bathroom.

"I don't know. I'll see if I can get someone out." Clemens put on his holospecs and gave search commands to locate a local repairman. As he scrolled through search results he kept ignoring the notifications coming in from local news sources, until the headline *No Water for Winnipeg* caught his eye and he selected it. He opened the link and shared it to the living room holoscreen.

"Well, there you have it," Esther said. "I guess this pretty much decides it then. We really do need to get out of here."

They both looked at James who was sitting on the couch with his arms crossed.

"I can feel you looking at me," he said without turning his head.

"It's not just this, son," Clemens said. He sat next to him on the couch and looked him in the eye. "Listen to me. Someone upstairs is making threats to our family. I think I might have pushed it a little too far this time. Now I'm in their crosshairs and so are you and your mother. I know it's not fair. It's not. But our lives are in danger if we stay any longer."

"What do you got on 'em?" James asked, allowing curiosity to break him out of his pouting.

"It's bad."

"You can tell me, dad. I'm not a little kid."

"Sex trafficking," Clemens said.

"No shit?"

"Jimmy!" Esther scolded.

"Some of the higher execs are involved," Clemens continued. "So as you can imagine, they're not too happy I know about it."

Jimmy nodded silently. "Can I say goodbye to Eric and Pia?"

"Of course!" Esther said.

James got up and padded to his room.

"I've got it all planned out," Clemens said after James closed the door to his bedroom. "I think we should leave tonight."

"Tonight!?" Esther exclaimed.

"It's the perfect time. Look!" He turned up the volume on the news report where mayhem was unfolding in the streets.

"The Guard has their hands full. They're going to be too busy dealing with all of this," he said gesturing toward the shaky camera footage on screen. "It's the perfect opportunity to get out unnoticed."

Esther took a deep breath. "When are you going to talk to the guys?"

"I'll make some calls."

"I'll start packing."

"Just the essentials. We'll be traveling on foot."

Clemens stepped outside onto the covered back porch. A dusting of ash fluttered in the morning air that carried a whiff of smoke. He put on his holospecs and tapped the side. "Call Sylvia," he commanded. A moment later, Sylvia appeared in holographic form.

"Sarge," she answered. "You're not going to believe the morning I've had!"

"Are you okay?"

"Yeah. Sort of. I got a strange message. A CPG officer delivered a jug of water to my doorstep with a note attached that just said 'Walk Away.' They wrote it on the back of a burned picture of my dad's house. Pretty creepy, right?"

"They threatened my family, too. I think we really stepped in it this time." He looked up as two helicopters flew overhead.

"What do we do now?" Sylvia asked.

"We get outta Dodge, that's what. I'm taking my family and leaving tonight with some of the other guys. I think you should come with us."

"Sarge, I can't leave. My dad needs me."

Clemens closed his eyes and let out a deep sigh. "Right. I forgot. Sorry." Sylvia's dad was in a wheelchair and in poor health. Clemens met him when Sylvia graduated from the academy.

"It's okay. I wish I could. I really do. He's all I got," she said.

"I understand. You're a good cop, Boone. It was good knowing you."

"You, too, sir. Good luck out there."

"Would you mind keeping this conversation between me and you?"

"Of course."

"Give your dad my best."

"I will."

Clemens disconnected the call and let out a deep sigh, brushing his weathered hand through thinning white hair. Sylvia would have been useful. She was dependable and sharp. He worried about how she was going to get by now that she was in the crosshairs. He took another look around his property. The drone from yesterday made him suspicious he was being watched.

SYLVIA BOONE HAD JOINED the CPG to get out from under its thumb. She didn't agree with their hostile tactics any more than her fellow Winnipeggers, among whom she was raised. Fortunately, she found herself under the scrupulous leadership of Sergeant Clemens, who offered an ethical sense of duty and fairness toward those he mentored and the citizenry he protected.

Two months ago, Sylvia and her team apprehended a local officer in South Winnipeg who was transporting women and children to a service center for involuntary sex work. The officer was taken into CPG custody and processed. She found out later, he'd been released.

"I don't understand," she told the Sergeant.

"Technically, there's no law against it," Clemens said.

"No law against sex trafficking?" Sylvia asked, shocked.

"No law against aiding and abetting by CPG officers."

"How is that possible? He was literally the one trafficking human beings, regardless of who paid him to do it."

Clemens shook his head. "He was suspended for five

days because he wasn't authorized to use a CPG vehicle off the clock."

"That's insane!" Sylvia exclaimed. "And what about the boss who hired him?"

"Poof," he said with a hand gesture. "Into thin air."

Human trafficking had always been widespread, but it was becoming clear that criminal activities on this scale could not be tenable without the aid of the local police. The Canadian People's Guard kept close surveillance of all travel throughout the region and trafficking required special access. The release of this officer caught red-handed and sent home with no more than a slap on the wrist got Sylvia's attention and she couldn't resist the urge to pull on that thread. She worked diligently for the next week until she thought she had enough evidence to bring to the Sergeant's attention.

"Sir, can I show you something?" Sylvia asked the Sergeant. She activated a holographic screen from her workstation. "Look at this list. Recognize any names?"

"Dear God," he said, looking over the list of names of prominent executives on the CPG council, along with incriminatingly sizable payments next to each name.

"These payments all came from a single offshore account —Crowe Industries, Inc."

"Any relation to Crowe Pharmaceuticals?" Crowe Pharma was one of the six corporations that made up the CPG.

"It's a subsidiary, established in 2082."

"The Minister of Order is on here," he said.

"I know." She bit the edge of her thumb. "How are we supposed to play this?"

Sergeant Daryl Clemens, the highest-ranking officer at

the 9th Precinct, brushed his hand over his ample walrus-style mustache. "Very carefully. We don't make any moves until this thing is air tight. You got that?"

And then what? Who are we supposed to turn them in to if they're at the top of the food chain? This is ridiculous! What are we getting ourselves into? She kept these thoughts to herself. The last time a CPG councilman was implicated in an embezzlement scheme, the prosecuting attorney was found at the bottom of Lake Manitoba—in pieces. "Does this mean the case is still open?"

"Unofficially," Clemens said in a hushed tone. "Keep digging. Quietly. Let's keep this between you and me, for now."

"Yes, sir." She turned to leave. "Boone."

"Sir?"

"Good work."

Sylvia nodded. She spent the next several weeks tracking financial transactions, identifying local and international players, and researching the history of trafficking activities worldwide. At first glance, it appeared that independent bosses continued to operate as they had in the past, aided by local police, yet there seemed to be another layer in their organizational structure, linking them to a single source: Crowe Industries, Inc. She only had a small piece of the larger puzzle, but her findings were consistent.

When she told her dad what she was working on, he advised her to leave it alone. "You won't get a conviction," he said. "Remember what happened to the last guy who blew the whistle." She was keenly aware of what happened to that guy. She wished she didn't know what she knew. But something inside her nudged her toward the flames, something righteous, perhaps reckless. She wished that it didn't.

AS SHE DROVE to her father's house on the northwest side of town, Sylvia wondered who had taken that picture and was that as far as it would go? Would they really drop the whole thing if she did what they said and walk away? She couldn't help but feel she would be on someone's list now.

She wondered what would become of her precinct. Who would replace Clemens? Some disreputable meathead with no regard for decency and justice probably. The bigger question, however, was whether you could even call it law enforcement if your superiors actively suppressed your efforts to enforce the law—because they were the ones breaking it. Without her trusted comrades, she would feel like a traitor working alongside common, unscrupulous guns for hire.

Sylvia arrived to her dad's house in an older residential part of the city with grass lawns and mature trees. Although the houses were built nearly a century ago, they'd been renovated and retrofitted with standard solar, smart utility and security systems that came standard on new builds. She placed her hand against the sensor pad on the front door and let herself in. Her dad was sitting in a wheelchair at the kitchen table, oxygen tank by his side, playing a game of chess against himself. Sunlight pouring in from the front window illuminated the white stubble on his unshaved face.

"Heya bug," her dad said in a gravely voice, keeping his eyes on the chessboard as he moved his rook with a trembling hand. His Parkinson's had been worsening over the last six months.

"Have you had anything to eat today?" Sylvia asked.

"I'm not that hungry."

"Dad!" Sylvia scoffed and went into the kitchen to microwave a cup of instant oats. She worried more and more about his deteriorating condition and ambivalence toward self-care. She sat the steaming cup and a spoon in front of him. "Eat. Please."

He pushed his oats to the side and grunted, keeping his focus on the chessboard. "Surprised they didn't call you in today," he said.

She didn't respond, trying to think of how to break the news. "Clemens is jumping ship," she blurted. She sat down across from him and studied the board. She took his knight with her pawn.

He looked at her for the first time since she arrived. "Jumping ship? What do you mean?"

"It's this trafficking investigation we've been working on. They must have found out we were onto them and they started making threats to his family if he didn't back off. I guess I don't blame him. We were so close to—"

"To what? Getting yourselves killed? I hate to say it, but they're untouchable." The word "untouchable" lacked the requisite force to fully form and trailed off midway through. He took another breath. "It's a no-win situation, Syl."

"Tell that to the victims." She didn't want to worry him with the sinister message she had received that morning. He had warned her about this and she didn't want to hear him say *I told you so.*

"So where's he going?" He took her pawn with his bishop. "Check," he added.

"The Sergeant and some of the other guys have this plan to migrate north into rural Canada, away from militia-controlled territories and start up a new settlement up there." She moved her king one space to the left. "They've been talking about it for a while now. I guess now's the right time since the CPG has their hands full with this water situation."

"You should see if you can tag along," he said. "If anyone can survive in the wilderness it's you. You're trained for this kind of thing."

"I'm not going to leave you here. Who's going to remind you to eat if I'm gone?"

"You have your whole life ahead of you, Syl. You have a much better chance out there than you do here if you ask me." He moved his queen. "Checkmate."

"I'm not having this conversation." Sylvia stood up.

"Sylvia! Listen to me."

"No! Dad, I'm not leaving you here! End of discussion." Sylvia rarely raised her voice to her father. Guilt crept into the silence as she searched for a change of subject. "Have you checked your rain barrels lately?"

He shook his head as he started resetting the board. Sylvia walked out the back door and over to the detached garage. She hoped to put together enough hose to reroute water from the rain barrels into the house. She knew he was right. Winnipeg no longer had anything for her. Her father was the only reason to stay. Plus, the cost of leaving might very well be her life. Then again, without water, both of their lives might as well be over.

CHAPTER 4

THE PLAN: MIGUEL

MIGUEL WAS SCHEDULED to work that Saturday. He donned his tactical uniform as news of the water crisis streamed from the holoscreen in the bedroom. Rebecca watched sitting cross-legged on the bed, hugging a pillow. She was vulnerable and Miguel worried about her safety. He considered calling in to stay home with her. The reporter gave accounts of break-ins and homicides, which happened regularly but had spiked significantly in the last few hours. Miguel sat on the edge of the bed to lace up his boots. "You want me to stay home?"

"No, I'll be okay. I don't go anywhere anyway."

"I can leave you my gun if you want."

She shook her head. "No, I'll be fine. I was planning to wash my hair, but I guess that's not happening."

"That's what you're worried about?" Miguel teased, tousling her slept-in hair.

"Stop it!" Rebecca smiled as she pushed him away. Then she pulled him to her and kissed him. "Be safe."

"Always." He kissed her forehead and left for the station.

Before working for the CPG, Miguel was a Texas Ranger, which had assumed power throughout the Southwest after the Republic of Texas dissolved due to oil depletion. The CPG was a disorganized rabble compared to the extensive reach and power of the Texas regime. It wasn't long into his service before Miguel realized that the Texas Rangers were nothing more than a far-reaching arm of the Mexican drug cartel. His conscience could not abide with such blatant corruption.

A champion of ethical law enforcement, Miguel turned to the CPG, who maintained an unblemished reputation by comparison. Or so he thought. Miguel flourished under Sergeant Clemens' mentorship. He proved himself among his peers and demonstrated integrity in his police work, even as corruption snaked its ways into neighboring precincts. He found solace in his aging mentor who held accountable every officer under his command. He became the Sergeant's right hand man and could be relied upon when *the plan* was to be carried out.

An incoming call flashed across the windshield. "Answer," he commanded and Sergeant Clemens appeared in holographic form on the dash.

"Sergeant, is everything okay?" Miguel answered.

"Some morning, eh?" Clemens asked.

"Tell me about it. I was just heading into the station." A message appeared on the windshield display: Re-routing. An ambulance was taking up most of the street he would have turned onto. Paramedics lifted a gurney into the back of an ambulance.

"Don't worry about it," Clemens said. "Listen, you know that plan we've been talking about?"

"You mean, *the* plan?" Miguel sat up in his seat.

"You still in?" Clemens' stoney-faced expression let Miguel know he was dead serious.

"Of course. When were you thinking—"

"Tonight."

"Tonight? Is everything alright?"

"They threatened my family. If they're bluffing, I'm not sticking around to find out. This water crisis is presenting us with a unique opportunity. This is our window. Are you in?"

"Yes, of course. Rebecca and I are in. We've already discussed it."

"I'm going to try to get Dutch on board." Dutch was a skilled marksman and built like a freight train. His former training involved covert, special operations missions with a mercenary outfit before joining their ranks as a police officer. Dutch's tactical skills would be a valued asset to their escape and survival in the wilderness.

"Dutch?" Miguel asked. "You think he'll do it?"

"If the money's right. His skillset would go a long way."

"Good luck. What do you need from me?"

"We're going to need food and medical supplies. We have more than enough firepower at the station." Clemens waited for Miguel to respond and finally interrupted the awkward silence. "Are you there?"

"Yeah, I'm just a little surprised to hear you suggest that." Miguel knew Clemens to be an honest man, incapable of stealing.

"They'd just use it against us anyway. I don't want to hand over a single bullet to those bastards."

"Well, when you put it that way," Miguel conceded.

"Alright then, let's get to it. Remember. Pack light. Only

the essentials. I'm sending you the location right now. Meet us there before sundown."

"Yes, sir. End Call." Clemens disappeared. "Re-route," Miguel commanded.

The car's computer voice prompted, *Where would you like to go?*

"Home." The car made a U-turn at the next intersection. "Call Rebecca," he commanded. After five rings, Rebecca's voicemail greeting prompted him to leave a message. He called back twice with no answer and his heart began to race. No way she would have gone anywhere after seeing the news this morning. He left a message after the final voicemail prompt: "Rebecca, where are you? Call me back."

Rebecca came into Miguel's life only four months ago. She was crossing into CPG territory with a convoy of refugees when they were attacked by bandits. Miguel and his team responded to the distress call. It was love at first sight for Miguel—her beauty unparalleled. He offered to take her in until she could get established in the territory, but as the weeks came and went, they had become somewhat of an item.

"Show Rebecca's location," he commanded. A map displayed across the windshield. The red pin showed that Rebecca was home. *That's weird*, he thought. She must have had her ringer off for some reason but he couldn't think of one.

When he arrived at the apartment, he rushed inside. "Rebecca!" Miguel called out. He looked in every room. She wasn't there. The apartment remained exactly as he'd left it— bed still unmade. He saw no sign of a break-in or anything out of the ordinary. Her holospecs were right there on the kitchen table. That would explain why her location was marked at home. *Was she taken? Were they holding her for ransom?* If that were the case, they would have left a point of contact or further instructions, so that didn't add up.

Did she leave on her own? Why would she leave her holospecs behind? She didn't have a car so wherever she went, she would have been on foot. *Surely she didn't go searching for water.* They watched the footage of mayhem together before he left and she commented that someone would have to be crazy to go out there and risk getting stabbed over a bottle of water.

Miguel paced around the apartment trying to solve the puzzle and decided to start searching for her. He got back in his car and drove slowly around their neighborhood in concentric circles, digitally enhancing the views in all directions. Looters entered a residence and gunshots rang out. He dashed into the ransacked grocery store a few blocks from their apartment, calling her name above the blaring alarm bells. After an hour, he returned home in despair.

Miguel collapsed onto the couch. His eyes filled with tears. If this was some kind of game, he didn't know what his next move was supposed to be. He wasn't going to leave without her. He hated to disappoint Clemens, but he wasn't willing to leave her here alone. Rebecca was not an official citizen and therefore had no vehicle registration. She also had no survival skills to speak of. He stood up to get a glass of water in the kitchen. When he placed the glass under the faucet nothing came out. He forgot. He looked up out the kitchen window and his world came to a screeching halt.

CHAPTER 5

DON'T LEAVE ME: REBECCA

"WE NEED TO STOP," Rebecca said, pulling her panties up around her thighs. "Maybe we should cool it for a while."

"You have a conscience all the sudden?" Malcom asked after exhaling a lungful of cannabis smoke. Malcom was their trusted single neighbor who lived across the hallway. He was not her typical choice in men, given his slight build and bookish interests, but he was convenient. It started out innocent enough. With Miguel working such long hours, the days would drag and she'd pop over for tea and crosswords. One thing led to another and they found themselves fornicating on Malcom's sleeper sofa, the same one Miguel helped him maneuver through his front door when he'd first moved in. It was all her idea.

"I gotta go," she said, pulling her long blonde hair from inside the collar of the t-shirt she'd just slipped on.

Malcom walked her to the door in his boxers and opened it. "'Til next time," he said with an impish grin.

She rolled her eyes and stepped out into the covered walkway between their apartment buildings. "We'll see," she said and kissed him passionately. She turned, flirtatiously flipping her blonde mane, and pranced back across the walkway toward her own apartment—technically, Miguel's apartment.

The twenty-six-year-old model/actress from Chicago sought asylum in Canada after ending a relationship with a highly influential public figure. Although Rebecca didn't come from money, her modeling career positioned her to circulate in high society. She enjoyed the material excesses that were made available to her when she was in his company —jewelry, fancy parties, travel. This was fun for a while until she realized she no longer had a choice. He had the might of Chicago's police at his disposal, which made it especially challenging for her to leave.

As fate would have it, she did manage to escape and found herself in the protective arms of Corporal Miguel Estes, who valiantly rescued her from bandits near Winnipeg's border. Rebecca had quite the taste for adrenaline-fueled adventure. She was instantly taken with the chiseled peace officer. His searing brown eyes and irresistible dimples turned her to jelly in his strong hands.

He offered to let her stay with him until she could get on her feet. Winnipeg wasn't exactly the place to pursue an acting career and even if it were, she was paranoid her ex would find her and send his goons to reclaim his property. For this reason, she never applied for jobs or established legal residency within the territory.

When Miguel went to work, she stayed home, and when she did venture out under a cloak of scarves and darkly shaded holospecs, she was limited to walkable destinations because without residency, she could not register a vehicle.

She spent her days exercising, watching old movies, conducting home spa treatments and generally biding her time until Miguel returned home from work. As the weeks progressed however, and Miguel stayed later and later at work, Rebecca began to feel restless.

Rebecca screamed when she saw Miguel standing there in the kitchen like a statue, the color drained from his face. "What the shit! You fucking scared me! What are you doing home?" He didn't move. "Miguel?" A wave of heat engulfed her face. "Did you see . . . oh my God. Babe, I can explain." She sidled up to him and pulled on his shirt. "Please, say something."

"Are you cheating on me," he managed to inquire, "with Malcolm?" She shook her head silently, not to deny it but because she couldn't formulate the right words. "No, you're not?" he attempted to clarify. She pushed her forehead into his chest still clutching his shirt. "You *are!*" he cried, pushing her away. "How long has this been going on?" His face turned red.

"Not long. It was just sex, that's all," she explained. "It's nothing. You have to believe me. He means *nothing* to me. I swear to God! Please! I love you, Miguel. I'm such an idiot!"

"I'm going to kill him!" Miguel shouted and started toward the door.

"No! Miguel, no." She positioned herself between Miguel and the door, both hands on his muscular chest. "Let me explain, please."

"I don't understand. I thought we were happy. I thought *you* were happy."

"I *am.* I am happy. I'm just . . ." Rebecca clenched the air with closed fists. ". . . so stupid!" She burst into tears.

"Malcom? I don't get it."

Rebecca shook her head and shrugged as if to say, *I don't either.* She tried to gain her composure long enough to reply but when she opened her mouth to say something, a wave of sobs emerged.

"I'm waiting," Miguel said, crossing his arms.

"I was just . . ."

"Just what?" He said in a commanding voice that sent chills through her body.

". . . bored."

"You were bored? What does that mean? I'm boring?"

"No! This isn't about you, Miguel," she said in a raised voice—courage arising from somewhere. "I'm alone! All day. I don't have a job. I don't have friends. I just wait around all day for you to get home. And lately, you've been too stressed or tired to hang out when you do get home." She found herself pacing around the living room. "I'm not the girl you want me to be, okay."

"I'm such a fool to think you were," he said in a defeated tone.

Her heart sunk. "No, you're not. Please don't say that. This is on me. I made a huge mistake and I hurt you and I couldn't hate myself more right now. This is totally on me. Let me make it up to you." She placed her hand on his face. He brushed it away.

"No need," he said. "I'm leaving. You can keep the apartment."

A wave of panic washed over her and her heart caught in her throat. "No! Miguel, don't leave. This isn't *over.*" She grabbed both his arms with each hand. "I promise, we can get through this. Tell me what I can do."

"We're getting out. I'm leaving with Clemens and his family. We're leaving tonight."

"Wait. The Plan? It's happening? I'm ready. Take me with you." They had discussed *the plan* on numerous occasions like couples do when dreaming of a someday vacation. Always ready for a new adventure, Rebecca was on board from the jump. "This is our chance to start over. We can just put all this behind us."

Miguel looked at the floor and let out a deep exhale. This was a good sign. Maybe he could be persuaded.

"Don't leave me," she pleaded. "You can't leave me here. I won't make it here on my own! Please! We'll work through this. Please, take me with you."

Miguel stood in silence for an eternity. He couldn't even look at her. "I thought you'd been kidnapped," he said finally. "I thought I'd lost you."

"I'm so sorry. You must have been so scared."

"I was terrified. And right now I'm pissed!" He clenched his jaws and then softened. Massaging the back of his neck, he said, "But if I'm being honest, I still don't want to lose you. I still don't want to live without you."

"I don't want to live without you either!" She threw her arms around his neck and sobbed. "I love you. I really do," she said into his chest. She took his face in her hands. "I'm going to make it up to you, I promise." She knew she didn't deserve his forgiveness, but she was determined to earn it. She didn't have much of a choice. Without Miguel, Rebecca felt powerless to make it on her own.

CHAPTER 6

A GENEROUS OFFER: DUTCH

DUTCH WAS STILL in bed when his mother knocked on his bedroom door that morning. He hadn't heard any news of the water crisis.

"Dutch, honey. We ain't got no water," his mother said pulling wrinkles toward the center of her forehead.

"What?" Dutch sat up, still a bit groggy. The mattress creaked under his weight. "I'll go check it out." He pulled on a pair of pants and a tank top over his barrel-shaped torso. He walked into the bathroom to confirm the plumbing issue.

"Dutch! You have to come see this," his mother yelled from downstairs.

He came down to the living room where his mother was watching the news. "What is it?"

"The whole city's out of water!"

"Cyber attack," Dutch read out loud from the captions.

"What are we gonna do? I was gonna make a stew tonight."

"I'll go down to the market and see what they got," he said.

"Well, they say all the stores are gettin' looted."

Dutch laced up his boots as the news reported the mayhem outside. "Don't worry, ma. I'll find us some water. Stay inside."

He started walking toward the market, which was only a few blocks from the house. CPG drones whizzed overhead and sirens called in the distance. He could see smoke rising over buildings to the north. Dutch heard a motorcycle approaching fast from the direction of the market. The rider kept looking back over his shoulder like he was being chased and the bike wobbled unsteadily. When he got close enough, Dutch could see he had a secured two five-gallon water jugs to the backseat of the motorcycle with bungie cords.

Dutch stepped into the rider's path and extended his arm. He clotheslined the rider who flipped backward off the motorcycle. The motorcycle skidded, flipped twice, and crashed into a tree. The water jugs had come loose in the wreck. Dutch lifted the rider by his jacket and placed him on the sidewalk. Other than a skinned elbow, he seemed mostly unharmed. The rider removed his helmet and tossed it angrily to his side.

"You steal that water?" Dutch asked in a low growl.

The man noted Dutch's mass and answered carefully, "Yeah. Everyone is. It's a free-for-all down there."

"Is that so? Well, then you must have seen this coming." Dutch turned and walked to where the jugs had rolled to the curb, miraculously still sealed. He lifted them over his shoulders and walked back toward the house, leaving the dazed rider to fend for himself.

"Hey, ma! I got you some water," Dutch said as he entered the house. He unsealed one of the jugs and poured water into a pitcher so that his mother could manage it with arthritic hands.

"Oh, thank you. Now I can make my tea." She patted his tattooed forearm and reached for a cup on an open shelf. "They say it could be days before they get the water running again."

"Did they say who did it?" Dutch asked, taking a bite from a slice of pound cake his mother had recently baked.

"Nobody knows. I bet it was them damn Mexicans."

"You always think it's the Mexicans."

Dutch heard the tone of an incoming call and placed his holospecs on. It was Clemens.

"Hey, Sarge. You need me to come in?" Dutch asked. He walked outside to take the call on the front porch.

"No. Dutch, listen," Clemens said. "You remember that plan me, you, and Miguel talked about at Purdy's a while back?"

"You mean the great exodus?" Dutch's recollection of this beer infused conversation was that the plan was more of a pie in the sky fantasy than a real proposition. Everyone talked about getting out. But that's all it was—talk.

"They're making threats against my family. If we stay, we're dead. We're getting out tonight."

"How do you plan to get out of Winnipeg?"

"With this water crisis wreaking havoc in the city, the Guard will have their hands full. They're pulling their resources toward central Winnipeg and away from the borders. I figure it's now or never. We could sure use you out there. What do you say?"

"I can't. My mom's not doing great. Her meds are expensive. I have to work."

"I'll pay you."

Dutch paused in reflection. "How much?"

"I can pay you an advance on your salary for the next three months, maybe more. I'll have to check the numbers but we're barely into Q3 so there's plenty of funding left in the budget. Whatever's left, it's yours. Plus, I can cash in my pension and get you an extra 10K by the end of the week."

"Sir, I couldn't—"

"You don't get it. I don't need the money. I'm out, for good. I'm not coming back. I can take care of my family and live off the land once we get to where we're going, but I need someone with your skill and expertise to help get us there. I figure that might take four weeks, tops. Administratively, you'd take leave, which you have plenty of—I checked. When you come back, you can pick up right where you left off. That's six months of pay for one month of work. I'd say that's a pretty fair deal."

"It's a generous offer, sir. I can't argue with that."

"Well?" Clemens asked.

Dutch thought of his mother. He didn't want to leave her, but now she could finally get that procedure they could never afford before. "Alright, I'm in. When do we leave?"

"Tonight. Sundown."

"Tonight?"

"We have to strike now while the Guard has their hands full. This is our window."

"Where should I meet you?"

"There's an abandoned industrial complex over between Foxgrove and the 101. There's a field directly between two checkpoints along the highway. We just need to cross over the highway undetected, which should be pretty easy since they'll have a skeleton crew working the checkpoints if they're even staffed at all. What do you say?"

Dutch paused for several seconds. He knew the exact spot Clemens referred to. The plan did make sense and he could definitely use the money. "I'll be there."

CHAPTER 7

WANTED: SYLVIA

ON THE NORTHWEST side of town, Sylvia stood on a ladder in the detached garage behind her father's house. As she dug through storage bins in search of extra hose to re-route the water from the rain barrels into the house, she discovered a cardboard box with her name printed on its side. She tugged the flaps open to bestow a collection of volleyball trophies, report cards, a ceramic bowl she'd made in fifth grade, and other miscellaneous items of varying significance. She was surprised her father had kept all this stuff.

Sylvia found an open envelope and pulled out the birthday card tucked inside. She opened it to find a photo of her mother, who died giving birth to her. As a child, Sylvia had blamed herself for her mother's passing. Her father, who was not in the habit of expressing emotion, gave her this photo on her tenth birthday with a brief note explaining that her mother would be very proud of the young lady she was becoming. She was surprised at how much she resembled her mother. Besides her mother's long hair, they were hauntingly identical. Her mother would have been around Sylvia's age when she passed.

Sylvia's father raised her all by himself. He had been in the military before she was born and was honorably discharged when her mother died so that he could stay home and raise her. He was able to pay the bills and kept a roof over their heads, but there was rarely anything left over for vacations or extra-curricular activities. All of her clothes were handed down from an older cousin, a boy.

On weekends, when her father wasn't picking up extra jobs, he'd take her camping at Riding Mountain National Park. He taught her to fish, how to build a fire, and how to create potable water through boiling and filtering it through a T-shirt. It was during one of these camping trips when she got her first period. They'd been swimming in the lake and she was telling him what she was learning in History class about the decline of the national currency. She was drying her hair when she noticed the stunned look on her father's face. "Dad? What's wrong?"

He opened his mouth to speak but nothing came out. That's when she looked down and saw blood mixed in with the lake water, trickling down her leg. No one had ever sat her down to inform her of the changes her body would undergo at a certain age. In that moment, she was both scared and oddly ashamed, but she didn't know why. Tears came to her eyes and that's when her father finally sprung into action. He wrapped her in his towel and scooped her up in his strong arms repeating, "You're okay. It's going to be okay."

She loved her father more than anything in the world. Never quite fitting in at school, he was all she had. And when he fell off that roof during a routine service call and broke both of his legs, she was there to pick up the slack. She was fifteen and got a job bagging groceries after school and on weekends. While she accepted this role without reservation, it was challenging, and there were times she wished she had a different life. But she never blamed her father who remained grateful and kind.

She was staring at the photo of her mother when she heard the crunch of gravel in the driveway out front. She stuffed the photo into her back pocket and shoved the box back onto the shelf before sneaking around the side of the house. Two men in uniform walked up the front steps and knocked on the front door.

"Who's there?" She heard her father's raspy voice call from inside the house.

"CPG. We're looking for Sylvia Boone," the first officer said. Chills rippled down her spine. Were these they guys who took the picture of her dad's house?

"You got the wrong address!" her dad replied.

"That's her car out front, isn't it?" When her father didn't respond the officer ordered, "Open the door!"

"Fuck off!" Her father's voice was both menacing and impotent.

"Don't make this hard, sir. Either open the door, or we'll open it for you."

Sylvia knew they would and when she heard the high-pitched whir of their plasma rifles activating, she walked around from the side of the house with her hands up. "Excuse me! Hi. I'm Sylvia Boone. Who's asking?"

"Corporal Boone, our boss has some questions for you. Please come with us."

"What's this about?" She knew exactly what this was

about. They wanted to make sure the trafficking investigation was finally put to rest.

"You'll need to ask him."

"Please," she said. "My dad is sick. I need to be here with him."

"Sorry, ma'am. We need you to come with us now."

"Okay. Let me just say goodbye to my dad."

Her dad pulled open the front door. "You're not taking her anywhere!" He was holding a plasma shotgun and put a gaping hole the size of a cantaloupe through the first officer's chest. Blood sprayed onto the second officer and all over the railing along the front steps. Before her father could get off a second round, the second officer shot him in the head. Sylvia unholstered her sidearm and in one fluid motion, exterminated the second officer who fell backward off the front steps.

"Dad! Oh, Dad! No!" She ran to him and held his unsupported head in her hands. Sylvia wailed and fell to her knees. Kneeling by his wheelchair, Sylvia sobbed uncontrollably into his shoulder. Dark brown hair clung to her tear-stained face. Violent sobs took control of her body and she felt helpless to fight it. Regret washed over her as she played out alternative scenarios in her head. Maybe she should have taken them out first. Maybe she shouldn't have come over in the first place. Maybe she should have gotten out of law enforcement years ago when her dad first suggested it.

Sylvia heard sirens in the distance. It wouldn't be long before the CPG would be following up. They were expecting her to return into their custody and now two officers lay dead on her father's front lawn. She had to get out of there fast. Sylvia wheeled her father back into the house. She pulled the dog tags from around his neck and put them over her head.

She kissed his cheek one last time and covered him with a quilt. It didn't seem right leaving him this way, but she didn't have a choice.

Sylvia grabbed her pack and ran to the kitchen. Her father's refrigerator didn't have much more than hers. She managed to find some dry goods in the pantry—protein bars, peanut butter pouches, saltines, canned tuna, half a loaf of bread, and a carton of almond milk. She crammed it all into her pack. She knew she couldn't go back home, and she couldn't stay there. She ran back out to the garage and grabbed a sleeping bag and a pup tent. She secured them to her pack.

They already had her car's location so she would have to leave it. She couldn't take her dad's either since she was an authorized user and they would likely track it, too. The next door neighbor's green pickup was parked in the driveway. As a CPG officer, she had access to all registered vehicles but she would have to log in to the registry system, thus giving up her location. The sirens grew louder. As the first SUV rounded the corner, roof lights flashing, she ran into the backyard and climbed over the chainlink fence into the neighbor's yard.

She continued hopping fences through the residential neighborhood to stay off the streets. Her heart pounded in her chest as she scanned her surroundings. When she encountered a resident she flashed her badge and gun, which was enough reason to make way. They would probably assume she was going after a looter and welcome the intrusion onto their property.

Eventually, she reached a commercial section littered with storefronts and pedestrians, which made it even harder to find cover. She tried to enter a fast food chain but the doors were locked and a handwritten sign taped to the door read: NO WATER. She crouched down behind a garbage can to catch her breath and conceal herself as best she could from the busy street. She needed a moment to regroup before fleeing again to who knows where.

A red alert appeared on her holospecs with a photo of her in uniform. It read: WANTED: Sylvia Boone, 34-year-old female, armed and dangerous. 5,000 unit reward for any helpful information leading to her arrest.

An incoming call notification appeared in the corner of her visual field. It was Sergeant Clemens. She took the call and Clemens appeared before her.

"Boone! What the hell did you do?"

"I might have just killed a guy?" She said contritely in the form of a question.

"Jesus Christ! Guard?"

"They shot my dad!" Her voice constricted. "He's dead," she managed to eke out.

"Oh, Syl, I'm so sorry. Every cop in town will be after you now. Where are you?"

"I don't know," she whined pitifully, her cheeks wet with tears.

"Listen to me. They'll be looking for you at home and they're probably tracking your vehicle. You're not in your car, are you?"

"No. I'm on foot." She enhanced the view from her holospecs to read the nearest street sign. "Somewhere on Kingsbury—on the Northwest side."

"Send me your location. I'm sending a car to you. When you get in, do not pair your holospecs to it. In fact, destroy your specs as soon as we hang up. They could be tracking those, too. Let's hope they're not listening in already. There's only one way out of this, Syl, and that's with us. Are you in?"

Sylvia was out of options. She was out of excuses. It was only a matter of time before the CPG would have her in their custody and she'd be tried for murder. But given what she knew about the CPG's involvement in human trafficking, she would probably be exterminated before she had a chance to take the stand. She brushed away tears with the heel of her hand.

"I'm in."

REBECCA FELT as if she'd been given a second lease on life as she silently packed her most essential belongings into a single wheeled suitcase. It was the smaller one because Miguel told her if she couldn't carry it without using wheels for miles at a time, it would be too big. No dresses, no heels, no makeup—only what would be useful in the wilderness. Since her holospecs could be traced, she had to leave those, too.

The tension in their small apartment was palpable as they squeezed past each other in the walk-in closet without so much as an "excuse me." She wished they could have had more time to process what had just happened but she wouldn't have known what else to say. He had agreed to take her with him and perhaps it was better to not have the chance to spoil it by saying something stupid.

It was a long and awkward ride to the meeting spot. Miguel hadn't said a word the entire drive and Rebecca didn't want to push it. When they arrived, Rebecca forced a smile, hoping nobody would notice the tension. She couldn't escape the thought that somehow everyone knew of her indiscretions and she felt exposed. In addition to her rolling suitcase, she was carrying two shopping totes filled with food from their cupboards, mostly staples—cans of soup, rolled oats, peanut butter, dried fruit snacks, and a four- pound bag of lab-grown potatoes.

"Miguel! It's about time," Clemens said. "Help us with this rigging." Clemens and his son were working on a gang-line system to pull a small flatbed trailer.

"What's this?" Miguel asked looking down at the mess of tie downs on the ground.

"Well, we can't carry all our supplies on our backs, especially the firearms and ammo. It's way too heavy and we need to move quickly. We can pull it easier than we can carry it."

"So, it's like a dog sled but with refugees instead of dogs."

"Mush!" Clemens exclaimed with a smile and slapped Miguel on the back. He turned to Rebecca. "Rebecca, it's good to see you again."

"You, too, sir," she replied politely.

"Would you mind helping Esther organize the trailer?" Clemens asked.

"Of course." Rebecca walked over to where Esther was consolidating food into coolers.

"Rebecca!" Esther called warmly, "How's my favorite bride-to-be?" This was Esther's little running joke.

"Not bad. Considering." Rebecca did her best to feign a cheerful disposition. She held out the sacks of groceries.

"Oh, wonderful! You brought food. You know, we didn't think to bring any ice," Esther said with a hand on her chin, looking back and forth between the piles of food.

"There's an Esso just a few blocks from here. Want me to

see if there's any left?" Rebecca felt intensely uncomfortable making conversation after what had just happened between herself and Miguel. She was more than willing to go on a solo mission.

"That would be great," Esther said. "Here, take these." She helped Rebecca load the coolers into the back seat of Miguel's car. "Do you have a piece?" Esther asked holding out a bolt pistol by the barrel.

"No." Rebecca had not had much experience with weapons, even before they had become outlawed.

"Here." Esther handed her the gun. "Just in case. You have to flip this here to activate it," she explained pointing to a small switch above the grip near the trigger.

"Thanks. Hopefully, I won't need it." She shoved the gun into the waistband of her pants and got into the car. Once inside, the computer asked where she'd like to go. "Nearest Esso," she replied and the car pulled away.

When Rebecca arrived at the charging station, the large ice coolers out front were completely empty. She expected as much. She hesitated before entering the ransacked convenience store, florescent lights buzzing off and on overhead. Although there didn't seem to be anyone in the store, she didn't want to be there any longer than she had to. The refrigerated shelves had been stripped of bottled water. She looked around to see if she could find anything else that might prove useful on their journey and tossed them into one of the coolers—two bags of mixed nuts, two bags of elk jerky, a handful of protein bars, two four-pack rolls of toilet paper, toothpaste, two packs of wet wipes, and a large bag of assorted jelly beans.

A carousel of greeting cards remained near the register.

The words, "I'm sorry," caught her eye. That's all it said on the front with a hand-drawn bouquet of flowers. It was blank inside. She grabbed it and stuffed it into her back pocket.

Before she walked out, she noticed a large sign advertising the store's hot dog and fountain drink combo—carbonation effervescing above the rim of the big blue cup. She hadn't had anything to drink all day and was suddenly stricken with thirst. She turned back to the soda machines and extracted a 24 oz. plastic cup from its dispenser. Out of habit, she pressed the cup against the lever marked ICE, and out tumbled perfectly formed cubes of ice.

She'd filled three cupfuls of cubed ice into the second cooler before realizing she could scoop it directly from the source instead of waiting for it to dispense from the front of the machine. She'd filled the entire second cooler and the remaining ice filled in between the other items in the first. Rebecca was relieved not to have to return empty- handed. It was important to her that she be perceived as useful—that she could pull her own weight.

The ice-filled coolers rolled easily to the car on wheels, but Rebecca struggled to lift them into the backseat. She stepped back to catch her breath and reevaluate her strategy when she spotted two men approaching from across the street. They were poorly dressed and dirty, giving Rebecca the impression they might be vagrants or bandits, which were an ever-present blot throughout the city. There was something unsteady, shifty in their movements.

She was able to heave the first cooler onto the backseat, but struggled to slide it over to make room for the second. The men crossed the street in her direction. They seemed to be picking up their pace as they drew near. Flooded with desperation, she put her back to the first cooler to push it over while pulling up on the second one. She quickly realized she could not lift the second cooler from one side in this position. Sweat accumulated on her forehead.

"Here let me help you with that," the greasy, hairy-armed man said as he took one end of the cooler by its handle. "Two coolers of ice? Just for you, eh?" His lips were chapped and his hair matted. "You all by yourself?" Rebecca's heart thumped forcefully like a wild animal trying to escape her chest cavity. The man smirked and looked over at his partner. "I think this little kitty cat's all alone." His emaciated, methed out partner jumped up and clasped his hands together. His head whipped from side to side scanning for possible witnesses.

"Just take it," Rebecca said, her voice trembling.

"If you say so," he said, forcing himself into the backseat, pushing her against the first cooler. Under the man's weight, Rebecca could not muster enough breath to scream. He licked her neck and she shuddered with disgust. The bolt pistol, which was tucked into the back of her pants was pressing into her sacrum. Rebecca reached behind her and found its grip. She slid it out and pressed it into the sweaty perpetrator's ribcage. He backed away from her as she steadied her aim squarely between his fear-stricken eyes. He backed himself out of the car with his hands up and tripped over the second cooler on the ground. Rebecca closed the door and gave the voice command to lock the doors and return to the meeting spot. The car rolled away leaving the ice-filled cooler in the Esso parking lot. Rebecca looked back at the men rolling the cooler away and breathed a sigh of relief. And then she began to cry.

She returned with one cooler less than she brought with her. Miguel still wouldn't make eye contact after she returned —still angry. She had to admit he deserved to be and resigned to give him as much space as he needed, even though she desperately craved the comfort of his embrace after her encounter at the Esso. The tension must have been evident. Esther kept looking back and forth between them with that knowing expression of hers.

"You guys alright, sweetheart?" she asked as she helped her carry the cooler to the trailer. Rebecca nodded unconvincingly. "Let's talk later," Esther suggested. Esther was observant and a bit nosey. She was also warm and motherly and had a habit of giving unsolicited advice. "Where's the other one?"

"I'm sorry!" Rebecca said. "These guys came up on me and I was just so freaked out and I left it, I'm sorry!"

"Are you okay? What happened?"

"I'm fine, I'm fine," Rebecca assured her. She already felt like a huge burden and they hadn't even left. Of all the crew, Rebecca had the least amount of survival experience. She knew she would be dependent upon everyone else for her very survival. It occurred to her that she'd always needed protection and had to rely on others, usually men, to keep her safe. She hated to admit it and didn't want to give the impression right off the bat that she would need to be carried and protected. Rebecca handed the gun back to Esther. "Thanks. It came in handy."

"Oh dear. I should have gone with you. I'm sorry, hon."

"Don't be. I need to learn to take care of myself."

Esther squeezed her arm gently and looked her in the eye. "We need to take care of each other."

SYLVIA ARRIVED at the back end of an abandoned industrial complex facing an open field. The highway spanned the horizon in the distance. The sun hid forgivingly behind a blanket of cloud cover as it retired quietly from its daily burdens. Clemens waved her over to where the men worked diligently rigging some kind of harness system made entirely of ratchet tie-downs. When she closed the door, the CPG vehicle she'd arrived in reversed and left the premises to wherever Clemens had programmed it to go.

Esther approached. "Oh, honey! Come here." Esther wrapped her arms around Sylvia. "I am so, so sorry, dear." Esther held Sylvia several seconds longer than she felt comfortable. Sylvia was not the touchy-feely type. If it were anyone else, she might have pushed her away. But because it was Esther, the Sergeant's wife, she yielded to her embrace with a rigid posture, hands down by her sides. "You let me know if you need anything at all," Esther said. "I'm here for you. We all are."

"Thanks." Sylvia patted her awkwardly with one hand

on Esther's back. This was not the time for mourning. She had already cried in the car. Sylvia was eager to get moving. "I'll be fine. What's the plan? How can I help?"

"We just need to make sure all this is packed tightly and then we should be ready to go," Esther said. "Could you give Rebecca a hand there?"

Rebecca rubbed Sylvia the wrong way. Women like her usually did. Growing up, Sylvia wasn't into the same kinds of things other girls her age were into. She wasn't interested in who liked who or what the latest fashion trends were. She didn't put much effort into her appearance either. She kept her hair short out of practicality and she dressed for the outdoors. She always had a hard time identifying with women like Rebecca, who always seemed prepared for the runway or a camera.

Sylvia didn't know whether Rebecca knew anything about her history with Miguel, which is partly why she avoided conversation with her. Not that Sylvia felt she had done anything wrong, since the encounter between she and Miguel occurred on New Year's Eve, nearly two months prior to Rebecca's arrival. It wasn't so much that she didn't want Rebecca to know she had slept with her boyfriend in the past but she simply didn't want to talk about it. She didn't do "girl talk" and wasn't interested in giving her take on what she considered a one-time thing.

Miguel was undoubtedly an attractive man—tall, muscular, chiseled features, intense brown eyes. Any woman would agree. But unlike other women, Sylvia had no designs of pursuing any kind of relationship with Miguel. Moderately intoxicated and lacking her usual inhibitions, Sylvia simply succumbed to his attentiveness toward her that night in a moment of loneliness, which occurred from time to time. She neither cherished the encounter, nor regretted it—the physical act, that is. She did have regrets about how she left it.

When she woke up in his bed the next morning, she could smell coffee brewing and heard him in the kitchen making breakfast. She dressed herself quickly and considered leaping out the window instead of having to walk through the kitchen in order to leave through the front door like an adult. When she finally made her way into the kitchen, he asked, "Will you stay for breakfast?"

"No, I have to get going . . . uh, maybe next time."

"*Next* time?" He said with a grin.

"No, I mean . . . *another* time." She felt flush and he was still grinning in that irresistible and infuriating way. "Not that I'm saying there should be another time, exactly. I mean, I don't expect there to be another time, but you know . . ." She was babbling now. "If it's morning and there's breakfast—" His grin faded into a look of confusion. "I gotta go." And she left.

To preserve her dignity, the next day at the station, she pretended nothing had happened. He made an attempt or two to engage her in casual conversation around the office, but she always found an excuse to leave or change the subject. This was her way of bringing homeostasis to their professional relationship. As far as she was concerned, Miguel probably thought about it as little as she did six months later, especially given the company he now found himself blessed with. She hoped it was of little consequence to him that he would have no reason to bring it up with his current girlfriend.

James, carrying two Kevlar vests, approached the women

awkwardly. "Um, my dad wants us all to wear these." James handed Sylvia and Rebecca each a vest, somehow managing to avert his eyes.

"Thank you, Jimmy," Rebecca teased playfully and snickered as the boy scurried away. She looked over at Sylvia as if trying to make some kind of connection and break the tension, but Sylvia was not amused and pretended not to notice. *This is going to be exhausting*, she thought.

The sun lowered toward the horizon, setting the sky ablaze in orange and pink bands. As Sylvia secured and adjusted the newly fashioned harness to her torso and shoulders, Sergeant Clemens addressed the group. "Listen up. Once we get across this field, we'll be crossing the 101 at the midpoint between the two checkpoints. I can't guarantee we won't encounter some danger before getting out of the city. We'll need to keep our eyes and ears open. Once we make it to the river, we should be mostly out of harm's way. We're officially family now. You can count on me to have your back. And I'm counting on you to have mine. Any questions?" Sylvia had a million questions but didn't ask a one. After a long silence, "Alright then. Let's move out."

Sylvia's heart jumped up into her throat. *Are we really doing this?* The trailer was heavier than she thought it would be. The sound of artillery jostling within metal chests as they traversed over ruts and grooves in the fallow terrain felt conspicuously loud over the sporadic and distant whoosh of cars along the highway up ahead. When they arrived at the edge of the field, only a sagging barbwire fence hung between the highway and the gang of defectors. Clemens used wire cutters to snip through the fence and pulled it back so they could safely pass through onto the shoulder.

The traffic was sparse along the four-lane highway but it moved fast. They positioned themselves in the shoulder of the highway and waited for two cars to pass before sprinting toward the median. The trailer moved much more smoothly over the asphalt but by the time they reached the median, the trailer had built up enough momentum that it didn't stop when the crew stopped pulling. It pushed Sylvia and Esther into Miguel and Rebecca, who stumbled into Clemens and James, who nearly pushed Dutch into oncoming traffic. A horn blared and trailed off as the car passed, narrowly avoiding a sure fatality. After a semi barreled past, they hauled ass to the other side, but this time stayed ahead of the trailer and allowed the terrain to slow it down.

As they passed through ramshackle residential neighborhoods in the twilight, people watched curiously from their windows and front porches. Some might wave or nod, silently giving their consent. Others seemed less approving. Sylvia pulled the hood of her field jacket down over her face knowing it had been widely broadcasted to all of Winnipeg. One phone call would have been a death sentence, both for her and her co-conspirators who were aiding and abetting her escape. Sylvia thought about her father, her tears concealed by the darkness. She was devastated and terrified, yet she had no other options. There was no turning back now.

They took back roads up through farmland, where they would begin traveling alongside the river. The trailer pulled smoothly on paved roads but once they took it off-road, the load would shift and bounce, making it difficult to maintain a steady tension in the gangline. The harness was digging into Sylvia's shoulders. With some adjustments to the load and generally having to slow down, they were able to moderately reduce the amount of jerking and bouncing. By midnight they had only made it as far as the northeastern suburb of East St. Paul.

Sylvia was exhausted and hungry. She didn't know how long Clemens was expecting them to travel that night and she didn't feel it was her place to ask. She was relieved when they arrived at a public park.

"I say we make camp here," Clemens announced. "We have a better vantage here than in some abandoned building. Leave the tents. That way it'll be easier to pack up and get going before sunrise. I want to be out of this town before the first light of day."

Esther heated a bag of soup over a camping stove and divided meager portions into paper cups. It wasn't a lot but it was enough to warm her stomach after the long trek. When she finished, Sylvia unrolled her sleeping back over the soft grass. The weather was mild, so she didn't get inside it but stretched out on top fully clothed. The hard ground felt good against her sore back.

Sylvia couldn't sleep. Crickets chirped incessantly. Every sound reminded her of footsteps and every time she closed her eyes she saw the clean hole in her father's forehead. The look on his face, his open jaw, kept surfacing in her mind the harder she tried to shut it out. When sobs bubbled up, she wrestled them back down, but she couldn't stop the tears from welling. She was grateful that the darkness hid her grief from the others. It wasn't their problem anyway.

At 4:40 a.m. gunshots cracked through the still sky and Sylvia instinctively covered her head. The others were torn from their slumber and didn't bother to investigate the origin of the gunfire before packing up. By 4:47 a.m., they were packed, harnessed, and back on the trail. Within an hour, the natural cloak of darkness was beginning to give way to the exposing light of day. Sylvia hadn't slept at all.

"Do you hear that?" asked James. They stopped. The distinct buzz of a drone could be heard flying in the distance. The CPG made use of surveillance drones to patrol the neighborhoods. "There!" James cried, pointing in the direction of the small craft roughly a city block away.

Dutch cocked his sniper rifle and took it down in one shot.

"Nice shot!" Clemens said.

"Do you think it saw us?" Sylvia asked.

"I don't know but they'll know the location it went offline. They'll be in pursuit now. We gotta go." The troop picked up the pace and kept their eyes and ears peeled.

At one point along the river, they were in plain view of Highway 204, where they'd easily be spotted by anyone driving by. The troop had no choice but to keep moving, and quickly. Sylvia breathed heavily as they finally made it to where the highway veered east and out of sight. The sound of the river to their left grew louder as their distance from the road increased. Morning dew covered the tall grass, which reached Sylvia's knees. She looked behind her and noticed the conspicuous path the trailer had carved out through the grassy meadow. Up ahead, she could see an old farmhouse through the trees.

CHAPTER 10

FARMHOUSE: CLEMENS

"GET DOWN!" Clemens ordered. Everyone tried as best they could to conceal themselves in the tall grass. If they could see the house, whoever was inside could see them, too. He used thermal binoculars to detect any human activity anywhere on the property. "It looks pretty old," Clemens said. "I don't think anyone's been here in a really long time. Looks safe enough. Come on. I think we can hide out here for a bit."

A weathered wood barn, once painted red, slouched a short distance from the main house. Several of its slats had fallen or hung loose against its sides and its roof caved inward. They pulled the trailer into the barn to keep it out of sight and cautiously entered the main house, floorboards protesting under their weight. It must have been abandoned for decades judging by the amount of dust and cobwebs.

"Dutch, could you set up surveillance?" Clemens said, wiping the heel of his hand across the grimy front windows.

"On it," Dutch replied.

"Rest up!" Clemens advised. "Let's have some breakfast and then we need to keep moving." He didn't expect the

Guard to pursue anything beyond the East St. Paul city limits, but they were still too close for comfort. He wanted to get as far away from Winnipeg as possible in the first couple of days.

James plopped onto a recliner and a plume of dust rose, forcing him to cough and rub his eyes. His mother stood over him with her hands on her hips. When he opened his eyes again he startled at her admonishing stare.

"Would you like to offer your seat to any women present?" she asked scornfully.

"Sorry, mom." He said and began to get up.

"Not me," she whispered, softly swatting his elbow and gesturing with her head toward Rebecca who stood near the window stretching her hamstrings.

"Oh. I'm sorry. Would you like a seat, ma'am?" he asked Rebecca.

"No, you're fine. Just don't call me *ma'am*. I'm not that much older than you."

Clemens, watching the interaction from across the room, shook his head inconspicuously. James had always been inexperienced in social protocols with women. James looked to his father, presumably for any hints. Clemens grinned and shrugged.

"Go ahead and rest, son. I'll fix us a little breakfast," Esther announced and made her way into the kitchen. The stovetop was inoperable, so Esther scrambled eggs on a portable induction cooktop she unloaded from the trailer. She had obtained the fresh eggs from her chickens back home and started in on how they each had unique personalities and how it broke her heart to leave them behind. Real eggs were a kind of luxury since the meat industry had collapsed years ago. She handed out spoonfuls of scrambled eggs on paper plates with pre-sliced lab-grown apples and individual cold-brew coffee pouches.

As they scarfed down the meager helpings an alert sounded from the surveillance system Dutch had set up.

"What is it?" Clemens asked. He, Miguel, and Sylvia all rushed over to where Dutch had stationed himself at the front window to see what the surveillance screen had picked up.

Dutch scanned for activity through high-powered binoculars. "I see something." he announced. "Drone."

"Dammit! This was a trap!" Clemens exclaimed. Once the drones confirmed their presence, it would be no time before the CPG arrived--armed. All their artillery, including the laser cannon, was still in the barn. The Guard would no doubt search the house first. "Everybody, get back to the barn!"

"At the rate they're approaching, they'll be here in . . . less than two minutes," Dutch calculated.

They must have triggered an alert to the CPG in East St. Paul when he entered the house. He'd heard about a once commonly used strategy for trapping refugees looking for shelter, but it wasn't anything they'd ever concerned themselves with back in Winnipeg, where they dealt mostly with inner city matters. The CPG would find abandoned properties to lure refugees and installed triggers on the doors and windows that would alert them to an entry.

By the time the drones had arrived the troop had relocated to the barn loading weapons and assembling the newly acquired laser cannon. None of them had ever fired one before in this compact form. Miguel consulted the manual as he tried to ready the cannon. It required charging before use, which nobody had even considered. It was connected to an external charger and the charging progress indicator lit the first of ten bars. One blast from this particular model would have taken out the SUV entirely, but until it was fully charged, it would be useless.

The drone hovered in front of each window, scanning the interior for activity. Heat sensors would detect hot spots where people may have made contact with the walls or furniture. There was no doubt now that CPG were in pursuit.

"Miguel," Clemens said, "You got that thing activated?"

"Still charging," he replied. "Two bars."

"Ah, to hell with it. Listen," Clemens said. "We've done this a hundred times. We know their moves because they're our moves, alright? That puts us one step ahead. They're coming straight through that front door. We're going to flank the house on all sides and ambush them from outside in." He handed his wife a plasma rifle. She expertly loaded a new cartridge and slapped it tight. "Just in case. If all goes as planned, they won't even know you're here."

Clemens looked at Rebecca and gave an assuring nod. She had been wringing her hands and pacing the dirt floor, trying to stay out of the way. She nodded back and crossed her arms to stop herself from fidgeting.

They watched as an SUV barreled down the highway in their direction as they donned their Kevlar vests. It slowed as it approached the dirt road and turned left onto the property. A dusty cloud rose behind the SUV as it approached the house. Clemens steadied his breath to decrease his heart rate. He hadn't been in the field for many years now, but the instinct to exude strength and confidence to his team and to his family had not left him.

"I count four . . . five men," Dutch said, looking through binoculars.

"We got this," Clemens said. "Miguel! Sylvia! Head around to the northeast corner of the main house."

"Yes, sir," they clapped back and ran stealthily to their post.

"Dutch, take the southeast corner and make your way around to the front," commanded Clemens.

"Yes, sir."

The SUV came to a sudden stop at the end of the driveway and five men with assault rifles piled out. Two climbed the porch steps and entered through the front_door. The other three flanked the main house on either side. The barn was located on the southwest side of the property, where Clemens had a clear view of the SUV parked in front of the main house as well as the back door.

Four consecutive shots rang out. "Stay here!" Clemens commanded his son. "Do *not* leave this barn." He looked him directly in the eye for confirmation, and then to Esther who put an arm around her son and nodded. Clemens ran toward the backside of the house. He made it to the back deck and crouched down with his back to the dilapidated latticework along the decking. He gave a thumbs up to his son back in the barn, who had a look of terror in his eyes.

Clemens heard two more rounds at the front of the house. He needed to get eyes on his team. As he stood, he felt a crippling sting in his right shoulder that spun him back to the ground. The burn radiated to his fingertips and up to his neck. The shot must have come from the back door.

He heard his son call out "Dad!" Clemens winced in pain and motioned for him to stay where he was. Esther held him back. Clemens activated a fusion grenade and tossed it back over his head with his left hand toward the back door, which electrified the entire deck on impact. Clemens pulled himself up and ran to the northwest corner and around the side of the house where Miguel lay unconscious.

"Miguel!" Clemens checked his pulse. He was alive. He'd been shot in the chest. The slug remained embedded in his Kevlar vest. After slapping his face and shaking him a bit, Miguel came to. Clemens helped him to sit up against the house and placed his weapon in his hands. "Stay put."

Clemens ran around to the front of the house where he saw Sylvia enter through the front door. Two men lay dead on the front porch with clean holes in their foreheads. It must have been Dutch who took these two out. Clemens entered the front door and locked eyes with Sylvia who was crouched in the galley kitchen. She pointed in the direction of the den.

Clemens nodded and motioned for her to approach through the kitchen as he made his way down the hallway, dripping fresh blood onto the wood floors. When he got to the den, he braced himself against the wall with his sidearm raised. He took a deep breath and pivoted into the room with his gun pointing to every corner of the room.

He heard two more shots ring out and he made his way down the hall where Sylvia had taken out another trying to escape through the back door. Another man lay stunned from the fusion grenade blast. When she saw him move, she reflexively shot him in the head. She stood there breathing heavy and staring at the man's blood pooling and soaking into the thin rug underneath him. Clemens tried to remember if she had ever killed anyone in the line of duty, and then realized this would be her second kill in a twenty-four hour period.

"Syl, you okay?" Clemens whispered.

"Huh?" Sylvia asked as if coming out of a trance. "Yeah. I'm fine."

Dutch came in through the front door. Clemens motioned up to the second floor and they made their way up the stairs. By his count, there was only one left. When he arrived at the bedroom, which sat above the front porch awning, the window was open. He heard a thud where the last man had jumped off the awning onto the ground. Clemens ran to the window to see the last man get up with a limp and hobble toward the SUV.

Clemens' view was obstructed by a large oak tree, and he wasn't flexible enough to crawl through the open window, especially with an injured shoulder. He called to the others to get back downstairs and then heard a huge explosion outside. Clemens flinched and covered his head instinctively.

"I got him," came his son's voice from outside. He ran back to the window to see the SUV fall back down onto its side with flames pouring out of the hood.

"Woah! This thing is awesome!" James cried. Another explosion. Celebratory hollers erupted from the front porch where the others had convened.

A wave of dizziness came over him in that moment and he had to steady himself on the railing, which he held tightly to as he descended the stairs. His shoulder was bleeding through his shirt and onto the floorboards. James and Esther rushed in and met him halfway up the stairs and helped him the rest of the way down.

"Careful," Esther said. "Go slow now." They laid him

down on the living room couch. Esther assessed his wound and cleaned it with saline from the med kit. Luckily the bullet had cut straight through the muscle. It was less of a hole than a horizontal slice into his shoulder, which only required eight stitches to close up. Clemens refused anything stronger than Lidocain for the procedure itself and Taminol for the residual pain.

"That's not going to be strong enough, dear," Esther said.

"I don't want to feel drowsy," Clemens said. "We need to get back on the road."

"I swear. When it comes to taking medication, you can be stubborn as a mule."

"I'll be fine." Clemens tried to put his shirt back on and winced.

"Here. Let me help you," Esther said, shaking her head. After threading his arm through the sleeve, Clemens pulled the shirt down over his torso and tried to stand.

"Slow," Esther said, helping him to his feet.

The others were all standing in a cluster on the other side of the room, apparently trying to give him a modicum of privacy.

"Well? What are we all standing around for?" Clemens said. "Let's get moving!"

CHAPTER 11

JUST A SCRATCH: MIGUEL

IT WAS late June and temperatures got fairly warm during the day. Summers were getting warmer and warmer each year. Miguel powered through the mid-day sun, sweat dripping from his brow. The pain in his chest from the impact of the gunshot radiated along his ribcage. He worried he might have a broken rib. Thanks to the body armor, at least he wasn't dead. With each step, the pain intensified as the adrenaline from the battle faded. He adjusted the harness so that it didn't bear so much weight across his chest.

He could hear Clemens in front of him, grunting every few steps as he dealt with his own fresh wound. He kept an eye on Clemens' right sleeve to make sure blood didn't seep through the bandage. Although he was an older man, Miguel viewed the Sergeant as a powerful commander—invincible. It saddened him to see him in such pain.

Miguel wondered if the Guard would send additional men to hunt them down. Or would they cut their losses and look the other way? Perhaps they saw it as a waste of resources with the water crisis in full swing. It was impossible to make that call, but either way, he remained vigilant.

He caught Rebecca, walking directly to his right, glancing at him from time to time. He could feel her gaze but refused to return it. Although he longed for the comfort in that look of concern, he denied her the satisfaction of providing it. The debt she had incurred through her careless infidelity was too great to be absolved with sympathy. He knew it was childish but struggled to find a more constructive way to mend his injured ego.

"Are you okay?" Rebecca finally asked, reaching out to touch his shoulder.

"I will be," Miguel said without looking in her direction.

"Does it still hurt?" Her voice filled with compassion.

"A little. I'll be alright."

She touched his shoulder again and when he looked at her, she mouthed the words: *I love you.*

He wanted to believe her more than anything. Normally, he would have reciprocated that *I love you*, but instead, simply nodded. He wasn't ready to let go of his lingering resentment. Hanging onto it didn't feel great either.

"How you holding up, Sarge?" Miguel asked, in attempt to push away the burden of his romantic troubles.

"Ah, it's just a scratch! We're damn lucky, ya know?" Clemens said. "It could have been a lot worse."

"Yes, sir." Miguel knew Clemens was playing down the pain. He'd incurred bullet wounds before and knew first hand it was nothing to scoff at. But he appreciated the way Clemens always found a way to put a positive spin on things. They were alive and that was indeed something to be grateful for.

"If we can make it to Lockport in the next couple of hours," Clemens said loud enough for everyone to hear. "I know a guy who owns a restaurant there."

"How are we going to pay?" Miguel asked. Their crypto wallets could only be accessed through online accounts, and they had all left their holospecs behind, knowing they could be traced.

"Ammo," Clemens said. "That's another reason we brought so much of it." Firearms of any kind were illegal in CPG controlled territories, but the black market proved to be stronger than ever, especially when it came to personal protection.

"Are we ever going to get online again?" James asked. It couldn't have been easy for a kid to get ripped away from his friends and his whole life like that, without any notice. Even so, he hadn't complained or shown any signs of resentment towards his parents. He seemed to be taking it all in stride.

"As soon as we get settled, we'll create new accounts. But not until we know we're safe," Clemens said.

"Can they trace our crypto accounts?" Esther asked.

"No," Dutch said. He hadn't muttered a word since they left the farmhouse. He was busy monitoring a reconnaissance drone a kilometer ahead of them to make sure the coast was clear. "Crypto is untraceable."

"Well, that's a relief," Esther said.

Miguel had worked alongside Dutch on a number of missions, but he realized they hadn't ever gotten too personal. Miguel knew Dutch had fought in the special forces, which was all he ever really talked about. But after that, before he started working for the CPG, he was a mercenary—a paid assassin. Miguel wondered how many people he'd killed for money. It's not something you just come right out and ask a person, and definitely not a person as big as Dutch.

"Hey Dutch," Miguel said. "What are you going to tell everyone when you get back? You know they're going to ask where you've been."

"I'll tell them it's none of their damn business," Dutch said.

"That's it? What if they put two and two together and ask about us? You think everyone will think it's just a coincidence that we all left at the same time? You don't think people will be suspicious?"

"It's not up to me to know or care about what people think."

"So that's it? You'll just say it's none of their business?"

"Yep."

Miguel knew he wouldn't get much more from him. A part of him worried Dutch could be bribed into giving away their location. After all, he did join their crew for a paycheck. He didn't know the details of his financial arrangement with Clemens, but he assumed the CPG had unlimited bribery funds at their disposal. He didn't have much confidence that Dutch wouldn't sell them out in the end.

"How do you plan to get back to Winnipeg?" Miguel asked.

"I'm CPG," Dutch said. "I'll commandeer a vehicle."

"Right." Not exactly ethical, Miguel thought, but it was within his rights as an officer. Their badges came with advantages Miguel often took for granted. They could own firearms, for one, regardless of where they originated. In many ways, they were above the law and that fact was made clear with how so many officials got away with such nefarious illegal activities, including the ways in which they enabled human trafficking.

They walked in silence for the next half hour. The sounds of footsteps and labored breathing were all that could be heard. The soreness in Miguel's chest had abated somewhat, making way for the burning in his thighs and calves. He felt his vitality fading in the mid-day sun.

THEY ARRIVED in Lockport two hours later, sun-drained and famished. Lockport wasn't much more than a glorified rest stop, but that's exactly what they needed—rest. As they approached the town center, they arrived at an abandoned boatyard and pulled the trailer into an empty bay. Everyone took a moment to hydrate and catch their breath.

"Gaffer's is just up this road," Clemens said. "Who's hungry?" Six hands rose.

Most of the businesses along the main thoroughfare were boarded up and appeared to be long deserted. Gaffer's was no different except for the open sign in the window. Blue paint peeled in sheets from the clapboard siding. The rooftop sign, which took the shape of a large fish, laid facedown in the parking lot. Someone, presumably Gaffer, had placed traffic cones around its corners. Clemens wondered how long it had been laying there.

His reticence faded the moment he stepped inside the air-conditioned establishment. The interior of the restaurant boasted a nautical theme with rope nets hanging from the ceiling, large fish were mounted on the walls along with oars, life preserver rings, and a massive Canadian flag. It was surprisingly clean and well-maintained, which was unexpected based on its crumbing exterior. He could hear music coming from the kitchen, as if played from a portable speaker rather than the house system.

"Gaff??" Clemens called out. "Anyone here?"

An older gentleman, around Clemens' age but much more weathered, pushed through the swinging kitchen door into the lobby, drying his hands with a towel before flinging it back onto his shoulder. He wore a soiled white apron over an equally soiled white t-shirt. A nest of curly grey hair protruded from a red beanie and faded tattoos adorned his forearms. "Daryl Clemens? Is that you?"

A smile reached across Clemens' face. "Gaffer!" Clemens embraced the old man. "It's good to see you."

"Esther! How are you?" Gaffer asked her.

"Hungry!" Esther enthused with a pleasant smile.

"We'll sure fix that!" Gaffer looked to James. "This must be little Jimmy." James held out his hand and Gaffer shook it. "You were just a baby last time I saw you." Gaffer observed the others standing silently in the lobby. "This your entourage?" Gaffer asked with a raise of an eyebrow.

"Yeah, this is my crew." Clemens pointed at each as he called their name. "Miguel, Rebecca, Dutch, and Sy—" Sylvia shook her head quickly. "Uh, Sue," Clemens stammered, recalling that Sylvia was wanted for murder throughout Canada.

Gaffer nodded to the group. "Well, how have you folks been? What are you doing up this way, eh?"

"'Bout to eat some of Manitoba's best fish, I reckon,"

Clemens said, not wanting to give away too much information. "How's business?"

"Ah, it's not great," said Gaffer a bit solemnly. "It's a ghost town here lately. I got too much product. Can't move it. Everyone's either fleeing or dying!"

"I'm sorry to hear that," said Clemens sincerely.

"It's alright. At least I get to go fishing every day, eh?" Gaffer laughed. Gaffer was one of those guys who could always see the bright side.

"Can't beat that, I suppose," Clemens replied.

"I heard about Winnipeg. I take it you're flying the coop?"

"What?" Clemens asked nervously.

"Ah, come on Daryl, if I were you, I wouldn't stay either. You're doing the right thing. And don't worry. My lips are sealed."

"Thanks, Gaff. I'd appreciate that. Listen, I'd love to catch up, but my guys are starving! What's fresh today?"

"Just got a haul of jumbo crab legs. That's thirty units per pound. The usual catch is ten. Rainbow trout, walleye, northern pike. All caught this morning."

"Hey Gaff?" Clemens stepped closer to Gaffer and lowered his voice. "You willing to do a little trade? Ammo for fish?"

Gaffer looked toward the front doors and back to Clemens. "You got any plasma cartridges?"

"Sure thing." This was a generous offer since a box of plasma cartridges went for two hundred units on the black market.

"You got yourself a deal," Gaffer said with a wide grin.

Clemens turned to Esther and the group. "Rainbow trout

sound good to everyone?" Everyone nodded. "Let's get five . . . make that six pounds of the rainbow trout."

"Rice? Veggies?"

"The works."

"You got it! Make yourselves comfortable. Sit anywhere you like." Gaffer clapped his hands and returned to the kitchen.

Miguel and Dutch pushed two tables together and they all sat. It was a relief to be off their feet and in the air conditioning. Esther rolled up Clemens' sleeve and examined his arm.

"The stitches seem to be holding," she said. "Any pain?"

"Oh, just a little." Clemens was playing down his discomfort. "It's not too bad."

"Here. Take two more of these." She procured a bottle of Taminol from her satchel, and he took the pills without protest.

"Listen," Clemens started. "We've been through a lot already. I want to say how proud I am of all of you. I know I've been pushing you hard, but we had to get as far away as fast as we possibly could. We still have a ways to go, but look how far we've come. Nobody thought we could make it out and here we are! The worst is behind us now. Let's just take a few moments to enjoy this. You sure as hell earned it."

Gaffer sprung forth from the kitchen with two large trays of food and a wide-eyed smile on his face.

"Here you are, folks! I threw in some of those jumbo crab legs in there for ya, free of charge. Oh! Hold on . . ." Gaffer went back to the kitchen and came back out with two ice-cold six-packs of Moosehead Pale Ale. "On the house! Haha!"

Everyone joyfully tore into their feast and laughter began

to fill the dining room. James was eyeing the beer cans as his dad pulled them off one at a time and passed them around.

"What? You want one?" Clemens asked his son.

"I mean, uh, yeah? I mean . . . if that's okay," the boy stammered. He glanced sheepishly at his mother.

"I think you earned it, son!" Clemens announced proudly. "The way you fired that laser cannon. God damn! What do you all think, eh?"

"Cheers!" they cried as they raised cold cans. James proudly cracked open his first beer and took a large gulp. He immediately choked, holding his arm to his mouth to keep from spraying beer on everyone. More laughter erupted as they patted his back and welcomed him into their ranks.

WITH FULL BELLIES and raised spirits, the troop pushed on. They arrived in Selkirk three hours later, around dusk. It was a sleepy town with less than four thousand residents, large enough that the CPG maintained a presence there, mainly at checkpoints but otherwise drone-patrolled. Although they were well-hidden by trees along the bank of the river, Sylvia grew anxious.

"I hear traffic," Sylvia said.

"We're getting close to town," Clemens said. "We'll need to keep our wits about us. Once we get to LeBlanc's place, we'll be safe."

"Who's LeBlanc?" Sylvia asked. This was the first she'd heard they'd be meeting up with anyone outside the group. As far as she was concerned, anyone in the group might be liable to turn her in. For five thousand units, why wouldn't a complete stranger?

"He's an old military buddy. We served two tours together," explained Clemens. "Then he got promoted and I finished out my service. He went on to work in intelligence with CSIS. He's mostly retired now. Hell of a guy. He's expecting us."

"Does he still make that nasty homemade hooch?" Esther asked.

"Oh, I think he'd say he's perfected it."

"Well, you can count me out!" Esther laughed. "I nearly perished the last time I dared take a swig of that trash." They laughed and after a moment she added, "It's a pity about his wife though."

"Yeah, she was a good one," Clemens recalled.

"What happened," Rebecca asked.

"She got caught in a biochemical attack six years ago," Clemens said.

"Such a pity," Esther repeated.

"Let's take five," Clemens said. "Nature calls."

Clemens walked down near the riverbank. Sylvia sat on a fallen tree trunk and ran her hands through her hair. She rested her elbows on her knees.

"What's wrong, Syl?" Esther asked. She sat next to her.

"Nothing." The truth was Sylvia's heart felt like it was going to beat right out of her chest.

"You don't have anything to worry about. Look at me. Daryl would never put you in any kind of danger. LeBlanc's a good man. You'll see."

"Yeah, well you don't have a bounty on your head," Sylvia said. "Excuse me if I'm a little wary."

"Fair enough. You know, Daryl thinks the world of you. He was disappointed when you told him you couldn't come with us at first. Says he wished more cops were as dependable and courageous as you."

"Right," Sylvia said sarcastically.

"You don't believe me? Well, honey, believe me when I say, if anyone comes for you, you can bet they'll have to get through me first." Esther was one of those tough-as-nails mother hens. Sylvia had heard enough of her tales of growing up in rural Alberta on her father's barley farm before droughts forced them into Calgary, where she got into fist fights with bullies who picked on her two little brothers.

Clemens returned to the group holding up a handheld radio. "Let's saddle up! Good news is most of the Guard here have been dispatched to Winnipeg for reinforcement. Bad news is their drones are still patrolling and we're about to be in violation of the curfew. I think we can make it, but we gotta move."

As they trekked north toward the town, James flew his drone ahead of them to scout for any sign of CPG along their route. Sylvia privately questioned why they weren't bypassing the cities altogether. Was it worth the risk just to catch up with an old friend? But Sylvia was not the kind to openly question her ranking officer. It's how she was raised, and it was how she was trained. She kept her opposition to herself.

When they arrived, she saw an older man sitting in a rocking chair on the front porch as the troop arrived at the ranch. At least, that's how he referred to it. It was mainly a large swath of marshland with a cabin he inherited from his father. LeBlanc was a sixty-year-old tall, wiry man with thinning white hair and a patchy beard. He smiled from ear to ear as they approached pulling the trailer behind them.

"Where's Santa Claus? Ah ha ha ha!" His laugh devolved into a wheezing fit.

"Ha. Ha. Very funny, old man," Clemens said. "Don't hurt yourself, eh?"

After making introductions the troop hid the trailer out back under a tarp and came inside. LeBlanc had a stockpot filled with seafood gumbo he'd been simmering all day. The aroma of seafood and spices hung heavy throughout the house.

"Ya'll make yourselves comfortable. Mi casa, su casa, ya hear?" LeBlanc announced. "I got plenty of gumbo so don't be shy."

"It smells amazing!" Esther said.

"It's a family recipe. Me and my folks migrated from New Orleans after yearly hurricanes put it permanently underwater. My mama used to make this every Sunday in our house growing up. I hope you like the spice."

Terrence LeBlanc seemed sincere. He seemed to make everyone feel welcome and at ease with his lively sense of humor and engaging storytelling. Yet Sylvia remained guarded. LeBlanc and Clemens spent the next couple of hours telling hyperbolic tales from their military days.

"Remember Seattle?" Clemens asked, grinning widely.

"Do I remember?!" LeBlanc replied. "I have the damn scar!" He pulled his shirt collar down to display a two-inch scar below his collar bone. Clemens went on to tell another tale from their glory days. LeBlanc interrupted. "No, no, you're not telling it right. *You* were the one who wanted to meet that waitress after her shift. You're leaving out that very important detail. This was not my idea!"

"Alright, alright, but you wanted to meet her friend. Anyway, so we get to this dive bar in Pioneer Square. And we're not sure it's the right place. We check the address.

Yeah, this is it, right? But the girls aren't there. So Terrence here goes up to the bartender and asks if he's seen her, but neither of us remembered their names. So he's describing this girl to the bartender, right?" LeBlanc held his head in his hands and shook it from side to side. Clemens continued, "Says she's got this tattoo of a hummingbird on her upper thigh."

"Here we go," LeBlanc said.

"And the bartender says, 'You talking 'bout this girl?' And he pulls up his sleeve and has a tattoo of the girl's face on his bicep. Terry's eyes got big as saucers and the bartender goes, 'That's my effing wife!' Only he didn't say 'effing.' And before you know it, the dude has Terrence by his shirt collar and pulls him over the bar and starts wailing on him. So I jump over the bar and we're both trying to take on this guy, but he's like 230, 240, six-foot-four, easy. So we're not faring well, at all . . ."

"No, we did not stand a chance!" LeBlanc interjected.

"So I had a blade on me and I pull it out and take a swipe at the bartender but I miss. He takes two bottles from the shelf and breaks them on the bar like a psycho and we're like, 'Holy crap!' We jump back over the bar and that's when Terrence here got this lovely gash."

"She wasn't even that cute!" LeBlanc hollered. The gang was in stitches, except Sylvia. She had never seen her commanding officer in such a relaxed and jovial mood. Under different circumstances, she might have enjoyed the informal nature of his off- duty banter. Instead, she felt hardened and reticent. The loss of her father weighed heavily on her heart and it was physically impossible to show any sign of contentment.

James had fallen asleep and yawns were circulating the room. "Alright, I guess that's enough spinning yarn for one night," said LeBlanc. "You let me know if you need anything at all. I have two guest rooms made up, and those two couches there pull out. Bathroom's at the end of the hall."

"You're a lifesaver, Terry," said Esther. "Thank you."

"No need. You're family. Any friend of Daryl is family to me," said LeBlanc making eye contact with everyone in the room. "I mean that."

He passed out extra blankets and pillows. Sylvia claimed the couch and turned toward its back to avoid goodnight pleasantries.

THE FAMILIAR DRIP from the coffee machine and the sizzle of bacon entered her consciousness before she opened her eyes the next morning. Sylvia had slept on the couch with all her clothes still on from the day before. Her bolt pistol sat on an end table within reach. She woke up with a thin blanket covering her body, but she didn't remember going to bed with one. Somebody must have covered her while she was asleep and that made her feel uneasy.

James laid sideways in a leather recliner under a throw. Dutch took the pull-out sofa, which struggled to support his weight. Miguel and Rebecca took one of the rooms and Clemens and Esther took the other. Sylvia sat up, cracked her neck, and allowed the smell of coffee to lure her toward the kitchen. Terrence LeBlanc whistled mirthfully while making bacon and homemade waffles. He wore a white apron with a red maple leaf printed on the center pocket. "Good morning, dear," he said cheerily as she shuffled into the kitchen and perched onto a barstool.

"It's morning alright," she grumbled as she poured herself a cup of coffee. "I hope the couch was comfortable enough," LeBlanc said. It wasn't. But Sylvia had too much on her mind to sleep soundly anywhere. Every sound she heard startled her into a mini panic attack. Plus, Dutch snored like a congested rhino.

"So you were like a spy or something?" Sylvia asked and took a sip of coffee.

"Something like that. I'm mostly retired now. They call me in for desk work from time to time. I'm too old for all that 007 shit." He chuckled.

"What do you do around here?"

"You're looking at it, kid." LeBlanc held up his spatula and gave it a spin.

Sylvia nodded slightly, pulling the corners of her mouth in and narrowed her eyes just enough to offer the faintest presence of emotional expression. "You ever get any trouble from CPG?" Sylvia asked.

"No, not out here. They're mostly stationed downtown and at different checkpoints. Long as I pay my taxes, they don't mess with me."

"Sounds nice." There was a lull in the conversation and Sylvia sipped her coffee.

"I heard about your pop," he said. "Daryl filled me in. My condolences."

"Looks like we've all lost people," Sylvia said.

"Yeah. That does seem to be the case here lately. So how long have you lived in Winnipeg?"

"Born and bred."

"Cool. Cool. I moved here with my parents after New Orleans finally got buried. I only have a few memories of it." He chuckled to himself. "I remember going to Mardi Gras one year when I was maybe eight or nine years old. I never seen a lady's breasts before. Funny what sticks with you."

Sylvia accidentally broke a smile.

"Oh, well now! Will you look at that? I don't think I seen you smile since you got here. It's nice."

She ignored his observation. "New Orleans? Was that in the American South?"

"Yeah, it was long gone by the time you got here. Where were you when Canada fell?" This had been a common conversation starter her entire adult life.

"I was still in high school. My dad was on the list to get bionic legs through the VAC, but when the government collapsed, so did his benefits. He took it pretty hard."

"What happened?" LeBlanc seemed genuinely interested.

"He was in solar maintenance and repair. Fell off a roof. He was paralyzed from the waist down. I was fifteen when that happened. I took care of him. I did everything. At the time, I thought it was really unfair. Other kids were going to dances and parties and I was stuck at home, cooking, cleaning, dressing him. He got really depressed. He'd been waiting for two years to get new legs. There was a time there when I was afraid he was going to take his own life so I couldn't leave his side. It was a lot."

"He was lucky to have a daughter like you," LeBlanc said.

Sylvia felt a knot forming in her throat, so she didn't respond.

"Good morning!" Esther said and took a seat at the large kitchen island, her hair still wet from the shower.

Sylvia nodded.

"Good morning!" LeBlanc replied.

"You boys were up pretty late last night," Esther said. Terrence and Clemens had retreated to the back porch after everyone else had gone to bed to sample his newest batch of moonshine.

"Yes, ma'am. It was that husband of yours. He twisted my arm, I swear," LeBlanc chuckled.

"Oh, and I'm sure you put up a big fight," she said jokingly.

"It's so nice to see the two of you. It's been too long."

"Terrence, I'm so sorry about Carol." Her tone turning warm and sincere. "How are you holding up these days?"

"Oh, I still miss her terribly. Not a day goes by I don't think about her. But you know, she told me once that if she ever went first, she'd want me to live my life to the fullest. She made me promise to always look for the beauty hiding in plain sight. So that's what I try to do. Everyday I wake up in this crumbing world and I start looking for the beauty. Some days that's harder to do, but the more you look, the easier it is to find."

"That's a beautiful outlook. She really loved you, Terrence."

"Yes, she did. I don't know what I ever did to deserve it, but she sure did," he said with a big smile.

"I'm sorry we couldn't have been there for you more when it happened."

"It's okay. You're here now and I couldn't be more grateful."

Sylvia sat quietly throughout this rather saccharin exchange, which she felt she had no business being a part of. It would have been rude to get up in the middle. Better to wait it out and hope for a change of subject. Luckily, she was the only one to witness smoke rising from the waffle maker. "Waffles!"

"What?" LeBlanc asked.

"Your waffles are burning!"

"Oh damn!" He tended to his culinary duties. "I never could do more than one thing at a time." He chuckled at himself. "Who ordered well-done?"

Sylvia was caught between a conciliatory smile and a vapid eye roll. The smile was for him. The eye roll was for her, because she smiled. There was something comforting about LeBlanc, something disarming, but Sylvia would not allow herself to be comforted.

CHAPTER 14

COLD SHOULDER: REBECCA

REBECCA SAT UP AND STRETCHED. The guest room was cozy. It reminded her of an Aspen ski lodge, right on down to the bear-carved wooden lamps and the moose and pine tree printed curtains and throw pillows. She looked over at Miguel who had slept facing away from her the whole night. He had fallen asleep quickly the night before, so they hadn't had a chance to check in. She was starting to feel impatient with the cold shoulder but also felt responsible for creating this situation in the first place.

Rebecca reflected on her transgressions with Malcom. She had no feelings for him whatsoever. She never did and acknowledged that she was only using him to pass the time. She wasn't attracted to him and wasn't particularly satisfied with the sex. It was the thrill of getting away with it that drove her to continue down that path. *What is wrong with me?* she thought. *Why am I like this? So selfish.* She'd made similar mistakes in previous relationships, but none mattered all that much to her. Miguel didn't deserve this. He was a good man—the only good man she had ever been serious with.

The man she was with prior to Miguel was a billionaire from Chicago. He was also married, which didn't bother her as much as it should have. She didn't love him anyway, but the lifestyle he bestowed upon her was enough to keep her interested. He showered her with gifts and vacations. She had gained a certain amount of notoriety in her own right as a model, which is how she found herself among the elite. It was fun for a year or so, but there was no real substance between them and eventually, she got bored.

That was her problem, Rebecca realized—boredom. She was always in search of the next adventure. And this is exactly what happened with Miguel. Once she was safe in his protective bubble, there would be no more adrenaline-fueled escapades. If she had only known that escaping the city illegally would be in her very near future, she wouldn't have bothered with Malcom. He wasn't worth it. Look where boredom got her this time. She was determined to make it right. Miguel began to stir.

"Do you want some coffee?" Rebecca whispered. The smell had now reached them from the kitchen.

Miguel sat up and groaned. "I'll get it."

"How's your chest?" Rebecca asked with that look of pained concern.

"It's better today." He raised his left arm and rotated his shoulder. "Still sore but it's getting better."

"Miguel," she said. She got up and grabbed her pants off an armchair and reached into the back pocket. "I didn't have anything to write with, but . . . here." She managed a cautious smile and handed him the empty greeting card she'd taken from the Esso station back in Winnipeg.

Miguel took the card and glanced at the front, then opened it up to the blank inside. "I know," he said flatly and handed it back to her.

Rebecca's face warmed. She felt supremely stupid for making such a hollow gesture. *I should have signed it at least.* "Babe?" she asked cautiously. "Are we going to talk about this?"

"I thought we did," he said. He was sitting on the edge of the bed, his head hung between his shoulders staring down at his feet.

"Yeah. No, I mean . . . like, when are we going to be normal again?"

"I don't think anything is ever going to be normal again."

"Right. But like, you and me. Do you think we'll ever be the same? Do you think we can get back to how it was before?"

"I think it's going to take some time," he said after a moment, not once looking in her direction. "Come on. Get dressed." He stood and picked his pants up off the floor.

"I'm sorry," Rebecca offered.

"You don't have to keep saying that." He finally turned to face her. "I believe you. It's just not enough." He pulled a t-shirt over his head, wincing a bit as his arm extended over-head. "We're just going to have to take it day by day."

It might have been a trite response, but in that moment, day by day was the only thing that made sense anymore. Nothing was ever guaranteed, but especially now. As much as she would have loved to hear platitudes and reassurances, day by day was the only thing that made sense and she was grateful for the honesty. She vowed to make it a good day. She knew she couldn't control anything beyond that.

CHAPTER 15

COURT OF PUBLIC OPINION: CLEMENS

CLEMENS AWOKE before anyone else that morning. He strolled down to the water's edge and felt a heavy sense of duty to protect his family and the men and women in his crew. Early morning sunlight reflected off the surface of the water, which reminded him that a peaceful life was possible. He was eager to get back on the trail but not to part ways with one of his oldest friends. LeBlanc would have urged him to stay an extra day but they were still too close to Winnipeg for comfort.

When he returned to the house everyone seemed to be in better spirits after a good night's rest. LeBlanc was joking with the guys and he even thought he saw Sylvia crack a smile—a rare sighting indeed. Clemens came into the kitchen to pour himself a cup of coffee. When he tried to lift the pot, he winced and involuntarily dropped it onto the stone counter. Luckily, the carafe didn't break but coffee spilled all over.

"Oh! Hon, let me get that!" Esther jumped up to help him. LeBlanc followed her around the kitchen island to assist.

"You alright, Daryl?" LeBlanc asked.

"Yeah. I just made a mess, that's all," Clemens said.

"Just leave it, man. I'll take care of it." LeBlanc said stopping the overflow of coffee onto the floor with a kitchen towel.

"You want me to take a look at that arm?"

"No, it's fine," Clemens said. "Esther stitched it up good. Just hurts a little."

"Let me get you some Taminol," Esther said.

"Taminol?" LeBlanc said. "You gonna need something stronger than that! Hold on, now." LeBlanc disappeared into his bedroom and returned with a pill bottle. "Here. They gave me these when I tore my knee up last year."

"What is it?" Clemens said holding the bottle up to the light. "Hydromethelate. Does it make you sleepy?"

"A little. But you ain't going anywhere. You need to rest anyway."

"Oh, I don't know."

"Daryl, please take it," Esther said. "Let's just see how you feel." She poured some water into his empty coffee cup and placed it in his left hand. She placed the pill in his mouth. "Thank you, Terrence. I swear, this man is so stubborn when it comes to taking medicine."

"I just don't want to feel all loopy, that's all." Clemens didn't like people fussing over him.

"You be alright. It ain't morphine," LeBlanc said. "It'll just take the edge off. What you really need is some of these waffles. Come on now. Before Dutch here has himself a fourth helping."

He joined his crew at the table. Clemens had been ruminating on a plan to strike back at the corrupt Guard who threatened his family and who killed Sylvia's dad. He'd been pondering its details over the last two days and wanted to make sure it was solid before introducing it to the troop. He cleared his throat. "Listen up." The room fell silent. "Now that we're safely out of the city, I think it's time we finish what we started." Clemens said looking directly at Sylvia.

She looked to her right and left and back at Clemens. "What?"

"You worked your ass off trying to expose those bastards and now what, they just get away with it?"

"Yeah, well, what's new?" she said. "What are you getting at?"

"Before we left, I transferred all the trafficking files to this drive." He removed a small device from his shirt pocket. "I say we release it all to the media and expose those bastards. There's enough there to hit 'em pretty hard."

"I don't see how," Sylvia said. "Who are we going to turn them in to anyway? The magistrate himself is in on it."

"Haven't you ever heard of the court of public opinion? The way I see it, the only way anything is ever going to change is if the people rise up. If we can provide solid evidence that their suspicions are true, they're not just going to sit around and take it. There'll be a rebellion. Your hard work could be just the thing to push it over the edge."

"Or get us killed," Sylvia said. Her hands were shaking.

"Yeah. If we played it by the book, you're right. It would have gotten appealed or dismissed, and we'd all pay for it. But isn't that why you're here? Isn't that why we're all here? To get out from under that corrupt machine? Besides, they can't touch us now. What do you say?"

"Accept they can touch us," Miguel said. "We might have

gotten lucky this time, but who knows if they'll decide to pursue this after the water starts running again? Kind of feels like poking the bee's nest."

"I'm telling you," Clemens said, "Winnipeg is on the brink of collapse. Leadership is losing control and they have been for years. It wouldn't take much to push it over the edge."

"I still have to live there," Dutch said. "I'm not sure I want to burn it all down just yet."

"I don't want that either," Clemens said. "What I want is for the people to hold them accountable. It's the only way anything is going to change."

Sylvia grew pale and stood up. "I need some air." She stepped out onto the front porch.

"It's alright," he said to the others after Sylvia was out of earshot. "She's been through a lot. As far as I'm concerned, she did her part."

The CPG killed Sylvia's father. Clemens took some responsibility for that. He knew it was foolish to pursue this from the very start. But now, what more did they have to lose?

After a few minutes, Sylvia walked back in with a look of resolve. Everyone got quiet and turned in her direction. "You're right. What was all this for, anyway? Let's do it. Let's expose the bastards."

The end product was a work of art. They had compiled evidence against a dozen CPG ministers and councilmen, all tied to enabling and even directly funding trafficking operations in the region. They designed interactive graphs and charts to illustrate the flow of payments, all either directly or indirectly linked to Crowe Industries. The ready-to-publish file was sent to the twelve most followed journalists in Winnipeg and other major Canadian cities.

"Hey, are you guys seeing this?" James asked from the living room recliner. He was watching a news report on LeBlanc's holoscreen in the living room.

A reporter stood in front of a burning building in central Winnipeg and reported on the mayhem that continued to devolve overnight. The public reaction to the water crisis stirred up unchecked violence throughout the city. Dead bodies laid in the streets. Gunshots and emergency sirens could be heard in the background. A mass exodus was underway as thousands risked their lives to break the lockdown mandates, which had been implemented in response to ill-contained rioting and looting throughout the city.

"Looks like more refugees may be coming our way," Clemens said. "We probably need to keep moving."

"Where ya'll headed exactly?" LeBlanc asked. "I mean, you must have some idea."

"Potentially. I guess we'll see it when we see it."

"I had an idea, if you don't mind" LeBlanc said.

"Go on."

"Any of ya'll ever been to Churchill?" Churchill, Manitoba perched on the northeast edge of Manitoba on the Hudson Bay, roughly two thousand kilometers from Winnipeg.

"There are no roads to Churchill," Clemens said.

"Exactly. And the railroad's been out of commission for years. Only way to get there these days is by air or sea."

"You have a plane?" Miguel asked.

"No. But I know this guy up in Thompson," LeBlanc said. "Use to be a tour guide up there. Took folks up to see the polar bears before they became extinct. Anyway, he has an arctic rover, big enough for all of you, and he owes me." Thompson was on the north side of Lake Winnipeg. It was the last town in all of northern Manitoba that maintained any sizable community.

"Well, how do you propose we get all the way up to Thompson while avoiding the roads?" Clemens asked.

"I'm glad you asked," LeBlanc said with a toothy smile. "I have a boat. It was my dad's. He bought it second hand from a junker. It was his retirement project to restore it, but he died before he could get it sea-worthy."

"I didn't know you were a boat guy," Clemens said.

"I am now. Listen, if you're looking for a place where nobody can get to you, Churchill has everything you need. It's a ghost town with infrastructure, water, solar, plenty of good fishing and hunting. It's self-contained. Best part about it," he continued, "ain't no Guard up there. In fact, nobody lives up there anymore, besides a handful of First Nation families. You'd basically have the whole town to yourselves."

"That does seem pretty ideal," Clemens said.

"So what do you say?" LeBlanc asked. "Shall I prepare the boat?"

CHAPTER 16

PONTOON: LEBLANC

LEBLANC COMPLETED some last-minute repairs to the newly sea-worthy vessel. The twenty-four-foot fishing pontoon could comfortably seat all eight passengers. However, their gear, food supply, and artillery would have to be balanced across every square inch of the deck to maintain stable weight distribution. He had installed 12" plexiglass barriers around the rails of the boat for additional protection from potential gunfire. The lake wasn't CPG patrolled the way roads were, but looters were everywhere.

The passengers seemed a bit apprehensive at the sight of the decades-old makeshift watercraft. Duct tape held in more of the filling in the original vinyl seating than did its seams. Rust and amateur welding held much of the craft in place. The carpet was hopelessly stained and smelled strongly of mildew. The one element of which LeBlanc was particularly proud was a large wooden plaque bearing the name of his beloved wife, Carol, which he had hand-carved and installed securely onto the boat's stern.

"Well folks, here she is!" LeBlanc said proudly as the

passengers gingerly boarded the pontoon. "I know what you're thinking. She may not look like much, but trust me, she'll get us across the lake."

"You sure this isn't too much weight? You know, with all these guns?" Esther asked as she stepped over crates of ammunition.

"Oh, I'm sure it's fine," replied Clemens, as if trying to convince himself.

LeBlanc's property bordered a small tributary that led into a chain of smaller rivers and lakes before emptying into Lake Winnipeg, the fifth largest Canadian lake spanning 416 km from north to south. With a push of a button, LeBlanc started the two solar-powered EV engines, and they were off. It was quiet as they cruised across the still waters, the sun disappearing beyond the tree line. The sounds of frogs and locust reverberated among the trees. They traveled without lights to maximize their stealth and navigated by satellite.

LeBlanc remained mostly silent as he observed the hushed murmurs from his new crew. Excitement, perhaps some wariness, definitely vigilance, buzzed through the troop with darting eyes, nervous laughter. He was happy to have been reunited with Clemens. They'd fought side-by-side during the Tech Wars and watched the world deteriorate before their eyes. Younger generations never knew what real freedom was. That term had been bastardized and reclaimed by authoritarians who enforced its very opposite. Clemens had always been a loyal friend to LeBlanc and he felt proud of how his life had turned out—beautiful family, respectable career.

The big guy, Dutch, seemed quite knowledgeable on matters of firearms and military strategy. The shear mass of his hulking form made him an intimidating opponent. He could see why Clemens had procured his services.

LeBlanc could sense tension between Miguel and Rebecca. She sat next to him on the starboard side, her arm slid through the crook of his elbow. Miguel remained silent, looking directly away from her. LeBlanc thought if he had a woman like that on his arm, it wouldn't have been possible for him to look away. Although he seemed wound a bit too tight, he could sense Miguel's loyalty to Clemens, which earned him respect in LeBlanc's eyes.

Sylvia was an interesting character. She was pensive and serious. His heart went out to her in light of her recent loss. He understood her vigilance, given the bounty. As a former spy, he knew the feeling. He couldn't quite put his finger on it, but something drew him to her. He wanted to protect her, to look after her in a fatherly way. LeBlanc never had children of his own but imagined this is what it might feel like if he had. He sensed a hidden potential stirring inside her like a heavy cloud amassing before the storm.

For the last hour, he'd been observing silently. A lull in conversation gave LeBlanc the opportunity to continue his game of *Where were you when Canada fell?*

"James, you probably don't remember it at all."

"No," Esther interjected. "He was born the same week our healthcare disappeared. Just our luck!" She laughed. She patted his cheek. "But he was worth it."

"Miguel?" LeBlanc moved on. "How old were you?"

"When was that, 2070? I was what? Nineteen, Twenty? I was still living in San Antonio at that time. The Republic of Texas had already collapsed by then, and the U.S. was well on its way, just a few years after that. I remember not being all that upset about it. I think we all saw it coming, especially after all the oil dried up. The Rangers were pretty much running things anyway, so it wasn't a huge transition."

"I was seven?" Rebecca said eyes directed upward as she calculated in her mind. "All I remember is getting in trouble once for playing outside by myself. I didn't understand because I always used to play outside and one day it wasn't okay anymore. And then at some point, probably that same year, my parents pulled me out of school. After that, I don't remember ever being unsupervised. Not until I started traveling for modeling work."

"None of you guys remember phones, eh?" Clemens chimed in. LeBlanc and Esther chuckled. The younger generations shook their heads. "Before holospecs we used to carry around phones. They were 'bout this big. The whole screen was this big." He demonstrated the size with his fingers. "And you had to charge 'em up every day." Holospecs and similar consumer wearables charged kinetically.

"Were you around when you had to drive your own car?" Rebecca asked.

"I remember when I was a kid, my dad used to have one of those cars," Clemens said. "But by the time I was old enough to drive, they weren't street legal."

"That just seems so dangerous!" Rebecca said.

"I'm pretty sure it was," LeBlanc said. "I think it was like the number one cause of death. When self-driving cars first came out a lot of people were very resistant to getting them."

"Why?" Rebecca asked. "I don't get it! Weren't they tired of dying in car accidents?"

"They didn't trust 'em. You got to remember this was brand new technology and a lot of people were afraid of robots taking over the world. People back then had some pretty cuckoo ideas about things."

"Yeah, like they didn't believe in climate change," James said. "They thought scientists were just making it up or something."

"That was just an excuse," Dutch interjected. "Governments were always reluctant to spend money on things that weren't going to affect them in their lifetimes. And corporations didn't want the governments interfering with their profits. So it wasn't necessarily that they didn't believe the scientists. They just spread that lie to maintain economic and political power."

"Well doesn't that sound familiar?" Esther said. "You'd think they'd learn their lesson after all that's happened. Doesn't seem like much has really changed in that regard."

"Well, that's why we're here," Clemens said. "We're not playing by anyone else's unjust rules anymore. Out here, we say what's what."

"Hear, hear," Miguel said, raising his water bottle.

"Shh, shh!" Sylvia interrupted. "Look!" She pointed in the direction of a smaller fishing boat up ahead. It perched unassumingly in the middle of the still lake like an unflinching predator. Everyone grew silent as the potential danger loomed.

Looking through his binoculars, Clemens identified two fishermen, a father and son presumably. Many fishermen had taken to night-fishing to avoid bandits.

"These guys don't look dangerous," said Clemens.

"But they could be armed," Miguel said. "And if they think we're dangerous, that makes them dangerous."

LeBlanc proceeded slowly and gave them a wide berth.

When the pontoon came into view of the fishermen, the younger one dropped his fishing line and turned to grab a rifle.

"Everyone put your hands in the air!" LeBlanc ordered as the fisherman raised his weapon.

"What?!" exclaimed Miguel and shot Clemens a look.

"Do as he says!" Clemens ordered sternly.

Everyone raised their hands. The boy slowly lowered his rifle as the pontoon passed slowly downriver.

"How did you know he wasn't going to shoot?" Miguel asked once the fishing boat was safely behind them.

"Aw, that boy wasn't gonna shoot nobody. He just wanted to protect his livelihood. I can understand that. Most people don't want to kill nobody. We're all the same, see? We all just want to live our lives and protect what's ours. We just want peace. Unfortunately, we live in a time where peace is something we got to fight for. Now that's messed up, ain't it? Everything's backwards these days. I hope wherever ya'll end up, ya don't have to fight so hard to be at peace."

They remained silent, pondering what LeBlanc had said. Gentle breeze rustling through the tree leaves, the burbling sound of water against the bow, and the occasional creek of the boat were the only sounds to be heard.

CHAPTER 17

A LONG TIME AGO: REBECCA

ANOTHER HOUR HAD PASSED and although it was very late in the evening, nobody was relaxed enough to sleep. Rebecca had been conspiring to get on Sylvia's good side since the beginning of the trip. Miguel wasn't much for conversation after having discovered her affair. He was talking with the guys about things she had no interest in—police stuff, mostly. If things didn't pan out between she and Miguel, she was going to need an ally. Now was as good a time as any to approach her, seeing as how they had vast stretches of lake to cross in the dead of night for who knows how long. She opened a bag of Elk jerky and sat across from Sylvia at the stern of the boat.

"Want some?" Rebecca asked.

Sylvia appeared circumspect. "Sure," she yielded and took a piece.

"I was hoping you and I could get to know each other a little better," Rebecca ventured. She gathered her blonde hair, pulled it to one side and began examining the tips for split ends. "I mean, we're probably going to be stuck together for a while. I mean, not *stuck,* I don't mean it like it's a bad thing." Rebecca was sinking and Sylvia offered no reassurance. Sylvia took another bite of jerky. Maybe it was best if she just cut to the chase.

"Can I be honest?" Rebecca continued, "I've always felt a little intimidated by you. Or maybe, like I've done something to offend you?"

Sylvia raised her eyebrows and shook her head. "I'm not offended," she offered, still working on her previous bite of jerky.

"Oh, good," Rebecca said, not fully satisfied. "Listen, I know you've known Miguel like, forever and you're probably pretty close—"

"It happened one time," Sylvia blurted in a forced whisper, "and it was way before you even got here."

"Wait. What?" Rebecca didn't know what she was talking about.

"What?" Sylvia's face became pale.

"What happened one time?" Rebecca asked.

Sylvia turned her head. "Nothing."

Rebecca turned toward Miguel at the other end of the pontoon, cutting up with Dutch. "Wait. Did you and Miguel …"

"It was a long time ago."

"How long is a long time ago?" Rebecca asked.

Sylvia took forever to answer. "New Year's."

"New Year's, *this* year?"

"It was a drunken mistake, and it didn't mean anything—to either of us."

"Wow," Rebecca said. "He never mentioned it."

"Probably because it wasn't worth mentioning. Are you going to be weird now?"

"No. I'm still trying to wrap my head around it. It's fine. I mean, of course he's had partners before me—"

"We weren't partners," Sylvia reiterated. "Please don't make a big deal out of this."

"I won't. It's cool." Rebecca flipped her hair in a show of confidence, although she was feeling anything but. Why would he keep that from her? Sylvia was fair game at the time. It's not like he'd done anything wrong. Then again, she'd never disclosed her past with Miguel either. She would have talked about it, but it was almost as if he didn't want to know, like he didn't want to spoil his image of her. She was fine with that.

On the other hand, she wasn't traveling across Canada with any of her past lovers. She could see what he might see in her. Sylvia was attractive and cool—like in an action movie femme fatale kind of way. She looked like she could hold her own in hand to hand combat with men twice her size. Miguel probably thinks that's pretty badass.

"So obviously, that wasn't what you were going to ask about," Sylvia said. "What did you want to ask me?"

"Oh. Well, it seems silly now. You've probably noticed Miguel and I are kind of not really talking. I was hoping maybe you had some advice. Like, should I be worried?"

"I'm not the one you should be asking for relationship advice," Sylvia said. "I'm the single one, remember?"

"It's fine. We'll figure it out. It's probably nothing," Rebecca said, trying to convince herself more than anything.

"Yeah. It's probably nothing. Good," Sylvia said. "Listen,

I'm going to try and get some sleep. It's been a long day." Sylvia laid her head back on her seat and closed her eyes.

"Oh, totally, yeah. Thanks for the talk," Rebecca said. It finally made sense why Sylvia didn't like her. She used to wonder if she was like that to everyone or if it was just her. Solving that puzzle didn't bring her any more comfort.

Rebecca moved over to where Miguel was sitting on the other side of the boat. He'd already fallen asleep. She placed her head on his shoulder, careful not to wake him. She wondered if their time was up. She began to lose hope that she could ever make up for her transgressions. Rebecca couldn't help but wonder if she hadn't begged Miguel to bring her along, would he have ended up with Sylvia? They definitely seemed to have more in common, both being tough cops. Was she going to have to compete for Miguel's attention? She'd never had to do that before.

CHAPTER 18

GULL HARBOUR: CLEMENS

BY 1:00 a.m. most of the crew had fallen asleep. Clemens had taken the helm and was struggling to stay awake. He suggested they dock somewhere and get a few hours of sleep. According to the navigation charts, they were coming up on Gull Harbour, which had once been a lively recreational destination with hiking trails, campgrounds, a golf resort, and a marina. Now it lingered on as an eerie ghost town. Its iconic lighthouse remained unlit now for thirty years.

Clemens used to go camping with his parents at Gull Harbour when he was a kid. He reflected on his youthful days as a child. They would go fishing and rent jet skis at the marina. Afterward, they'd have lunch at the Lighthouse Inn. Although they never stayed there, the two-story, 12-room inn was always booked. Now, it stood completely deserted.

"Why rough it, when we could spend the night at a hotel?" Clemens proposed as they pulled into the docks.

"Do you think it's safe?" Esther asked.

"Do you think it's *clean*?" Rebecca asked.

"Oh, I'm sure it's fine," Clemens said with an air of glee.

He was thrilled to be back in his nostalgic childhood vacation spot and hurried to moor the boat. Nobody lived on the island itself. It was purely a recreational destination. No reason CPG should have any business there. *Maybe this is far enough*, he thought. It was an isolated island that nobody was allowed to travel to anymore. It had infrastructure—plumbing, solar. It was on the water so they'd always have fresh fish. The inn could accommodate the entire crew. Originally, he'd planed to travel further north, but this place might just do. He kept these musings to himself. Best to investigate further.

They docked the pontoon. "Dutch, come with me to do a sweep of the building. You guys stay here and start unloading."

The front doors to the inn were locked. They headed toward the back to find two other entrances, also locked. From the back of the property, they spotted three private cabins tucked away among the trees.

Using Robbie's thermal binoculars, no human activity could be detected in any of the cabins. Although the front door to the first cabin was locked, a quick search around the building revealed a bedroom window that had been left unlocked. Dutch entered and did a thorough sweep of the cabin. The two-plex cabin had two bedrooms on each side. The adjoining door was locked. However, it was not equipped with smart locks like the front doors, but with traditional deadbolt hardware on the other side. Dutch kicked in the adjoining door with little effort.

To their surprise, the island still had electricity and running water. The furnishings and fixtures had been recently updated prior to going out of business. Except for the dust, it seemed like a brand new model home on the inside, which contrasted starkly with the rustic exterior. On the coffee table laid a restaurant menu, some brochures for local recreational activities, and a greeting card with the light-house logo, propped up against a dusty bottle of wine, which read: *Thank you for staying with us! Please make yourself at home.*

THE NEXT MORNING, Clemens woke to the sound of birds chirping outside his window. He sat up and stretched. His dreams had brought him back to childhood vacations and he was eager to explore the familiar grounds. Esther stirred beside him. Not wanting to disturb her, he quietly placed his feet on the floor but when he stood, the mattress creaked and Esther awoke.

"Where are you going?" Esther asked sleepily.

"I didn't mean to wake you up," he whispered. "I was just going to go for a little walk."

"I'll come with you," she said, throwing back the covers.

"You sure you don't want to sleep in?"

She was already pulling on her hiking boots. Morning walks had been a luxury they hadn't got to experience in some time. He welcomed the opportunity. Esther made coffee and filled a thermos for them to share on their walk. He loved that she thought of these things. A simple walk would have been just fine, but the coffee made it just a little better. He cherished that about her. She had a way of making everything just a little better.

The sun was barely visible as a thin, pale yellow glow over the tree line to the east, casting a pinkish film over the entire island. The air was crisp and cool from a soft breeze wafting over the sleepy lake. The ground was still wet with dew and he could see his breath in the morning air. He held her elbow as they descended the dewy wooden steps off the front porch. They sipped their coffee and chatted as they walked along the golf cart trail through the overgrown fairway. The lighthouse loomed in the distance. As a kid, he always wanted to climb to the top but never had the chance. "Hey, you want to go up there?"

"You're not serious?" Esther chuckled and swatted his arm.

"I've always wanted to see the view from up there." He looked into her eyes, which reminded him of their younger years when adventure always found its way into their hearts. "Why not? Who's gonna stop us?"

Esther laughed. "What about the others? What about Jimmy?"

"Let 'em sleep in. This . . . this'll be just for us."

Her eyes ignited with the recognition of a foregone era. "Lead the way, Captain."

They cut across the fairway and into a pine grove that separated the golf course from the campground where they were to meet back up with the main trail. "Are you sure you know where you're going?" Esther asked.

"I know this place like the back of my hand," he replied with confidence. At that moment they heard twigs snapping and fast footsteps approaching. It was Sylvia! She was half running, half crouching. If she was trying to be sneaky, she wasn't doing a very good job. Sylvia motioned for them to turn around and run the other way.

"Sylvia?" Esther called.

"Shhh!" Sylvia replied and made the *go back* motion

again with her hands, but they remained in place. When Sylvia reached them, out of breath, she said, "Someone's here."

"Where?" Clemens asked, craning his neck to see if anyone was following her.

"There's an RV parked at the campground." She rested her hands on her hips as she caught her breath. "I went out for a hike and—" She turned back in the campgrounds direction and pointed. "There's a satellite dish on the roof. Could be CPG."

"Did you see anyone?" Clemens asked.

"No, but there was a fire pit that—."

"I'm sure they're just vacationers," Esther said.

"Maybe we should investigate," Clemens suggested. "I'm a little curious about what they might know. I mean, like how long they've been here. Whether it's safe out here."

Sylvia gave a sideways glance but didn't outright oppose the idea. The three of them walked through the pine grove into the campsite where Sylvia pointed out a camper parked in the RV lot. A mountain bike and two child-size bikes, one pink and one purple, leaned against a concrete picnic table. The paved driveway was covered in colorful chalk drawings.

"It's a family!" Esther said, picking up her pace. When they got to the camper, Esther knocked gently on the camper door. Clemens could sense Sylvia's hesitance and stood back with her at a distance. They could hear tiny footsteps scurrying inside.

"Hello? Anybody home?" Esther asked in a friendly sing-song voice. She stepped up onto the metal step and peered into the front door window, which was obscured with blinds.

"Hey!" A man in a corduroy jacket shouted from a trail leading into some woods. "Get away from there!"

They put their hands in the air and stepped away from the camper. Clemens cursed under his breath, wishing he'd brought his gun. A tall, mid-thirties man with long disheveled brown hair and full beard was walking toward them with a hunting rifle pointed at them. A dead rabbit hung from his waist.

"We're unarmed!" Clemens called out with his palms facing out.

"What do you want?" the hunter called as he approached them.

As the hunter neared the site, Clemens introduced himself, keeping his hands in the air. "I'm Daryl and this is my wife, Esther. And this is Syl—I mean, Sue. We didn't mean to startle anyone. Just wanted to introduce ourselves, that's all."

The hunter kept the barrel pointed at them as he placed himself between them and his camper. "What are you doing here? Who else is with you?"

"There's eight of us. We're just passing through. We stayed in one of the cabins last night, but we're leaving. We didn't mean to intrude, honestly."

The man lowered his gun. "Alright. You just never know these days." He untied the rabbit from his waist and tossed it onto the picnic table.

"We get it. Believe me." Esther said. She looked over at the bikes and asked, "Do you have kids?"

"Two. Two girls."

"Is your wife here, too?" Esther asked.

"No, it's just me and the girls. Their mom passed last year."

"Oh, I'm so sorry to hear that. How old are they?" At that moment the door cracked opened. A little blonde-headed girl sheepishly poked her head out.

"I said stay inside!" he ordered, and the tiny head quickly disappeared behind a closed door.

"Oh, it's okay. I'd love to meet them," Esther pleaded. Two heads could be seen peering through the blinds. Esther waved playfully at them. She loved little kids and babies.

"Come on out, girls!" the man surrendered. The two barefoot girls warily exited the camper and clung to their father. "This is Coral. She's seven. Say hello, Core."

"Hi," she squeaked, almost inaudibly. The slender girl had striking blue eyes and wavy blonde hair to the middle of her back. She sniffled and rubbed her eye with the heel of her palm in a twisting motion.

"She's been a bit under the weather this week. And this little bunny here is Mabel. She's four." Mabel hid behind her father, clutching his pant legs.

"Aren't they just adorable!" Esther beamed. "And I didn't catch your name."

"Name's Ethan," he said. "I used to come up here every summer with my folks as a kid before . . . you know. Anyway, we came up here after the water crisis in Winnipeg. We have clean water and good fishing."

"Why aren't you staying in one of the cabins or at the inn?" Esther asked.

"We like it out here," Ethan explained. "It's been home now for a while. Plus, if anyone does come around, they're probably going to scope out the marina first, so it feels a little safer tucked away back here."

"Have you had any run-in's with CPG?" Clemens asked.

He was quiet for a beat. "I *am* CPG."

Sylvia froze and then tilted her head downward to let her hair fall in front of her face. Surely, he would recognize her from the wanted postings.

"At least, I was," he continued.

"You defected?" Clemens asked.

"You could say that. My supervisor was into some shady stuff. I'm not even sure what all he was into. I didn't want to know. But he kept trying to get me involved in a lot of under the table jobs that had nothing to do with police work. When I kept refusing, he turned against me. He rejected any promotions or advancement opportunities I was due for. So when the water crisis hit, I just said, 'Fuck it, I'm out.' Excuse my language."

"So you're not connected with them at all anymore?" Clemens asked, hoping to ease Sylvia's apparent fright.

"Hell no. I only joined the Guard as a last resort. I couldn't get any work for a long time, and they offered benefits and a steady paycheck. It kept my family fed. But most days I couldn't stand it. All these guys are on a power trip. They have no regard for the law, or the safety of the people they're supposed to be protecting. I couldn't sleep at night."

"Aren't you worried they'll find you here?" Esther asked.

"Shit. They got their hands full with this whole water crisis. First thing I did after we got here is I blew up the bridge that connects the island to the main road. At least they can't get here by land."

"Smart," Esther said.

"Hey Core, go make you and your sister some pop tarts," he said. When they climbed back into the camper, he looked directly at Sylvia and continued. "Look, I know who you are. 'Corporal Sylvia Boone, age 34, armed and dangerous.' Don't worry. I'm not going to turn you in. That guy you killed? Lester Atwood. He was an asshole."

"He killed my dad," Sylvia blurted in defense. Tears welled in her eyes.

"Like I said, he was an asshole. I'm glad he's dead. If murdering your dad wasn't enough of a justification, you should know, that guy was trafficking kids."

"What?" Sylvia said.

"You did the world a service. Your secret is safe with me."

"Listen," Clemens said. "Would you like to join us? We're headed up to—"

"No! Don't tell me. It's better if I don't know. Thank you, but we're doing just fine right here. We have well water, wildlife, and honestly, as long as I have my girls, that's all I need. If I could give you a piece of advice, stay on the water. There's a mass exodus happening right now. Roads aren't safe. Good luck."

SYLVIA FELT agitated and ill at ease after their encounter with Ethan. Clemens and Esther seemed annoyingly delighted at having made Ethan's acquaintance and made light of the near miss. She couldn't believe Clemens was so willing to invite Ethan, a complete stranger, to join them. The shock of being so easily recognized still reverberated throughout her body and she felt no safer just because everything worked out this time. She was eager to get off that island and away from civilization altogether.

Everyone seemed a bit more energized after a full night's sleep and hot showers, but it took several hours for Sylvia's mounting anxiety to dissipate. They hadn't seen a single human on the lake that day, which helped ease her mind.

A flock of geese took flight from the western shore. Clemens took advantage of the moment and aimed his rifle into the sky as they flew over the lake to the east. He fired two shots in a row and one of the geese tumbled back down into the lake. "That's dinner!" Clemens announced, quite happy with himself.

"Nice shot," Dutch said. "I would have gotten it in one shot, but that was pretty good."

"The first one was just to get his attention," Clemens said without missing a beat.

They made it to Reindeer Island as the sun slowly knelt into the horizon. Reindeer Island was the largest uninhabited island on Lake Winnipeg. It had been declared an ecological reserve for the past hundred years. Sylvia remembered this from an eighth grade geography assignment. That made her think about her dad who helped her with it. She still couldn't believe he was gone. Gone.

Sylvia imagined they might have been the only humans to have ever stepped foot on this island in some time. There were no docks or human structures of any kind. Dutch and Miguel began gathering firewood since the remaining daylight was dwindling and the temperature rapidly dropping. Sylvia helped LeBlanc build a fire pit with large rocks. Clemens de-feathered the goose he'd shot earlier to roast over the fire, demonstrating his technique to his son. Rebecca and Esther were deep in conversation about something that hadn't registered as remotely interesting or relevant to Sylvia.

The night sky was ablaze with stars and the landscape was pitch black except what was immediately illuminated by the campfire and LED lanterns scattered around the site. It was the most remote place she had ever been, which felt eerie yet safe. Now that she wasn't panicking about being discovered, her mind turned toward her father. She looked up into the starry sky in search of her father's presence, but it only made her feel more isolated and lost. The camaraderie and laughter emanating from the crew wasn't enough to sustain her spirits.

"Well, I'm gonna turn in," Sylvia said, chucking a piece of kindling onto the fire.

"The goose is almost done," Clemens said. The aroma from the roasting bird was not appetizing in the least.

"Oh, yeah, no that's okay. I'm good," she said trying not to offend.

"Alright, then. Sleep well," Clemens said, followed by goodnight wishes from others.

"Hey," Miguel said jogging over. "You need help with your tent? Let me give you a hand."

Sylvia didn't need help putting up her tent. She could do it with her eyes closed but she didn't want to be rude, so she passively accepted and he followed her to a small clearing. She made sure to choose a spot close enough that they were never out of sight from the others, and particularly Rebecca.

"So do you think we'll see any reindeer?" Miguel asked. "I'd rather have venison than that trash bird he's roasting over there."

"There's no reindeer on this island. It's an isolated preserve," she explained. "Here. Can you hold my light?" She felt like she should at least give him something to do.

"Then why do they call it Reindeer Island?"

"They call it that because . . ." Sylvia shook her head.

"Because why?"

"It's stupid."

"Tell me," he said, smiling.

Sylvia sighed. "They use to say this was a rest stop for Santa Claus on Christmas Eve."

Miguel laughed. "Seriously?"

"Yeah. Stupid right?"

"What? You don't believe in Santa Claus?"

She shook her head, not to answer his question but to dismiss it. "All done."

"Oh. Well, I guess you didn't need much help after all." Miguel flipped the flashlight in the air with a flourish before handing it back to Sylvia but he missed the catch and it fell to the ground. They both reached down for it and bumped their heads together.

"Ow!" Sylvia said.

"Sorry. Are you okay?"

"Yeah, it's fine," she said rubbing the side of her head. "Well, thanks for the assist. And the minor concussion."

"Sorry about that. I'll see you in the morning. Sleep tight."

"You, too," she said reflexively without making eye contact. Sylvia zipped herself inside. She kept her bolt pistol aimed at the opening, and her 8" tactical knife under her pillow. She sat up and pulled the photo of her mother from her pack. There was an easy look in her eyes, as if there was nothing to fear in the world. This must be what people looked like before the fall—light and carefree. She wondered what that must have been like. She wondered what her parents might have been like together before she was born. Were they in love? What would her father have been like if she had survived?

She tried to remember a time when she'd seen him happy. The memory of her dad on a boat came to mind. She must have been eight. This was the fishing trip where she got that scar above her right eyebrow from a fishing lure. She tried to remember every detail of that memory, tracing it back to the beginning and filling in every detail along the way. The look of pride in her dad's face as she held up the first fish she ever caught. She cried silently until she finally drifted into slumber.

CHAPTER 20
EVEN STEVEN: MIGUEL

MIGUEL, feeling slightly snubbed by Sylvia's abrupt retreat, returned to the campfire where Clemens sliced the cooked goose into strips.

"Try some of this bird," Clemens said, handing Miguel a piece. Rebecca, who was standing behind Clemens, silently shook her head and made an X with her index fingers. Miguel, ignoring her dissuasion, placed the greasy sliver in his mouth. He was unable to conceal his immediate displeasure.

Esther laughed. "You thought it was going to taste like turkey, didn't you? It certainly does not!"

"It's a bit gamey," Miguel said with his fist to his lips, trying his best not to offend the chef.

"Needs more seasoning," Clemens said, as if salt would have redeemed the awful flavor.

Rebecca handed Miguel his water bottle and he took a gulp to wash the lingering taste from his mouth, but a greasy film remained despite his efforts. Rebecca pulled him by the arm away from the group toward their tent.

"What were you guys talking about?" Rebecca asked.

"Who?" Miguel was confused.

"You and Sylvia."

"Oh, I asked her about why they called it Reindeer Island." He smiled. "Apparently, they use to think this was a rest stop for Santa Claus." He chuckled to himself. "That can't be true, right?"

Rebecca's eyes narrowed.

"What?" Miguel asked, not sure what she was getting at.

"That's it?" Rebecca pressed.

"Yeah. Why?"

Rebecca shook her head. "Nothing."

Then why aren't you looking at me? he thought. *Is she jealous? Of Sylvia?* "Wait. What's wrong?"

"It just looked like you were laughing about something."

"Yeah. I just told you." Miguel was starting to feel irritated.

"Okay," Rebecca said, feigning indifference.

"You sure?"

"Yeah. Whatever." She shrugged and shook her head.

"Rebecca, where is this coming from?" His tone hardened. "What are you accusing me of exactly?"

"I'm not—"

"Like you have room to talk!" Miguel surprised himself with his tone. He could feel heat rising into his neck and face.

Rebecca stormed off. Miguel regretted alluding to the infidelity. He had managed to think about it less over the course of the day. But with the injury fresh in his mind again, his anger rekindled. He decided to give her, and himself, some time to cool off. He took in a deep breath and let it out before joining the others by the fire.

"What's wrong with her?" Dutch asked.

"Who knows?" Miguel said.

Esther raised her eyebrow.

"What?" Miguel asked.

"It's none of my business," Esther said.

"Did she tell you something?"

"I just noticed the two of you haven't been especially close lately. You're usually a very lovey-dovey couple. Is everything alright?"

"I don't know." Miguel didn't want to get into their relationship issues in front of everyone.

"Maybe you should find out," Esther suggested.

Miguel nodded dismissively. When he looked up he caught Esther's stare with one raised eyebrow. "What? Now?" He tossed a dried up pine cone onto the campfire and walked over to where his girlfriend stood by the shore. The moonlight infused her blonde hair with an otherworldly glow. Whatever happened between them could be fixed—it had to. The whole reason she was here on this journey with him rested upon the premise that she had promised to make it up to him. He had to give her that chance.

"I'm sorry," he said. "That wasn't cool what I said back there."

"I'm never going to live it down," she said. "No matter what I do, you can always throw that in my face. It's not fair."

"Fair? Is it fair that you get to betray me and I have to just pretend like it didn't happen?"

"No, of course not! But I'm not going to just be in your debt for the rest of my life. I was wrong, okay? I feel terrible about it. But I'm never going to be able to make it up to you. Nothing you do will ever be as awful as what I did, so if I ever call you out over anything, you can just say, 'well at least I didn't fuck so and so,' and you get to come off smelling like a rose."

"I can't believe this. So you can full on cheat with some other dude, but I'm not allowed to even flirt with anyone?"

"So you *were* flirting with her!"

"No!" Miguel pressed his fingers into his forehead in bewilderment.. "But . . . how can you not see this double standard?"

"What? You want to even the score? You want to go fuck Sylvia so we can be even Steven?"

"Oh my God. You're insane!"

"Fuck you, Miguel! I'm done. I'm not going to grovel day in and day out just hoping that you'll forgive me one day. I said I was sorry. I hate myself for what I did to you. I don't know what else I can do. It's obvious you're never going to let it go."

"Let it go? Are you kidding me?"

"Don't misconstrue this, Miguel. I'm not trying to get out of anything. I take full responsibility for ruining this relationship. I did it, okay? It was my fault. But let's be real. It *is* ruined."

"I can't believe *you're* breaking up with *me!*"

"I can't be with someone who isn't willing to forgive."

"Well, how convenient for you."

"Fuck you," she said softly, wiping tears from her cheek. She pushed past him and retreated to their tent. She threw out his sleeping bag and backpack, and zipped herself inside.

Miguel returned to the campfire with his belongings in his arms and sat on a rock, dazed. *What just happened?* Whatever conversation was happening before he got there ceased the moment Miguel joined them. Dutch stood next to him shoveling trail mix into his mouth, some of which fell onto Miguel's shoulder.

"Hey! Do you mind?" Miguel barked.

"She kicked you out, eh?" Dutch asked.

"Obviously."

"You guys break up?"

"Dude!"

"You want to sleep in my tent? Plenty of room."

"You better not be hitting on me."

"You're not my type, Broseph. So does this mean Rebecca's single?"

"You wish."

CHAPTER 21

SIDEARM: SYLVIA

THE NEXT MORNING Sylvia emerged from her tent and stretched her back and shoulders. She could see her breath in the chill morning air. A low fog covered the still lake and the sun was nowhere to be seen, making the morning light diffuse and dreary. She zipped up her jacket and pulled a beanie over her ears.

"Morning!" LeBlanc called from the campfire where he boiled a pot of water. "You want some coffee? Should be ready here in just a few minutes."

Sylvia approached LeBlanc and sat on a boulder while LeBlanc stoked the fire with a stick. She reached her hands toward the low flame to warm them.

"Where's the Sergeant?" Sylvia asked.

"He and Esther went for a morning walk. They have a very special relationship, don't they?"

"I guess so." Sylvia had never really thought about it. She didn't feel qualified to answer that question.

"What about you?" LeBlanc asked. "Did you have anyone special back home? Sorry if that's too personal."

"No. No, I'm not with anyone."

"I don't mean to pry."

"No, it's okay. I'm not upset about it. Relationships just haven't really worked out for me."

"Ahh, lone wolf," LeBlanc said, putting a positive spin on her situation. "There are advantages to the single life."

"Like what?" Sylvia almost wished she hadn't asked.

"Well, for one, you don't have to confer with anyone else to decide how you want to spend your free time. You can come and go as you please. Don't have to sacrifice your personal passions to make room for someone else's." He'd been counting on his fingers as he listed these so-called advantages and now, he seemed to be stumped. His eyes cast downward.

Sylvia's heart sank. "You don't believe any of that. Do you?"

He smiled. "No."

"How long has it been?" Sylvia asked. She was surprised to hear herself ask.

"Six years."

"I'm sorry. Does it get any better?"

LeBlanc smiled again but his eyes moistened and filled with sorrow. He shook his head. "No. I mean, no, the hole doesn't get any smaller. But you get used to it over time. You just get used to having a hole. Right here." He patted his chest.

Sylvia wanted to say something to ease his pain in that moment, but suddenly felt inadequate. So she said nothing.

Miguel and Rebecca simultaneously stepped out of their respective tents. When Rebecca saw him, she turned and stalked away toward the woods with a roll of toilet paper under her arm.

"Uh oh," LeBlanc said just loud enough for Sylvia to hear. "Looks like trouble in paradise."

Miguel skulked over and nodded at Sylvia. "Hey."

"Hey," Sylvia replied, keeping her eyes on the fire. Whatever had happened between him and Rebecca the night before was of no interest to her and she didn't want to play into their drama by way of associating too closely with either one of them. She most certainly didn't want to provide any solace or comfort to Miguel, like some kind of emotional stand-in. Whatever it was, it was probably Miguel's fault. Because—men.

"You sleep okay?" Miguel asked.

"I know you didn't." Sylvia said.

"What do you mean?" Miguel asked nervously.

"I could hear Dutch snoring all the way from my tent."

"Oh. Yeah. It's ridiculous. He's like a big bear."

Dutch enjoyed a morning swim in the frigid lake. At that moment, he emerged from the water, naked as the day he was born.

"Or an elephant," LeBlanc said. "God damn!"

Robbie's dangling cock wobbled comically about as he stepped gingerly onto the rocky beach, oblivious to his non-consenting audience.

Sylvia turned away instinctively. "Jesus."

"Put that thing away you degenerate!" Miguel called out, hands cupping the sides of his mouth.

Dutch waved Miguel's comment away as he stepped carefully toward the rock where he laid his towel.

"I feel violated all the way over here," Sylvia said in a deadpan tone mostly to herself.

LeBlanc thumped Miguel's chest with the back of his hand. "Hey, you said he had an impressive side-*arm*." LeBlanc held his left forearm with his right hand and bounced it up and down.

This time, even Sylvia chortled. "That was stupid."

"You laughin!'"

"Alright fine," Sylvia said, trying to dampen her expression. "Can we please just drop it? What if he feels self-conscious?"

Miguel and LeBlanc erupted into raucous laughter. "Good one!" Miguel said, still laughing.

"I'm just saying . . . it's not normal," she said, unintentionally encouraging the moronic laugh-fest to continue. It finally abated when they noticed Clemens and Esther approaching from the woods.

"What did we miss?" Esther asked as they reached the campfire. By then Dutch had dressed himself.

"Nothing!" Sylvia blurted.

"No, yeah," LeBlanc started. "Dutch was just showing us his, uh . . ."

Miguel interrupted. "His sidearm," he said, putting every ounce of will into maintaining a straight face.

Sylvia trained their gaze on the campfire, imploring the universe to put a definitive end to the whole sidearm situation.

"Oh. Alright. So . . . what's the plan for today?" Esther asked.

"Well . . ." LeBlanc cleared his throat. "We're not far from Grand Rapids. I think we should be there before noon."

"What's in Grand Rapids?" Clemens asked.

"Absolutely nothing. But it's right on the highway. I have a feeling there's not a whole lot of traffic this far north. From there, it's just a three-hour drive to Thompson."

"Uh . . . we don't have a car," Clemens noted.

"Sergeant Clemens, haven't you ever commandeered a vehicle in the name of the law?" LeBlanc asked with a smile.

"No, but I suppose there's a first time for everything."

"Well, that'll be the end of the road for me. You've got Bishop's contact. He knows you're coming."

"I really appreciate all your help, Terrence," Clemens said.

"Don't mention it. It's been an adventure!"

Sylvia didn't expect she would miss Terrence LeBlanc. There weren't many people in this world she trusted anymore. He turned out to be one of them. She wanted to tell him so, but she didn't.

CHAPTER 22

HAZARD OF THE TRADE: MIGUEL

IT ONLY TOOK three hours to arrive at the long forsaken town of Grand Rapids, where the Saskatchewan River flows into Lake Winnipeg on the northwestern shore, just as the sun reached its highest position in a cloudless Manitoba sky. LeBlanc helped them unload their gear onto the dock and said his goodbyes.

"It was nice getting to know you, Miguel," LeBlanc said extending a veiny hand.

"Likewise. Thank you for your hospitality."

"Pleasure's all mine." LeBlanc shook Miguel's hand firmly and then pulled him in close and spoke quietly into his ear. "Don't let that one slip away," LeBlanc said motioning with his head toward Rebecca. "She's a keeper." LeBlanc patted his shoulder and gave him a wink.

"Yes, sir." Miguel hadn't had a chance to settle things with Rebecca that morning and she seemed to be deliberately avoiding him. He wondered how all this had gotten turned around on him. It seemed like everyone could feel the tension between them, but as far as he knew, nobody knew the whole story. For the sake of his pride, he hoped it would stay that way.

"Well, I wish you all safe travels," LeBlanc announced to the group. "Let me know when you get there. Can't wait to hear all about it!" Everyone said goodbye a final time and got in their last hug or handshake before LeBlanc fired up the engines and pulled away from the dock. Waving with his hat, he called out, "Take good care of each other!"

Miguel couldn't help but think that final admonishment was meant for him. He wanted more than anything to take good care of Rebecca. The thought of breaking up had never been a serious option, and only arose in anger. After all, that's why she was here. He'd made a commitment to take good care of her. This wasn't over.

They hiked inland until they could see the highway. Not a single car, not even a freight truck, passed in several minutes. They split up to search for a vehicle large enough to accommodate the seven of them and all of their gear up to Thompson.

"Rebecca, will you stay here with Esther and James, and keep an eye on our gear?"

She nodded. Miguel wondered if that was intentional, and if so, who was Clemens trying to protect?

"Dutch and I will take this road south. Miguel, you and Sylvia head north. Here's a wristcom. I'm on channel two. Let me know what you find."

"Yes, sir." Miguel complied, strapping the wristcom onto his arm. He worried what Rebecca might be thinking of him being alone with Sylvia after last night's debacle.

As they walked away from the main highway, Sylvia walked several steps ahead of Miguel. As much as he'd tried to befriend her, she never seemed much interested in conversation. He caught up to her and attempted to adjust the twisted gun strap on her shoulder. She pulled away and readjusted the strap on her own. Although his intentions were friendly, this felt like more of a rejection than it should have. He tried to think of something interesting to discuss as loose gravel crunched under their boots, but the harder he tried, the more he came up short.

They came across a plain-looking warehouse with bars on its few windows. An extended cab pickup truck was parked outside. It wouldn't be big enough, but Miguel checked the doors and peered inside anyway. The truckbed could accommodate their gear. Then they'd just need a second vehicle for whoever couldn't fit in the cab.

"Hey! Get away from there!" An older man, sun-weathered with facial scruff crawling down his neck and thin, greasy, grey hair atop his head, stepped out of the building with a rifle aimed directly at Miguel.

"Drop it!" Sylvia commanded, her own gun aimed at the man's head. "You've got to the count of three . . ." The man slowly lowered his rifle and placed it on the ground.

Miguel slowly approached him. "Listen, I think we got off on the wrong foot. We're not looking for any trouble. We're CPG." Miguel showed him his badge. He hoped this would put him at ease rather than on edge. It could have gone either way.

"Staff Sergeant McDonald." He slowly removed his own CPG badge, which did little to allay Miguel's suspicion.

"We're from Winni—," Miguel started. Sylvia cleared her throat and shook her head, giving him the look of death. He had completely forgotten about her bounty and that every

CPG in the region would have her photo in their inbox. "We're headed up to Thompson and we need a vehicle."

"Well, that one's mine," McDonald said pointing at the truck with a crooked finger. He didn't seem to recognize Sylvia.

"Of course. We're actually looking for something a lot bigger. You know where we might find a van or—"

"Well, I guess you all better keep moving then," McDonald said with a snap of impatience. He wasn't going to be much help.

"Yeah, I guess we should probably head ba—" Miguel thought he heard something coming from inside the building —a voice?

McDonald loudly blurted as if trying to conceal whatever noise was coming from the building, "Tell you what, why don't you let me give you a ride back into town."

"What was that?" Miguel asked, looking toward the building. He shot a look at Sylvia who seemed to have heard it, too.

"Alright, let's get going now," McDonald said nervously, attempting to corral them away from the building toward the truck.

Miguel heard a muffled banging. A faint voice called from inside the building,

"Help!"

Sergeant McDonald reached for his rifle and Miguel kicked it out of his reach toward Sylvia's feet. Miguel shoved him against the side of the building, pressing his forearm into his neck. Sylvia picked up the weapon and pressed its barrel against the man's temple.

"Stay with him," Miguel commanded. "I'm going in."

Miguel entered the dimly lit office with his bolt gun extended in front of him, darting to each corner of the room as he advanced toward the back. The office was sparsely furnished —a desk, a few file cabinets, a floor fan. He couldn't tell what kind of business operated out of the nondescript workspace.

He followed the voice to a locked conference room and kicked in the door. Four teenage girls, gagged with their hands zip-tied behind their backs, sat trembling in a corner, tears streaming. One of them, the oldest one, had managed to remove her gag. Her forehead was bleeding. He noticed the window that she must have been trying to break was also smeared with blood.

Miguel called_Clemens using his wrist com. "Clemens. Come in, Clemens."

"Miguel, good news," Clemens replied. "We found a school bus!"

"That's great, but . . . Sir, you're not going to believe this. We stumbled upon a trafficker, and he's got four girls trapped here. We might need some backup."

"Where are you?"

"It's a warehouse, right off the main road before it turns back toward the highway."

"Don't move. We're on our way."

Miguel tried to reassure the girls they would be safe. None of the girls spoke and the younger ones continued crying while the older ones held them. He had the feeling the girls might feel apprehensive around men, so he had Sylvia take them outside and wait with them until the rest of the crew arrived. Miguel dragged Staff Sergeant McDonald back inside and handcuffed him to a metal desk.

"You don't know who you're messing with!" McDonald

shouted.

"Tell me," Miguel said. "Who am I messing with?"

"You don't want to cross these guys. They're bad news."

"Who are they?" Miguel pressed through gritted teeth, shoving the barrel of his pistol firmly against the man's forehead.

"Gideon. They're called Gideon. It's just code for their operation, not a real person."

"How is CPG involved?"

"They just hire some of us to transport their workers. Get 'em across checkpoints. I'm just a fucking babysitter." McDonald started to cry. "They're gonna kill me! If you take these girls, I'm a dead man! Do you hear me? I'm fucking dead!"

"I think they call that a hazard of the trade," Miguel said flatly.

"Please! I can pay you. I'm getting four thousand units from this job. It's yours as soon as they make the transfer, once they claim their product."

"I got a better idea. We take the girls and you get what's coming to you." Miguel turned and walked out of the building while McDonald continued to plead through sniveling sobs.

Clemens and the rest of the crew arrived a few minutes later in a yellow school bus. The girls were given water and first aid. Two of them were still crying and begging to go home. Esther took the lead in talking with the girls. She had a gift for talking to kids.

"My name is Esther," she said in a sweet, nurturing tone, placing her hand on her chest. "That's Miguel and Sylvia. You met them already." She pointed at the others as she named them. "That's my husband Daryl and my son James. This is Rebecca. And that big ol' friendly giant over there, that's Dutch. What are your names?"

"Hannah," replied one of the older girls with the injured head.

"It's nice to meet you, Hannah."

"Ataksak," said the other.

"Ataksak," Esther repeated slowly. "That's beautiful. Is it Cree?"

The girl smiled and nodded. She looked to be around sixteen years old.

Esther turned to the younger ones, who looked closer to twelve or thirteen, and strikingly similar—sisters probably. "And what are your names?" At first, they just looked at each other. Esther smiled and prodded, "It's okay, you can tell me."

"Kaylie," said one of them between sobs, and then looked at the other.

"Briana," she said, almost inaudibly.

"Are you sisters?" Esther asked.

They both nodded in unison.

"Where are you from? Where do your parents live?"

"I'm from Toronto," Hannah said. "These two are from Winnipeg."

Esther shot Miguel a look before asking them, "How long have you been away from home?"

They looked at each other and Kaylie answered, "About a week or so?"

They didn't know. Miguel wondered how they were going to get them safely home with all the riots going on.

"Can we go home?" Kaylie asked.

"Let's see if we can't get a hold of your parents," Esther

said. "Miguel, can you see if the com panel works on this ol' bus?"

"On it." Miguel pulled up the on-board communications panel on the bus. "Looks good," he called.

Esther ushered the girls onto the school bus and had them dial their parents' numbers. The sisters' parents' line went straight to voicemail. They tried again with the same results. Unfortunately, these were the only numbers they'd memorized. Hannah's mother's line had been disconnected. Ataksak's father answered and appeared holographically against the windshield.

"Daddy!" Ataksak cried. A tear fell down her cheek.

"Ataksak! Are you okay? Where are you?"

"I don't know," she said and looked at Esther.

Esther positioned herself into the video frame and addressed the man. "She's in Grand Rapids, Manitoba. Do you know where that is?"

"Yes! I'm at a work site about two hours from there. I am coming there now."

"We'll wait here with her until you get here. I'm sending you our location."

"Is she safe?"

"She'll be safe with us. I can promise you that," Esther said.

"I got your location. Thank you! I'm on my way!" His image disappeared.

Ataksak wiped her tears of joy from her face and then noticed the younger girls sitting together, crestfallen. She sat with them and held them close. Esther sat next to them. "Don't worry. We'll keep trying." Hannah sat on the other side of the isle looking out the window.

Miguel stepped off the bus to consult with Clemens. "We got a hold of one parent. He's on his way. How are we going to get the other girls home? Two of them are from Winnipeg."

"That's what we were just discussing," Clemens said. "If we take the main highway it'll take four and a half hours to get back to Winnipeg, but we'd have to avoid the checkpoints."

"What about Gaffer?" Sylvia said.

"Gaffer?" Clemens asked.

"Doesn't he make deliveries into Winnipeg? He could smuggle them in."

"That could work, if he'll agree to do it. It's risky. We still need to get a hold of their parents to coordinate a plan though. And we can't stay here much longer. Who knows when those traffickers will get here?"

The girls stepped off the bus, followed by Esther. Ataksak stood between the younger girls with an arm around each of their shoulders.

"I've invited the girls to stay with me and my family on the reservation," Ataksak said. "At least until we can get a hold of their parents. They will be safe there."

"Are you sure it's okay with your father?" Miguel asked.

"Yes. I called him and he agreed," she said.

Hannah, who had been sitting on the bus steps, stood. "I want to come with you guys," she said.

"Don't you want to go back home? To your mother?" Esther asked.

"My mother had stage four pancreatic cancer the last time I saw her," Hannah said. "She only had a two to three months to live. That was two years ago. That's why her line was disconnected."

Miguel and the rest of the crew glanced at one another. Hannah appeared to be around James' age, and he had proven to be self-sufficient and an overall asset. Hannah looked like she could hold her own. He couldn't imagine the horrors this girl had been through, like glass shattered over and over again. How was she still standing? Miguel looked to Clemens who nodded.

When Ataksak's father arrived, he sobbed and embraced his daughter, repeatedly kissing the top of her head. He was dressed in worker's attire, a cowboy hat and denim shirt buttoned to the middle of his sun-darkened chest, hands calloused by hard work. He removed from his neck an intricately beaded necklace with an eagle's talon at the center.

"I am forever grateful to all of you for reuniting me with my precious daughter. I cannot fully express my gratitude, but I am forever in your debt. Please accept this necklace. It was my grandfather's. The eagle represents vision and strength. The eagle can see more broadly from incredible heights. May your spirits soar high above the madness of this world."

Miguel accepted the necklace on behalf of the group. His throat tightened as he delivered his thanks. Working for a corrupt regime, it wasn't always clear whether his efforts ever resulted in positive outcomes. He'd arrested bad actors connected to human trafficking in the past, but as far as he could tell, the charges never stuck, and they would be released within a week. He never witnessed what happened to the victims once they returned home, if they remained safe or for how long. He could only pray these girls stayed out of harm's way as they climbed into Ataksak's father's dented work truck.

HANNAH WAVED as the girls drove away—dust rising from the truck's tires. Even though she'd only known them for a couple of days, she felt bonded to them. They had all experienced such an unlikely emancipation. At the same time, she felt ill at ease as she found herself in the custody of strangers. What had she just singed up for? Would she be able to pull her own weight? She tried to remind herself that anything would have been an improvement on where she'd been the last two years.

A wave of chills shook her and her teeth began to chatter. Her legs felt weak and she feared they might fail to support her. She felt nauseous.

"Are you cold?" Sylvia asked her.

Hannah nodded slightly, and she held her arms across her stomach.

"Are you hungry?" Sylvia asked.

Hannah shook her head. The shivering continued. Sweat beaded on her forehead, and her saliva took on a metallic taste.

"You don't look so well," Sylvia asked. "Do you feel sick?"

Hannah nodded slowly.

"Esther," Sylvia called. "Can you check Hannah? She's sweating. A *lot*."

"Oh, dear. Let me take a look at you." Esther came over and felt her forehead.

She checked her pulse. "Your heart is racing. I think you have a fever. Syl, can you get her some Taminol from the med bag? And a cold, wet towel?" Esther brushed her hair from her forehead. "What hurts, dear?"

"Stomach. Head. Everything." Hannah held out her hand which was shaking uncontrollably.

"Did they have you on anything? Drugs?" Esther asked.

Hannah nodded.

"I think you're in withdrawal. Do you know what they gave you?"

Hannah shook her head.

"Pills?"

Hannah nodded.

"Probably benzos, maybe opiates. Honey, I'm afraid we just have to wait this out. What do you need?"

Hannah proceeded to vomit where she stood. She was too ill to feel embarrassed about it.

"It's okay, hon," Esther said and pulled her hair back while Hannah threw up a second time, mostly bile. "You're okay. Let it out."

Sylvia hurried back with the meds and wetted a towel with a water bottle and held it on Hannah's forehead. She wiped tears from Hannah's eyes and offered her the water bottle to rinse her mouth and take the Taminol.

"Let's get you on the bus so you can lie down," Esther said and then called out to Clemens, "Are we ready?"

"Yeah."

"I think we need to get moving. Who knows when those traffickers will be back."

"I think you're right," Clemens said. He announced to the rest, "Let's load up! Time to roll!"

Sylvia helped Hannah onto the bus. She pulled an ammunition crate into the isle so Hannah could prop up her feet and lay sideways across the seat with her head resting in Sylvia's lap. Hannah continued shivering. Esther covered her with a blanket.

Clemens stood at the front, facing everyone while the bus pulled away. "I just got off a call with Bishop. He's preparing the rover for us. His place is up at Mystery Lake, just northeast of Thompson. It'll be dark when we get into town, so I say we check into a hotel for the night, get cleaned up, have a good meal—I think we could all use it. First thing in the morning we'll head out to Bishop's."

The adults continued talking, but Hannah failed to follow the discussion. Something about the Guard and their limited jurisdiction this far north. Something about Churchill, wherever that was. She stopped paying attention as the voices blended into the sound of the road, and her mind drifted far away.

She thought about her mother, who she was fairly certain had passed while in captivity. She tried to remember what her mother looked like before she got sick. Shame crept in as she recalled the many, many times she'd been warned never to go out unsupervised—how she would roll her eyes and dismiss what she had become background noise along side *make good choices,* or *drink water. Never go out unsupervised.*

Hannah remembered the sterilization clinic where she'd initially been taken after being kidnapped. She remembered waking up in a hospital bed with her wrists and ankles secured to the bed frame. She looked to her right and her left, where five other girls, laid in various states of consciousness. One girl was screaming profanities and thrashing her body— she must have been only twelve or thirteen. A pale, wrinkled woman entered the room, walking calm and steady toward the bucking teen. The old woman filled a syringe with a light blue substance and swiftly injected it into the girl's thigh. Within seconds the girl's appendages fell limp and she was back to slumbering, drool oozing from the corner of her mouth.

An ache pulsed in Hannah's right arm where two small stitches pulled reddened lumps of skin together. She looked to her left to find another girl, roughly her same age, staring at her.

"Where are we?" Hannah asked.

"Hell," the girl said in a half-whisper through cracked lips. "We're in hell."

"What is this?" Hannah asked attempting to show the girl her arm, which was shackled to the bed frame.

"That's your bar code."

"Bar code?"

"It's also a tracking device."

"What for?"

"What do you mean, what for?" The girl laughed, but Hannah could see tears in her eyes. "It's what we've always been warned about. It's why we don't ever go anywhere unsupervised—the worst thing that could ever happen. The life we knew is over. We're their property now." A tear trickled down her cheek.

Hannah's left arm contained an IV. Her vision was blurred so she couldn't make out the writing on the bag and she was too afraid to ask. The girl must have seen her trying to make it out.

"Infertiline," said the girl. "I hope you weren't expecting to have a baby ever." The girl turned and faced the ceiling. "I didn't want babies anyway," she said.

Procreation was culturally frowned upon, especially among youth. What could be more irresponsible? Hannah had officially bought into this rhetoric, but now that the option was removed, felt the sting of having been unjustly plundered.

The machine beeped when the IV bag had emptied. A nurse came in to turn off the machine and then injected another medication through her IV line.

"What's this?" Hannah asked.

"Oh, just something to help you relax," the nurse said.

"What's going to happen next?"

"You're going to take a long nap."

Hannah's memories from this point forward remained hazy and broken. They kept her heavily medicated so that she could no longer delineate day from night, or place events in chronological order. Hannah had no idea how long she'd been in the transport vehicle or how long it had been since leaving the sterilization clinic.

"Keep your eyes on the ground until we get into the building," ordered one of the men after the transport lurched to a halt. The back doors creaked open and light poured in from outside.

Hannah was curious about where she was. Was she still in Toronto? When she stepped down from the vehicle, she looked around at the surrounding buildings, forgetting what she had just been instructed..

"I said keep your eyes down!" The man yelled and shocked Hannah's ribs with his taser wand. He pushed her head down and through the building's entrance.

Hannah learned quickly to follow orders and keep her mouth shut. They herded her and five other girls down a long hallway with doors on each side into what appeared to be a cheap hotel room, except the windows had been blacked out and an inconspicuous camera had been installed in one corner or the ceiling.

"Everyone get showered up. Someone will be by with lunch shortly," the man said.

"Wait—" one girl started, but the man ignored her and walked out the door, locking it behind him.

The girl Hannah spoke to at the sterilization clinic, a short-haired brunette, turned on the holoscreen and tried placing a call, but a message appeared stating the communication gateway had been disconnected. The girl sat on the bed and began to cry. Hannah didn't know what to say to console her. The whole situation was surreal and she didn't fully believe any of this was really happening. Hannah sat next to the brunette on the bed and put an arm around her.

The girls each took turns showering. While Hannah was in the shower someone had brought them lunch—one 12 oz. strawberry protein pouch each and a bottle of water. It had been hours since Hannah had had anything to eat and she squeezed every ounce from the pouch.

"Does anyone know how this works?" one of the girls asked.

Hannah shook her head. They hadn't been given any further instructions. A man entered the room—the same man who tased Hannah outside the building. She froze. He had a key card attached to his belt and a taser wand in one hand. Hannah was too afraid to look up at his face.

"You, with the short hair." He pointed with the taser wand at the girl Hannah had tried to console earlier. She started crying again. "Let's go," he said as he raised the wand. The girl stood, head bowed, and left with the man, sobbing.

"She won't remember it," said a tall redhead after the door locked. "They'll sedate her first."

"How do you know?" Hannah asked.

"This isn't my first day," said the redhead. "They'll take her to a service room, like this one. They'll give her some pills, strip her, and when she can't remember her name, they'll bring in the John. When he's done—he gets a half hour, but they usually don't take that long—then they'll bring in the next one, and the next one, for the next four hours. Then she'll get a meal break, a shower, and another dose. And then it starts all over."

"I heard Johns are not allowed to leave any marks," another girl said to the redhead. Rumors about service centers were a popular topic among the uninitiated. "Is that true?"

"That's one good thing," said the redhead. "If they do, they get charged—get this—a 'mishandling fee.'"

"How long do we have to stay here?" Hannah asked.

"Depends. Not more than a week or two. Then they'll ship you somewhere else. They call it 'rotating the stock.' We're nothing more than merchandise to these pricks."

The door opened. "You." He pointed at Hannah. "Your turn."

Hannah's stomach leapt into her throat. She looked at the tall redhead with pleading eyes, as if there was anything she could do. The girl gave her a reassuring nod, as if to say *it'll be okay*, but Hannah felt no comfort in it.

He walked Hannah down the hall and up a flight of stairs. When they got to room 311, the man used the key card, attached to his belt on a retractable string, to open the door. He pushed her through the door and then shut it behind her.

A plump middle-aged woman stepped around the corner holding out a paper cup with two pills inside. "Here. Take these." She handed Hannah the pills and a bottle of water.

"What are these?" Hannah asked.

"Your only saving grace," the woman said with a complete lack of sympathy.

Hannah regarded the blue and white capsules for a moment. *Pills for forgetting*, she thought to herself. She tossed them into her mouth and took a swig from the water bottle.

"You can leave your clothes in these drawers," the woman said. "Then you should lie down. These drugs work fast." And then she left, locking the door behind her.

Hannah sat on the bed holding her arms. She couldn't bring herself to undress. Within a few minutes, Hannah's eyes grew heavy. She looked down at her shoes.

Hannah did not remember what came next. Due to her sedated state, she didn't remember many details of the abuses that befell her that day and over the next two years. Penetration commenced without protest. She recalled hands groping and clutching at her body, repetitive thrusting, the smell of sweat and stale breath, but never faces. Her thoughts drifted to happier times—birthday parties, pizza with her parents at Rosati's, or the fantasy worlds of middle-grade books—while Johns panted and grunted their way to quick completion.

IT WAS dusk when they entered the town of Thompson, which was more populated than Sylvia had expected. It was a refreshing scene as cars traveled unhurried along the roadways. People walked freely along sidewalks and gathered in parks and cafes. It was like nothing Sylvia had ever seen except maybe in old movies. Sylvia scanned vigilantly for any signs of CPG but there were none to be found.

"It's like stepping back in time," Esther remarked.

"This must be what society looks like when it isn't under authoritarian control," Clemens said. He turned to Sylvia. "You don't have to worry about CPG up here. They have no jurisdiction up this way. You can breathe."

"Are there no police at all?" Sylvia asked.

"Thompson is an anarchist community," Clemens said.

"Doesn't look like anarchy," Sylvia said.

"Just means they govern themselves. Looks like they're doing a pretty good job of it, too."

Hannah woke up from a three-hour nap with sleep marks

on her cheek. "Hey," Sylvia said quietly like she didn't want to startle her. "How do you feel?"

"Hungry."

Sylvia and the others smiled. It was a good sign. "That's good. What do you want?"

Hannah's eyes lit up. She smiled. "Pizza?"

"I think we can do that," Sylvia said. She turned in her seat. "Everyone else good with pizza?"

Everyone enthusiastically concurred, happy to oblige their new crew member. They checked into a chain hotel in the center of town and booked two double rooms, one for the women and one for the men. They figured Hannah would be more comfortable with that arrangement. Both Esther and Rebecca seemed excited to have a girl's night, which is something Sylvia had never had as a girl. It sounded stupid but upon seeing Hannah's delight, agreed to play along.

Pizzas were delivered to their room and Sylvia was delighted to see Hannah voraciously devour her first two slices.

"You were really hungry, huh?" Rebecca asked.

Hannah nodded with a mouthful of pizza. Sylvia smiled and handed her a napkin to wipe her greasy mouth. When she finally swallowed, Hannah said, "I haven't had pizza in two years! Come to think of it, I haven't had any solid food. They made us eat protein pouches. So gross."

"Really?" Rebecca asked. "Every day?"

"Three times a day. Different flavors though." She started in on her third slice.

"So," Rebecca ventured, "I mean, if you're not ready to talk about it, that's totally fine, but like, what happened? How did you get captured?"

Sylvia gave Rebecca an admonishing glare but she didn't seem to notice.

Hannah nodded as she swallowed what was in her mouth. "Basically, I went to the movies." She wiped her mouth and took a sip from her can of soda. "You know the movie *Quantum Force*?"

Sylvia and Rebecca nodded.

"Well some of my friends were going to go see it on opening day and I begged my parents to go. At first they were like, no it's not safe, which, everybody knows, right? But even though everybody says that all the time, I never felt like I was ever in danger. Looking back, that's because I was always with my parents. Anyway, I kept begging like a little brat and my stepdad said he'd go with me, but—" Hannah's voice caught in her throat. Her face reddened and tears welled in her eyes.

"It's okay," Sylvia said. "Take your time."

"I should have listened to them. But instead I accused them of not trusting me and that they were being unfair. Anyway, they finally gave in, but they said they had to take me there and back, I had to keep my holospecs on the whole time, and I had to carry pepper spray. So they dropped me off and I did everything they said. It was such a good movie. Have you seen it?"

Sylvia and Rebecca nodded.

"Anyway, when the movie ended, we were all waiting for our parents outside the theater. I noticed this little girl, maybe like four years old, standing in the middle of the parking lot. She was crying and holding a stuffed lamb. I was a like, 'Oh my God! Wait here, I'll be right back,' and I ran over to the little girl and knelt beside her. I tried to ask her if she was lost and where were her parents, but she didn't answer me. I remember the look of terror in her eyes, so vividly. Like she was about to witness something terrible. At that moment, a van pulled up between me and where my friends were standing. The door slid open and two guys pulled me into the van and sped away."

Sylvia held a hand over her mouth. "They used that little girl as bait?"

Hannah nodded. "Yeah. And stupid me fell for it."

"Don't say that," Sylvia said. "You weren't stupid. You were fifteen. And you were trying to help that little girl."

Hannah sighed. She put a hand on her belly. "Ugh. I think I ate too much."

"Hey," Sylvia said. "You're safe now. We won't let anything happen to you."

Hannah smiled and nodded.

"What do you say we paint our nails?" Rebecca said. She pulled three bottles of nail polish from her suitcase, one a dark shade of red, another light pink, and one in robin egg blue.

"Oooh, I'll take red," Esther said in a way that implied she was doing something naughty.

"You packed nail polish?" Sylvia chided. Sylvia hadn't worn nail polish since she was in the seventh grade, and even then it was black to match her angst.

"You never know," Rebecca said.

"Can I try the blue?" Hannah asked.

"Of course!" Rebecca said cheerfully. "What about you, Syl?"

"Oh, no, I'm okay."

"Can I do yours?" Hannah asked Sylvia. Her youthful eyes simply could not be refuted.

"Wh—uh. Yeah, sure," Sylvia conceded.

"Blue?"

"Okay."

Hannah took Sylvia's hand and opened the nail polish bottle with her teeth. She had done this before, Sylvia thought. Hannah scooted a little closer on the bed and raised the sleeves of the thermal pajamas Rebecca had lent her for the night. Sylvia noticed a scar on her right forearm.

"What's that?" Sylvia asked, pointing to the scar.

Hannah gasped. "Oh my God! Oh my God! I forgot. I'm so sorry!"

"What?" Sylvia said wide-eyed. "What is it?"

"It's a tracking device!" Hannah shrieked.

"There's a hospital right across the street," Esther said, "Let's get over there, pronto!" Esther called Clemens next door from the holoscreen. "Daryl, we have a situation," she said when he appeared on the screen.

"What's wrong?" Clemens said.

"It's Hannah. They put a tracking device in her arm. We're taking her to the hospital across the street to see if they can get it out."

"I'll just need to get dressed—" He grunted as he stood.

"No, it's okay. We'll be fine but we need to leave right now. I'll call you from the hospital with an update."

Sylvia, Esther, Rebecca, and Hannah ran across the street into an empty ER at Thompson General Hospital. It was a small hospital but appeared clean and modern. The receptionist desk was unmanned.

"Hello?" Esther called out. "Hello! We have a medical emergency!"

A young, black-haired doctor stepped out from a nearby office masticating a turkey sandwich and wiping mustard from his mouth with a paper napkin. "So sorry," he said, still chewing. "Didn't hear anyone come in. I'm Dr. Malloy. How can I help you?"

"This child has a tracking device in her arm. She needs it removed immediately," Esther commanded.

The doctor discarded the napkin in a waste bin, extracted two pumps of hand sanitizer from a wall-mounted dispenser and slathered his hands with it. He removed the holospecs from his breast pocket and placed them on his head. "Let me take a look-see here." He took Hannah's arm and examined it through the X-ray setting of his medical grade specs. "Ah, yes. There's the little bugger. How'd that get in there?"

"That's not important right now! Can you please just get it out?" Sylvia asked. She was perturbed by the doctor's lack of urgency.

"Oh, yes. It's a simple procedure, really. I can have you in and out in half and hour."

"Will it hurt?" Hannah asked.

Dr. Malloy bent slightly at the waist to look directly into Hannah's eyes. "You won't even feel it." He went on to describe the procedure. "You'll place your arm into a white tube. An inner sleeve contracts around the upper arm, sealing it off from the air in the room. Then you'll feel a little pinch. That's the local anesthesia. I promise that will be the worst of it. A robotic arm will locate the device and place the smallest possible incision, remove the device, and then seal the incision with the latest grafting technology. You won't even have a scar."

Sylvia rubbed Hannah's back. She looked pale and clammy. "Are you okay?"

Hannah nodded unconvincingly.

"Okay then," Dr. Malloy said. "I'll have you all wait in here until we get the surgical room prepared. I'll have someone around in a few minutes to get the paperwork started. "

"Please hurry," Esther said. "She could be in grave danger."

"We'll have her out in no time." He opened the door to a small waiting room with burgundy upholstered chairs and a vending machine. A holoscreen projected against one wall, providing facts about heart disease and stroke.

Hannah curled up on a couch and closed her eyes. Rebecca sat next to her and rubbed her back. "Are you getting sick again?" Rebecca asked. Hannah didn't respond.

A few minutes later another faculty member entered with a tablet, preloaded with the required intake forms. "Who is Hannah?" Hannah summoned the strength to raise an index finger. The staff walked over to her and scanned Hannah's retina with a handheld device and asked who the responsible guardian was. Sylvia looked at Esther and then Rebecca. "We aren't technically her legal guardians," Sylvia said.

"That's okay. We just need an adult to sign off on the procedure." She brandished the retina scanner with a disarming smile.

Sylvia wasn't willing to have her retina scanned in case

that information somehow got back to the CPG, revealing her current location. Esther must have sensed her trepidation.

"Give 'em here. I'll do it," Esther said and walked up to the nurse.

The nurse scanned Esther's retina and handed her the tablet with a smile. "Thank you. It shouldn't be too long now," she said and left the room.

Esther started filling out the intake forms, asking Hannah for medical history, allergies, etc. Under current medication, she added that Hannah may be suffering from opioid addiction and requested a drug test to know for certain. Hannah held her stomach and Rebecca pulled a waste basket over. "Just in case."

Sylvia felt a chill. She looked up in the corner of the room at the CCTV camera, which seemed to follow her, even though it was in a fixed position. She instinctively hid her face.

Esther completed the intake forms just as the nurse entered the room with a wheel chair. Hannah, curled into the fetal position, was clutching her stomach, shivering, and lightly moaning with each exhale. Rebecca helped her to a sitting position and the nurse assisted in getting her into the chair.

"I'll take it from here," said the nurse. "We'll have her back in no time at all."

"Can I come back with her?" Esther asked.

"I'm sorry, we can't have anyone in the surgical room." Hannah's head flopped to one side as the nurse wheeled her out.

"Poor girl," Esther said, standing at the door watching her disappear down the hallway.

Sylvia paced back and forth, chewing her fingernails. "They're not really treating this like an emergency. Every second she has that thing in her, the closer they are to finding her."

"I know," Esther said. "Hopefully they—" Esther was interrupted by four men in street clothes and guns running past the waiting room. "What the hell?"

Sylvia jumped up and tried to get a look. She heard voices in the hall—raised voices. Someone said, "Sir, you can't be in here with firearms," and "Sir, sir, excuse me, sir," and then in a gruff voice, "Open this door!" They were demanding to enter a secure area. "Now!" Two gun shots reverberated through the halls. Screams followed.

Sylvia jerked up and down on the handle. "It's locked!" She slapped the door with the palm of her hand. "Let us out!"

"It's a safety protocol," Esther explained. "When a gunman is present they lock all the interior doors to keep the patients safe."

Hannah's captors had finally caught up to her. Had they brought Hannah in an hour earlier, she would have had the tracker removed and they would have been safe back at the hotel painting their nails. A rage awakened in Sylvia. Rescuing Hannah had given her a sense of closure, a small token of justice that she could cling to in light of everything she'd been fighting for. And now that was being ripped away from her. In the past, she might have given up hope, but now, a righteous flame grew inside her and she wasn't going to let it burn out.

CLEMENS WAS GETTING ready to turn in and had just finished showering when the call notification from the hotel room's holoscreen woke him up. "Answer," he said and Esther appeared on the screen.

"Hey honey. How's it going down there?"

"Not good!" Esther answered. "They found Hannah!"

"What?!"

"These guys blew in here with guns and they might have shot some people. We couldn't see. We're locked in a room."

"How many?"

"Four, I think."

"We're on our way! End call."

By the time Clemens and the rest arrived, Esther was in a heated discussion with the Dr. Malloy in the main foyer. Sylvia stood with her arms crossed, seething, while Rebecca paced the floor.

"Esther! Are you okay?" Clemens called out as they ran through the automatic sliding front doors.

She ran to her husband and embraced him. "They took her! They took her!" Esther cried.

Dr. Malloy was visibly shaken. "I am so sorry."

"How did this happen?" Clemens demanded.

"They appeared out of nowhere with guns. They shot an attendee and used his access card to break into the surgical unit." His lip was trembling. "She hadn't even been prepped for the procedure. She . . . she was pretty out of it. I was with another patient when they busted in. They were brandishing their weapons and I got on the floor." The doctor started blubbering as tears streamed down his face. "I was s-s-scared."

Clemens felt sorry for the young doctor. "It's okay." He placed a hand on the doctor's shoulder. "It's okay. Look at me. Do you have any idea where they took her?"

The doctor shook his head.

"Did they say anything at all?"

The doctor thought for a moment. "One of them said something about needing to charge up."

Of course. If they were leaving town tonight, they would need a full charge to get back to Winnipeg, if that is where they were headed. "Where's the nearest Esso?" Clemens asked.

"Oh, no. They didn't drive here," the doctor said. "They came in a helicopter. They would have to charge it at—"

"At the airport," Clemens said, finishing his sentence. "Come on, gang." He turned to thank the doctor and then said, "We're going to bring her back here and you're going to get that damn thing out of her. Got it?"

The doctor nodded. "Yes, sir. Good luck!"

They piled into the school bus and Dutch started loading and distributing weapons to his fellow officers as the bus navigated toward the airport.

"Do I get a gun?" James asked.

"No, son," his father said. "I need you to stay on the bus with your mother. Understood?"

"Yes, sir," James said, sounding dejected.

"He could fly a drone." Dutch said. "Might be good to keep an eye in the sky."

"Sh—yeah, can I, dad?"

Clemens looked to his wife, who didn't offer up any opposition. "Alright." The boy did know how to fly a drone and it wasn't a bad idea to have another pair of eyes on the situation, especially since it was dark and the drone had night vision.

The airport was dark and desolate. Since the grounding of all commercial flights throughout the region, the only flights in and out of Thompson were freight deliveries. While it was easy enough to locate the helicopter, it was going to be a challenge to approach it unnoticed in a bright yellow school bus. They would have to enter from the north end of the airport, away from the main road, and conceal the bus before approaching their enemies on foot.

The flight service station was a rectangular building that jutted out from a row of hangars with a helipad and charging docks on the other side. It had once been a full service lounge with food service and a small bar. Now it was an empty seating area with a restroom and an empty vending machine.

"There they are," Clemens announced looking through thermal binoculars. Clemens, Dutch, Miguel, and Sylvia had gathered in a nearby hangar approximately fifty meters to the north of the charging station. "Okay, listen up," Clemens said. "We definitely have 'em outnumbered. We're gonna to need to draw 'em out. We can't just go in guns blazing and risk them getting away. We have to keep 'em on the ground."

"Can you see Hannah?" Sylvia asked.

"No. It's too dark. Wait, wait. Two guys are getting out. Both armed. They're walking toward the service station. Probably going to take a piss. Miguel, Sylvia, make sure they don't leave the building. Go in from the back. Dutch, you come with me."

Miguel and Sylvia ran toward the back entrance of the flight service station. Clemens and Dutch crept around the side of the building to get a clear shot of the helicopter on the pad.

One man was standing at the charging pod, apparently monitoring the status of the charge. Another was standing guard outside the helicopter door on the far side, so that they could only see his legs. Clemens couldn't see inside the helicopter but his thermal binoculars confirmed a fifth person inside—Hannah.

Gunshots blasted from inside the flight service station, which caught the attention of the two men outside.

"Go see what that was about," said the man standing guard.

As the second man ran toward the building, Dutch took him out in one shot and he fell to the tarmac like a sack of rocks. The man standing guard climbed back inside the helicopter and shut the door. Within seconds the rotors began to turn.

Clemens started to run toward the helicopter when one of the men from inside the building stepped out with a gun to Sylvia's head. "Stop! Drop your weapons now or she dies!"

"Syl!" Clemens cried out.

"Drop your weapons *now* and get on your knees!"

Sylvia had a look of terror in her eyes. Clemens and Dutch dropped their guns and kicked them over. The rotors were spinning fully now. The man walked Sylvia toward the helicopter with his arm around her neck and a gun pressed against her temple as wind from the rotor blades pounded down upon them. Clemens was powerless to act.

Dutch nudged Clemens. "Look!" He motioned with his head toward the sky. The sound of the rotors was deafening, which is why nobody heard Jame's drone approaching overhead. The drone approached Sylvia and her captor from behind as he dragged her toward the helicopter. Once it got within a few meters, the drone delivered a tranq dart into the man's neck and Sylvia dropped to the ground under his weight.

The helicopter lurched upward and wobbled. With the interior lamps now illuminated, Clemens could see inside the hull where Hannah could be seen in the cockpit struggling with the pilot. The helicopter rose up and spun to the left before crashing back down nose-first onto the helipad. Clemens rushed over to Sylvia and helped her to her feet.

"Are you okay?" Clemens asked her.

"Yeah. Come on!" She took the incapacitated man's gun and they rushed to the fallen bird. The pilot was struggling to free himself from the safety harness and Clemens shot him before he had a chance to beg for mercy. Hannah had been thrown against the hull and was passed out, bleeding from her nose. They carried her out and laid her on the helipad.

"Where's Miguel?" Clemens asked.

Sylvia shook her head. Tears filled her eyes. "He's gone. They got him. It's my fault. I hesitated in there."

"No! Don't do that, Syl. It's not your fault, okay?"

Sylvia shook her head slowly. She turned her attention to Hannah, who was starting to moan.

"Hannah! Wake up, Hannah!" Sylvia said through her sobs.

Hannah opened her eyes and blinked. Her eyes widened when she saw Sylvia who wrapped her arms around the girl. Hannah rested her head on Sylvia's shoulder and looked at Clemens. "You guys came for me."

"Of course we did!" Sylvia said. She held her by her shoulders and looked her in the eyes. "You're one of us now."

"That's right," Clemens said. He put his hand on Sylvia's shoulder.

The bus pulled up in front of the service station and Rebecca ran out. "Miguel! Where's Miguel?" Dutch motioned with his head toward the building and Rebecca ran inside. Clemens and the others followed. Rebecca knelt beside Miguel who laid on the floor with blood covering one side of his head.

"No!" Rebecca cried. She laid her head on his chest and sobbed.

Miguel coughed.

"Miguel?"

Miguel winced and sat up. He held the side of his head with one hand. "Motherfucker shot my ear off!"

"Oh my god, you're not dead!" Rebecca squealed enthusiastically.

"What?" Miguel asked.

"You're alive!" She wrapped her arms around his neck. "You're alive!"

"What?!"

THEY RETURNED DIRECTLY to the hospital, the whole troop this time, where Dr. Malloy removed Hannah's tracking device and also tended to Miguel's head wound. He'd lost quite a bit of blood, in addition to most of his left ear. To keep the bandage in place, his whole head had to be wrapped, leaving a small oval opening for his face and one for his right ear so that he could still hear. Miguel was comforted by Rebecca's attentiveness as she sat by his side while the nurse applied the dressings. She certainly didn't have to stay with him. *Does this mean she's taking me back?* he thought.

It had never been a question for Miguel. He'd gone over their fight a dozen times since it happened and never did he conclude he would be better off without her. He regretted his defensiveness and hostility toward her and he wished he could take it all back.

"You look like a mummy," Rebecca said with a tender smile after the nurse momentarily left the room.

"Yeah? Like in a good way?"

Rebecca smiled briefly and averted her eyes. There was a

comfort in their familiarity but also, undeniably, a sense of unease. She was visibly in turmoil—trying both to be supportive and emotionally guarded.

"I'm sorry," Miguel said. "For the things I said yesterday. That was harsh."

"You were still processing. I get it."

"You know, maybe this is just part of me getting over it. Maybe we could start over?"

Rebecca looked down and fiddled with the zipper on her sweatshirt. "I'm not so sure."

"Really?" Miguel struggled to comprehend her dubiousness. *Over a stupid fight?*

"I'm not sure this is something we can get past."

"Of course we can," Miguel said tilting his bandaged head.

"I don't know if it's something *I* can get past. It'll always be something hanging over my head. I'll always be indebted to you, and I don't know if I can be happy like that."

"Even if I forgive you? Because I do. I forgive you." Miguel knew immediately that he was giving lip service. It's not as if he didn't want to forgive her. He wasn't certain that he had, or even if he knew how, and he could tell she wasn't buying it.

Rebecca rested her head against the back of her chair and exhaled deeply. "I don't know. Obviously, I didn't think this all the way through. I didn't plan this out. I think we both just need some more time."

Miguel sat in silent bewilderment for a moment, letting it sink in. *More time, or never?* he thought. "I mean, yeah. We have plenty of time, I guess."

"As long as you don't get your head blown off," Rebecca quipped with a smile.

Miguel attempted a smile but the bandages, which wrapped all the way around his chin, suppressed his full expression so that his cheeks bunched forward quite comically and Rebecca failed to contain a giggle. Miguel remained hopeful, despite the ambiguousness of Rebecca's concerns and not knowing exactly what she needed from him if forgiveness wasn't the answer.

The nurse came back into the room with a container of salve and extra dressings to take with him. She dismissed him with a warning to "be safe out there." Rebecca walked with him toward the lobby where the rest of the gang were waiting.

"You look like a mummy!" Dutch said.

"Yeah, I've been getting that a lot," Miguel said. "Where's Hannah?"

"They're just finishing up with her now," Esther said. "They took out the device. The doctor was right. No scar! So now she's getting an infusion."

"What kind of infusion?"

"It's this new treatment. The doctor says he's had a ninety percent success rate with preventing relapse. It's a one-time infusion and then a regiment of this new medication that she takes for twenty-eight days. The dosage decreases each week until she's down to barely anything at all. It's supposed to drastically improve her withdrawal symptoms in the very first week."

"That sounds amazing," Rebecca said. "I hate seeing her like that."

"She's a tough girl," Esther said. She turned. "Well, speak

of the devil!" Sylvia and Hannah came down the hall. Hannah was bright-eyed and nearly skipping. She smiled as everyone stood to greet her, taking her in their arms and letting her know she was welcome and loved.

Miguel put his hand on her shoulder. "Good to have you back, kid."

She examined him. "You look like a—"

"Like a mummy. Yeah, yeah. Where have I heard that before?"

THEY RETURNED EXHAUSTED to the hotel around 4 a.m. Miguel had the pleasure of sharing a double bed with Dutch who occupied sixty percent of the mattress and who snored loud enough to wake himself at times. After a particularly disruptive and sputtering inhale, Miguel threw back the covers and jumped out of bed. He stared angrily at Dutch whose respiratory cadence had fallen back into the normal range. He looked over at Clemens and his son who were sleeping soundly in the other bed. How did they do it?

Miguel pulled on a pair of pants and a t-shirt, stretching out the neck to accommodate the bandaging around his head. He walked outside where Sylvia stood leaning against the railing and looking out over a well-tended courtyard.

"Hey," he said.

"Hey." Sylvia glanced at him for a moment and returned her gaze toward the night sky. If Rebecca was hard to read, Sylvia was a complete enigma. They hadn't spoken on a personal level since their one-time New Year's fling, before Rebecca had come into his life. He assumed she had completely forgotten about it—perhaps because it was just that forgettable to her. To preserve his ego, Miguel chose to conclude it was her devotion to work that made it necessary for her to move past it. Since they worked on the same cases, it behooved them both to keep their relationship strictly professional. Yet, he couldn't help but hope for some kind of closure, some acknowledgement that it did happen and that it wasn't utterly trivial to her. His recent breakup had hurt his pride and he found himself seeking some kind of validation.

"Couldn't sleep?" Miguel stood beside her and placed his elbows on the railing, leaning forward.

"No. Not really." She stepped back from the rail and crossed her arms. "Listen, I wanted to apologize."

"For what?"

"Back at the airport. I hesitated. I had a clear shot and I hesitated and that's why you got shot. I won't let that happen again."

"No, I don't blame you, Syl. Are you kidding me? You did good back there. Not your fault, alright? Seriously."

Sylvia nodded. She turned back toward the courtyard and clasped the railing.

"Are you still worried about the bounty?" Miguel asked.

"Wouldn't you be?" Sylvia snapped. She seemed offended, but that wasn't anything new.

"Yeah, I guess I would," Miguel said, trying to appear empathetic. "But I don't think you need to worry about it all the way out here. And once we get to Churchill, I think we're pretty much in the clear, right?"

"I don't know. Yeah. Maybe." She looked preoccupied—distant.

Miguel wondered if there was something else. He wondered if she ever thought about him. Surely she wasn't harboring negative feelings about how that all ended, not that it ever really started. He wondered if Rebecca hadn't come along, if they would have ever hooked up again. He couldn't see himself in a real relationship with Sylvia. He was attracted to her physically, and they did have common interests, but Sylvia was guarded—bottled up. Then again, he never really got a chance to know her.

"You know we never talked about New Year's," he ventured. She didn't respond right away so he couldn't tell if she heard him. "I feel like maybe we should have talked about it, you know? Instead of just pretending it didn't happen."

"What's there to talk about?" Sylvia asked. "You have Rebecca."

"Do I?" He waited for her to respond, but she didn't. "It's probably not going to work out."

Sylvia looked at him briefly and quickly averted her eyes. "And so now you want to talk about it." She scoffed—then laughed, but in a way that felt disingenuous, mocking even.

"What?" He wasn't sure what he said that was so funny.

"Now that Rebecca's not an option, you think—" She didn't finish her thought but shook her head.

"No! No, that's not—"

"I'm not going to be some consolation prize."

"No! I don't think that. Look, I like you, Syl. I've always liked you."

"Are you being serious right now?" She said with an incredulous smirk.

"I tried to talk to you afterwards, before Rebecca even came along. Remember? You always found a way to shut it down. You're not the easiest person to talk to, you know."

"Okay, so let's talk. What do you want to say about New Year's?"

Miguel felt put on the spot. He hadn't really thought about what he wanted to say as much as he wanted to hear what she had to say. "I . . . uh, I guess I've been wondering if . . . I don't know. If that night meant anything to you? I mean, it's fine if it didn't. I just wonder if you ever still think about it."

"Do you?" She was looking directly at him now, a hand resting on her hip. *Dammit.* She did it again. "I . . . yeah. Okay yeah, I do . . . sometimes."

"Really?" She asked dubiously. She tucked a strip of hair behind her ear and crossed her arms. She turned to him, giving him her full attention now.

"I mean, yeah. I thought it was . . . great. I thought it was amazing actually."

Her face reddened. "Really?" This time more sincere.

"Yeah, didn't you?"

Sylvia turned away—blushing. It wasn't like her. "I guess," she said, looking away.

"You guess?" Miguel smiled. He brushed her shoulder with the back of his hand and she didn't pull away. He drew a few inches closer. At that moment, a door opened behind them. Rebecca stood, frozen for a moment, stunned, assessing Miguel and Sylvia's physical proximity and then she stepped back into the room and closed the door.

CHAPTER 27

AND ALL WE GOT WERE THESE LOUSY BULLET HOLES: SYLVIA

SYLVIA AVOIDED Rebecca and Miguel the rest of the morning. She couldn't deny that part of her hoped Miguel's bid for connection the night before might be more than some attempt to secure a backup as she had originally assumed. Then again, even if it was genuine, now wasn't the time to get into unnecessary complications. As far as Rebecca was concerned, she didn't feel as though she owed her any kind of explanation. After all, she hadn't done anything wrong.

She heard a pitiful wrenching coming from the bathroom. She went in to check on Hannah. Esther tended patiently to the poor girl and had removed her shirt, which was stained with vomit. Sylvia went through her pack and pulled out clean shirt and brought it back to Esther.

"Maybe we should stop and get her a few changes of clothes. I think I saw a clothing outlet just up the street," Sylvia said.

"That's not a bad idea," Esther said.

There was a knock at the door. Sylvia looked through the peep hole. Clemens. She opened the door.

"Is everybody ready?" Clemens asked. "Bishop is expecting us at 9 a.m."

"Hannah's feeling sick." Sylvia said with pained expression. The sound of Hannah vomiting could be heard in the doorway.

"Oh, uh . . . Well, I tell you what. I'll just take James to go pick up the rover. Shouldn't take more than an hour to get there and back."

"Okay. You need me to come with?"

"No, no, you stay here with Hannah. In fact, if she's feeling better, I thought maybe you could take her to pick up a few changes of clothes. I saw an outlet just up the street."

"I was thinking the same thing."

"Oh, they're serving breakfast downstairs until 10 a.m. Comes with the room." He took another glance at the bathroom door and winced before leaving.

The toilet flushed and Esther stepped out of the restroom.

"Was that Daryl?" Esther asked.

"Yeah, he and James are going to get the rover. He said we should stay here with Hannah take her shopping if she's up to it."

"Shopping?" Hannah said, emerging from the restroom wearing Sylvia's clean shirt.

Now that she could access her crypto wallet online, Esther looked up the name of the clothing outlet on the holoscreen and transferred some credits directly to the store. Sylvia had forgotten people still did that anymore. She'd only ever paid for anything via holospecs.

The rest of the crew met downstairs for a continental breakfast of bagels and runny oatmeal. Color had returned to

Hannah's face and she had reclaimed her appetite. She seemed to have bounced back from that wave of withdrawals much faster than before. When they finished breakfast, they all walked to the outlet store together.

"You're going to need a jacket. It gets pretty cold up there," Esther told Hannah. "Try these on." She held out two options for her to try on. "And boots! You aren't getting much farther in those sad old sneakers."

Hannah looked down at her shoes, which were separating at the toe.

Sylvia helped Hannah pick out some basic tops and bottoms, a couple of base layers for cold weather, a new package of socks, underwear, and three bras. They even found a pair of genuine graphene leggings. Graphene was a higher end material and usually prohibitively priced, but due to an unnoticeable manufacturer defect, these were astonishingly affordable.

"Aren't you getting anything?" Hannah asked Sylvia.

"Not today. Maybe after we get settled in Churchill." She already felt indebted to Clemens and didn't expect him to buy her clothes.

"This would look good on you," Hannah said holding up a thermal hooded pullover. She leaned in and whispered, "I'll get it for me and you can borrow it whenever you want."

Sylvia looked around to see if anyone had overheard and then looked back at Hannah who was nodding with a mischievous and irresistible grin. Sylvia smiled back. She couldn't help it.

"I'm walking away," Sylvia said, showing her hands to indicate she could not be held responsible.

When they returned to the hotel, Clemens and James

were organizing their supplies in the arctic rover, which looked sorely out of place among the rest of the cars in the parking lot. It was painted white and had six forty-two-inch off-road tires. Black lettering across the sides and back read: ARCTIC ADVENTURE TOURS.

"She used to be a military transport vehicle," Clemens said. "All these windows are bulletproof. It's fully armored. It's got satellite and everything!"

"And he just handed it over?" Esther said, taking a look inside.

"Yep. Said we could keep it as long as we needed it. I asked him what LeBlanc had done to deserve such a big favor, but he wouldn't tell me. 'That's top secret,' he said."

Dutch seemed especially enamored with the vehicle. "Can I drive?" If Dutch were a vehicle, he'd be this monstrosity.

They drove east for nearly four hours on paved highway until they reached the decommissioned railroad, where they began the off-road leg of their journey. Once Dutch shifted it into 6X6 mode, he had to operate it manually as the rover crawled onto the permafrost from the paved road. The front cab was separated from the rest of the passenger seating by a partition with a small sliding window. Sylvia rode shotgun to avoid Miguel and Rebecca.

"You ever driven one of these before?" Sylvia asked. She had never spoken to Dutch at length about anything remotely personal. He was surprisingly friendly for such hulking ex-mercenary.

"No. It's awesome. You wanna try?" Dutch said with a touch of glee.

"Maybe later." She peered out the windows at the vastness of the frozen tundra. The tips of evergreens in the distance faded into a low fog. She reflected on what Miguel had said last night—about her not being easy to talk to. "Hey, can I ask you a question?"

"Shoot."

"Am I hard to talk to?"

"Ha! That's an understatement."

Sylvia gasped. "You're the second person who's said that today."

"You know . . . you're just . . . you're just not the most approachable person."

"I'm not approachable?" Sylvia was genuinely befuddled.

"Come on! I thought that was your whole deal."

"That is not my whole deal. So does everyone think I'm this cold bitch?"

"Woah, I never said that! No, it's more like a vibe, like a 'nobody better fuck with me' vibe."

"Sounds like a cold bitch to me."

"Why are you surprised? Personally, I think it works."

"You do?"

"Sure. As long as I'm not on your bad side."

Sylvia couldn't tell if she was offended or flattered. "I mean, I know I can be a little stand-offish sometimes. Maybe that's why nobody asks me out."

"I wouldn't."

"It's really that bad, huh?"

"Oh, it's not because of your vibe. It's your body."

"Excuse me?!" She couldn't believe he just said that. *Rude! What's wrong with my body?*

"I'm into dudes," he said looking straight ahead.

"Get. Out! I've known you for like five years. How did I not know that?"

"You never asked."

"Does everyone know but me?

"I don't know what other people know or don't know. It's not a secret. But then again, it's not as obvious as your cold bitch vibe."

She feigned offense with a dramatic gasp. "I knew you thought I was a cold bitch!"

"Bitch, please," he said with a grin.

Sylvia laughed and shook her head.

Clemens knocked on the partition separating the cab from the passenger section. Sylvia slid the partition open. "What's up?"

"Do you guys hear that?" Clemens asked, eyes scanning the rover's ceiling.

Dutch rolled down the driver's side window. "Sounds like a chopper."

"Can you get eyes on it?" Clemens asked.

Dutch peered into his side mirror. "Yep. It's a chopper and it's gaining on us." There was no tree coverage or anywhere to hide. They were traveling parallel to the railroad on their right. Nothing but open tundra on their left.

"Keep going!" Clemens turned to the others. "Help me get the laser cannon ready." Miguel and James got to work assembling the weapon.

Sylvia could hear the chopper getting closer.

"They're closing in on us!" Dutch called.

"Go faster!" Clemens yelled.

"How do we know they're after us?" Rebecca asked.

A smattering of bullets perforated the roof of the armored vehicle and everyone instinctively ducked their heads.

"Does that answer your question?" Clemens yelled.

The helicopter slowed as it caught up to the rover and hovered. "Pull over!" came a voice from a bullhorn up above.

"You think it's the traffickers?" Sylvia asked.

"It's got to be," Dutch said. "We're too far from Winnipeg for it to be Guard." He reached behind her seat to grab his sniper rifle. "Hold the wheel!"

"Are you fucking kidding me?!" Sylvia protested.

Dutch cocked the rifle and took aim at the door gunner who fired off another dusting of rounds across the driver's side door. Dutch remained steady as he peered through his site and calmly pulled the tigger. A slug pierced the gunner's forehead and he fell to the earth with a crunch.

Clemens and Miguel assembled the laser cannon and mounted it at the back end of the rover so they could fire it through the open cargo doors. They needed to get the chopper positioned behind the vehicle in order to get a good shot.

"Dutch, speed up!" Clemens commanded. "Put 'em in your rearview!"

Dutch sped up as much as he could given the uneven terrain, but the helicopter pulled ahead.

"Where's he going?" Sylvia asked. The helicopter accelerated a ways in front of them and spun around to face them head-on.

"I need you to take over," Dutch said to Sylvia.

"Oh, for fuck's sake!" She slid over into the driver's seat and took the wheel. Dutch pulled himself outside the open window and took aim at the approaching helicopter. As soon as he placed crosshairs on the pilot's goggles, the rover hit a large boulder and bounced sideways. Dutch lost his balance and nearly fell backwards out of the window but Sylvia grabbed a fistful of his utility vest and pulled him up with one hand while steering the rover with the other. The pilot fired the mounted Gatling guns, which peppered the grill and hood of the armored vehicle. A round chipped the windshield, but it did not shatter.

Sylvia hit the gas and positioned the helicopter behind them. Seconds later she saw the helicopter in her rearview burst into flames and scatter across the tundra, like a busted piñata.

They still had another four hours to travel across the wild terrain before reaching Churchill. Although they'd taken out their assailants, the feeling was anything but celebratory. Each time they thwarted their pursuers they increased the chances of retaliation. Each victory was an invitation for further reckoning.

"It's not over," Clemens warned.

"You think they'll send more?" Miguel asked.

"More men, more guns."

Hannah pulled her hoodie over her head and began to cry.

"We're okay. We're okay," Rebecca said reassuringly, putting her arm around her.

"This is all my fault," Hannah said.

"No, don't say that," Rebecca said, trying to comfort her.

"It's not your fault," James said. "Listen!" James turned up the radio.

In a recent article in the Sun, several councilmen in the Canadian People's Guard, including the Ministry of Order, have been exposed in a sex trafficking operation by whistle-blowers inside the CPG. A warrant has been issued for Corporal Sylvia Boone and Sergeant Daryl Clemens, who leaked their investigations to the press, citing treason. Sources say they may have fled the city. Officials from the CPG have declined to comment.

"So that was CPG?" Sylvia asked. She felt a lot more confident rescuing a trafficking victim from piece-of-shit traffickers, but that was only because they had no idea who she was. The CPG was another story. As far as they'd come, she still remained a target.

"We did it!" Clemens said, pounding on the partition. "It worked. We exposed those bastards!"

"Great!" Sylvia said sarcastically. "And all we got were these lousy bullet holes."

"You gotta admit though," Clemens said. "It does feel kinda satisfying doesn't it?"

"I'll let you know when we make it to Churchill in one piece," she said.

"See," James said to Hannah. "They're after us for a whole other reason!"

Hannah wiped tears from her cheeks with the sleeve of her sweatshirt. "That doesn't really help."

"I know you must be scared," Esther said. "But at least we have each other. We're a family now and we look out for each other."

"Plus," Clemens added, "We have something they don't."

"What's that?" Hannah asked.

"We have a purpose. We're the good guys. As long as we choose to stand up for what's right, we're going to be in trouble. As long as we're on the side of truth, the bad guys are going to have it out for us. That's just the world we live in. It's up to us to make things right."

Sylvia knew deep down, that as long as she was running, she would never be safe. Maybe it was time to stop running. Maybe it was time to fight back.

THE TROOP PRESSED ON, following the tracks to the train station in Churchill. They arrived well after nightfall. There were no street lights to welcome them into town and they only had one headlight since the other one had been shot out in the helicopter attack. They drove stealthily through the unlit ghost town until their one headlight illuminated a wooden sign that read: Lazy Bear Lodge.

"This place looks cozy," Clemens said.

"Looks abandoned," Esther said.

"Probably. Let's assume it isn't though."

The lights were off but the front door was unlocked. When they stepped into the lobby it was empty. Dark brown leather couches surrounded a stone fireplace. A large wood-carved bear stood majestically in one corner, which startled Rebecca when she directed her light toward it. Bear skins, antlers, and indigenous pottery adorned every wall of the lobby. If the place was abandoned, it hadn't been for long given the level of cleanliness and the faint smell of wood smoke that lingered in the lobby.

Dutch rang the call bell on the front desk.

"Shhh," Clemens said, muffling the bell with his hands. "Let's do a sweep before we start ringing bells."

"Fair," Dutch conceded.

Clemens' heart skipped a beat at the distinct sound of an old shotgun being cocked.

"Who's there?" called a slippered and robed woman with long, straight, grey hair. She cautiously descended the wooden staircase behind them with her head tilted against the comb of the shotgun, one eye peering along the barrel toward the troop.

Miguel instinctively reached for his bolt gun. Clemens gestured with an outstretched arm instructing him to put it away, then reached both hands up in surrender. The others followed suit. "We're just looking for a place to sleep," Clemens said. "Is this still a hotel?"

The woman scanned the intruders carefully and lowered her rifle. "I haven't had any guests here in over five years. Wasn't expecting anyone."

"We didn't mean to startle you, ma'am," Esther said, examining the rustic decor. "This is a lovely place you have here."

"It's been in our family for a hundred years. All the exterior timber was reclaimed from a forest fire and assembled with hand tools by my grandpa Wally back in the eighties— the nineteen eighties. I was checking in guests and helping my aunts in the kitchen since I was a little girl. My name's Marjorie."

"Nice to meet you, Marjorie. You've kept it up very well," Esther said.

"Well, thank you. Looks like you've been traveling a while. I bet you could use a hot meal."

"I could eat," said Dutch.

"No," said Clemens glaring at Dutch. "We don't want to be any more trouble."

"Nonsense," said Marjorie. "I just made a new batch of elk stew today. I can't eat it all by myself! Let's get you checked in and you can go up to your rooms and get unpacked. I'll have it ready in a half-hour." She handed them four physical keys, each with the room number branded into a wooden key chain.

They traipsed upstairs to their rooms, which were cozy and tight with two full-sized beds per unit and solid wood furniture. Each headboard was individually handcrafted from locally sourced wood. Antler lamps and paintings of fishing scenes and other frontier art adorned the walls. The nightstands were repurposed tree stumps.

They came downstairs after showering and getting settled in their rooms. Marjorie had lit the fireplace and pushed tables together in the dining hall. The table was set with candles, fresh linens, and wood-carved napkin holders. Marjorie emerged from the kitchen with a large ceramic pot of stew and set it in the middle of the table.

"I hope you're hungry," she said, placing bowls and silverware in front of each guest. She returned to the kitchen and brought out two baskets of sliced sourdough and two bottles of red wine. "Just leave everything there and I'll clean up in the morning. Breakfast will be ready at 8 a.m. Well, I'm going to turn in. I'll see you all in the morning."

They bid her a goodnight and then dined on the most savory elk stew Clemens had ever tasted.

"I bet she grows her own vegetables," Clemens said. "Can you taste the difference?"

"It's amazing!" Esther said. Heads nodded around the table.

"Once we get settled, I want to start a garden. Imagine eating fresh vegetables everyday," Clemens said. "No more of that lab grown imposter food."

"Is anyone worried about the fact that we just took out a CPG helicopter?" Sylvia asked, deflating the optimistic mood Clemens was trying to create. "They have to know we're in Churchill by now. Where else would we be heading to?"

"Yeah," Dutch said. "I'm not so sure we're in the clear."

"How did they find us, anyway?" Miguel asked. "You don't think Bishop put a tracking device on the rover somewhere. I mean, we don't even know that guy."

"Let's all just calm down," Clemens said sternly. "Are we completely out of the woods? Who knows? I know we pissed a lot of people off down there, but I can't imagine what would motivate them to go out of their way to track us down. I'd be very surprised if they wasted any more resources on us. I'm not ruling it out, but I'd be very surprised. Now, we came prepared. You all knew this wasn't going to be a walk in the park. If we encounter them again, we're prepared to fight back. In the meantime, we're going to proceed as planned. We're going to eat and get some rest. Tomorrow, I'm going to start looking for suitable properties around town. My plan is to move forward, and you can't do that looking back over your shoulder. Do you all understand me?"

Everyone nodded in silence.

"Now, what vegetables are we going to plant in my damn garden?"

. . .

THE NEXT MORNING the troop gathered in the dining hall again for breakfast. Esther remained upstairs with Hannah who was having a rough morning of withdrawal symptoms. Marjorie emerged from the kitchen with a fresh pot of coffee. She seemed delighted to have guests in the hotel again. "Who needs a refill?" Cups raised. "So where are you folks from?"

"Winnipeg," Clemens said.

"Oh, I'm so sorry. It's just terrible what's happening down there. Are you looking to relocate here in Churchill?"

"That's the plan," Clemens said.

"Well, there's plenty of properties up here for the taking, if you find what you're looking for. There's only a few other families that live out here anymore. Everyone's pretty self-sufficient."

"Maybe we'll take a look around today. See what's out here."

Marjorie took a folded map from a display case in the lobby and circled a few areas around town with abandoned properties she thought might still have working solar utility systems and running water. Clemens was grateful for the direction.

Esther came downstairs and entered the dining hall. "Good morning!"

"How's she doing?" Clemens asked, handing her a fresh cup of coffee.

"Thank you. She's resting. This medicine does seem to be helping. She just has a headache and upset tummy. Much better than it was in the beginning."

"Good. Marjorie here was just showing us where we might find some decent properties around town."

"Oh, wonderful. I'd love to come, but I think I better stay back with Hannah."

"Can I come with you?" James asked.

"Sure, son. Bring the drone so we can take some aerial shots."

"Need me to come, boss?" Dutch asked.

"Nah. Why don't you to stick around here and set up surveillance. I'm still not comfortable after yesterday."

"What happened yesterday?" Marjorie inquired.

"We had a little run in with CPG," Clemens said.

"All the way up here?" Marjorie asked, surprised.

"I don't want to alarm you, ma'am, but there's a chance they might be following us."

"What do they want?" Marjorie asked.

"It's kind of a long story."

"You can stay here as long as you need," she said with a resolute nod. "Those fascist numbskulls are not welcome in my house!"

Clemens and James took Marjorie's truck toward a cluster of properties with varying degrees of usefulness. They were well spread out but close enough to allow each family to have their own property and still maintain a semblance of community. They hadn't discussed it, but he assumed he and his wife would look after the girl, at least until she had fully recovered. James hadn't said much to the same-age co-ed. Clemens wasn't surprised.

"Have you had a chance to talk to Hannah?" He asked his son as he sat in a rocking chair on the porch of an old cottage they'd just explored.

"What? Hannah? No, not exactly," James murmured awkwardly.

"She seems like a smart kid, don't you think?"

"Smart? Yeah, I guess so."

"What's wrong? I would think you two would have hit it off by now. You know, being the same age and all. You probably have some things in common I'd bet. Music? Video games?"

James stared blankly into a distant space and Clemens was careful not to push too hard, lest the boy clam up again.

"Dad?" James said finally.

"Yeah, son?"

"Can girls that have been, well . . . girls like Hannah, you know, having been put through all that . . . abuse and whatnot." He paused again, as if allowing his thoughts to catch up. "If I were in her shoes, I don't think I'd ever want to see another man ever again."

Clemens smiled warmly and place a hand on his shoulder. "You know what they call that, son?"

James shook his head.

"Empathy. When you put yourself in someone else's shoes, that's called empathy. And I think you're right to consider how someone might feel, given what they've been through." Clemens gave him a minute to let that sink in. "You know what else? I'd imagine that girl has been very lonely for the last couple of years. I bet she hasn't had a single friend or anyone to talk to or to show her any kindness without expecting anything in return. What do you think about that?"

"So you think I should try to be her friend?"

"I think you should let that empathy that you have, that

kindness that your mom and I know so well, I think you should let that lead you."

James nodded. "Okay, dad."

"Okay." Clemens gave his son's shoulder a squeeze. "Come on. Where do you think we should go next?"

CHAPTER 29

SO MUCH FOR GIRL TALK:
HANNAH

HANNAH STIRRED as sunlight filled the room. She heard footsteps up on the roof and the low murmur of male voices. She looked at the alarm clock on the tree stump nightstand—10:04 a.m. Her headache wasn't completely gone, but it was no longer throbbing. Her tummy grumbled and she realized her hunger was growing stronger than her nausea. She sat up and felt the room spin so she laid back down again until it stopped. She took five deep breaths before slowly placing her feet on the floor and gently pushing herself into a sitting position. *That's better.*

Her throat felt like dry, cracked leather and she took a long drink from the water glass Esther had left for her on the nightstand, then wiped her lips with the back of her hand. She looked up toward the sound of footsteps and low voices above her. Hannah slowly rose to her feet and shuffled into the bathroom to relieve herself. A wave of dizziness came and she braced herself with both hands on the walls on either side of the toilet. It passed. She stood and approached the vanity mirror and gazed at her own reflection. *Has my hair always been this color?* As she peered into her own eyes, she could barely recognize the person she used to be. Was she in there? *Who is this?*

She walked down each step one at a time holding onto the carved wood railing. Sylvia, who had been reading one of the paperback novels from the lobby's bookshelf, noticed her and jumped up to help her the rest of the way down.

"Careful," Sylvia warned. "Go slow. I got you."

Hannah was immediately drawn to Sylvia, who never seemed to say much. There was something about the way she carried herself that made Hannah feel safe. It was a confidence, or maybe an indifference, she couldn't quite explain it — something about her mannerisms. Plus, she was tough. Sylvia's arms were well-toned and she liked the way her veins snaked from her hands and branched out around her forearms. She liked her short pixie hairstyle that fell into her face constantly and the way she reflexively pulled it behind her ear. Sylvia was the coolest woman she'd ever met—hands down.

Hannah sat at a table in the dining hall and Esther brought her a steaming bowl of hot oatmeal topped with brown sugar, sliced almonds, and golden raisins, which she burned her tongue on, even after being warned. She welcomed Esther's mothering and she strived to be a good patient, playing down her discomfort as best she could.

"How do you feel, dear?" Esther asked, feeling Hannah's forehead with the back of her hand.

"Better." She blew on her next spoonful to cool it down. "Are there people on the roof?"

Esther laughed. "Marjorie put Miguel and Dutch to work fixing one of her solar panels. She's not charging us to stay here, so it's the least we can do I suppose. I said we'd all help with dinner. You feeling up to it?"

"Yeah, sure." Hannah didn't know how to cook but she was eager for the chance to bond with her new family. She looked around the dining hall. "Where are the other two?"

"Oh, Daryl took James to look at some properties around here. They'll be back later. I'm going to see if Marjorie needs any help in the kitchen. Glad you're feeling better, dear."

Hannah noted that Esther was the only one who called him Daryl. He was Clemens to everyone else. They were a cute old couple, older than her own parents but not quite grandparents either.

"So," Rebecca said with a grin. She was painting her toenails at the end of the table. "What do you think of Jimmy?"

Hannah raised one eyebrow. "What do you mean?" She hadn't come to any conclusions about James. He was a lot like the boys she used to hang out with before being kidnapped. Cute maybe, but kind of clueless and awkward. He probably played hockey or lacrosse and he probably jerked off like ten times a day. The kid had no game, which was comforting somehow.

Rebecca blew on her toes, which were propped up on the edge of the table. "Do you think he's cute?" "Rebecca!" Sylvia chided.

Rebecca ignored her. "I'm just saying, you guys are the same age. Is he your type?"

"I don't know." Hannah blushed.

"Rebecca!" Sylvia gave her an admonishing stare.

"Does he even talk?" Hannah asked.

Rebecca laughed and shook her head. "No, I don't think he does!"

"He's just shy," Sylvia said.

"He's only shy around pretty girls," Rebecca said with a wink.

Hannah tried to hide a grin.

"Don't embarrass her," Sylvia said to Rebecca.

"I'm not! She's pretty," Rebecca said and then looked at Hannah. "You *are*."

"No," Hannah protested mildly. She did feel embarrassed, but she didn't mind.

"Isn't she?" Rebecca asked Sylvia.

"Well, of course she is." Sylvia rolled her eyes and shook her head, silently apologizing for Rebecca's behavior.

As much as Hannah enjoyed the compliments, she felt compelled to divert the focus away from herself. "So what's going on with you and Miguel?" Hannah asked Rebecca. Rebecca's smile vanished. Sylvia cleared her throat. Hannah felt like she'd just stepped on a landmine.

Rebecca put her feet down and sat up. "We're not together."

"Oh. Sorry." Hannah wished she hadn't said anything.

"No, it's fine. We were a thing for a minute and . . . He's moved on, apparently."

"What's that supposed to mean?" Sylvia challenged.

"Nothing. It's fine."

Hannah's eyes volleyed back and forth between the two and then she fixed her gaze on the table.

"What do you mean, *apparently*?" Sylvia asked.

"I saw you with him the other morning. It's fine. We're finished. You can have him."

"What do you think you saw, Rebecca?"

Rebecca sat silently shanking her head. Sylvia scoffed. Hannah sunk slowly into her chair, trying to disappear. So much for girl talk.

The tension was interrupted by a yell, followed by a crash outside. They ran to the window to see Dutch rolling off the back porch awning into a cord of stacked firewood, which gave way and tumbled beneath his weight and delivered him harshly to the ground where he sat, legs splayed before him. Three or four logs from the top of the pile followed him the ground and fell upon his massive bald head one at a time. The girls ran outside to help. Miguel called down from the roof, "Dude! Are you okay?"

Dutch rubbed his head and brushed bark and sawdust from his arms and chest. "I think so." He slowly got to his feet and tested his neck and limbs for mobility. He looked up and gave Miguel a thumbs up. "All good."

Dutch looked like he could tackle a grizzly bear in the wild and squeeze the life right out of it. His tree trunk arms didn't fall to his sides like a normal person.

"Jesus, Dutch!" Esther said brushing past the girls to look him over. "It's gonna take a lot more than falling off a roof to slow you down!"

"Yes, ma'am," he replied.

"Come inside. Let me take a look at that scrape."

Hannah was distracted by a sound up above. "Does anybody hear that?"

Everyone looked toward the sky. Helicopters.

CHAPTER 30

TRAIN STATION: MIGUEL

MIGUEL quickly and safely made his way down from the second story roof to find everyone assembled in the lobby. Dutch was peering through binoculars out the front window. Sylvia paced back and forth rubbing the back of her neck. Rebecca sat with an arm around Hannah, reassuring her everything would be okay. Marjorie came downstairs with her shotgun in one hand and a box of shells in the other. Esther kept trying to reach Clemens on her wrist comm, but couldn't get a clear signal.

"Dutch, what do you got?" Miguel asked.

"Two. I can see two of them and they're headed north."

The rover was parked out front and it stuck out like a sore thumb in the empty parking lot. Had there been snow, it might have blended in, but it was still summer and its white paint and massive scale would be a dead giveaway.

"We need to get the rover off these premises," Miguel said. "It's a huge target."

"Where are you going to take it?" Sylvia asked.

"Dutch and I will take the rover to the old train station. If they see us, at least we'll lead them away from here."

"I'm coming with you," Sylvia said.

"You're the one with the warrant, Syl. They're coming for you. You know that, right?"

"Yeah. I know."

Miguel could see that, for Sylvia, this was personal. They killed her father and she wasn't going to back down. He nodded. "Let's move."

Dutch drove while Miguel charged the laser cannon. Sylvia activated a case of fusion grenades and kept an eye out for approaching choppers. For the time being, it appeared as if they had flown toward the northern peninsula, but it was only a matter of time before they turned back toward town. The old train station was only blocks away from the Lazy Bear but far enough that the rest of the crew would be safe.

"I see them!" Sylvia said as she pointed east. They were still a ways out but headed toward the center of town. Dutch pulled onto the train tracks and parked the rover in front of the station where they hoped to establish adequate cover. They unloaded two footlockers of artillery and the laser cannon from the back of the rover. Dutch carried the laser cannon on his left shoulder and dragged one footlocker behind him with his right hand. Miguel and Sylvia took hold of either side of the second footlocker and hauled it inside the station.

"They're headed toward the Lazy Bear," Dutch called looking through binoculars.

"Shit!" Miguel said. "We need to distract them. Do we have any flares in there?"

"Way ahead of you," Sylvia said, rifling through one of

the footlockers. She loaded a flare and ran back outside. She shot one directly above them, and then another. Within seconds the helicopters seemed to have noticed and started heading west toward the train station. "Here they come!"

Dutch helped Miguel set up the laser cannon on the east facing windows and then got in position with his sniper rifle. Sylvia clipped three fusion grenades to her belt and activated a plasma rifle. The laser cannon was only capable of firing once every thirty seconds due to having to recharge between shots. "I'll take out the first one. You think you can get the pilot on the second?" Miguel asked Dutch.

"All day," Dutch replied smugly.

Miguel looked over at Sylvia. "You ready?"

"Ready."

An LED lit up when the laser cannon had the helicopter in optimal range and the fire button blinked red. "Eat shit, dickheads!" Miguel pushed the fire button. Nothing. He pressed it again. "What?" He pressed it a third time. "Piece of shit!"

"What are you waiting for?" Sylvia yelled.

"It's not working! Stupid thing is jammed!"

"What?!" Sylvia yelled.

"I got 'em," Dutch said. But before he could get off a shot, an explosion sent him flying backwards and into the ticket counter like a cannonball. Miguel, too, was thrown back by the blast and fell on his ass. He got onto his feet as the first helicopter touched ground and several men emerged, weapons drawn.

"Dutch!" Miguel called. "Dutch, are you alright?" Dutch didn't respond. He didn't have time to check on him before the men from the first helicopter, four or five of them, started shooting out the windows along the east wall.

The second helicopter landed on the tracks side of the station next to the rover. "You're surrounded!" came a voice from a bullhorn. "Come out with your hands in the air and you will not be harmed!"

"Yeah, right," Sylvia mumbled. She activated a fusion grenade in her right hand and looked at Miguel as if making an oath. Blue LED light pulsed from the grenade, indicating its readiness. She nodded and Miguel kicked the front door open. Sylvia chucked a grenade at the approaching men. The current spread like a net connecting their bodies, which convulsed as electricity flowed through them for several seconds and they fell to the ground like marionettes whose strings had just been snipped.

Rounds echoed in the empty station—glass shattering all around them. Dust from the explosion, and dirt kicked up from the helicopter rotors outside got into Miguel's eyes, obstructing his vision. He continued spraying automatic rounds in a random arc, not knowing if any were landing. He turned back and Sylvia was on the ground. He dove behind a rafter that had fallen from the explosion to reload, and when he stood back up was stunned by an invisible attack. His body tensed up in a snarled rigidity and he fell to the ground like a fallen statue.

When he opened his eyes, who knows how long later, Sylvia was gone. As his eyes tried to focus, he saw four men dragging Dutch away in the distance. He tasted dirt and blood, and then he saw black.

CHAPTER 31

RETRACTION: CLEMENS

THE NEXT PROPERTY Clemens was interested in was just east of Isabelle Lake. He noticed that the truck's battery was running low and thought it better to charge up before going much further. The closest charging station was near the Churchill Airport.

At the station, James hopped out to connect the charging cable while Clemens consulted the map. "Hey dad! Do you hear something?"

"What is it?" Clemens asked without looking up from the map.

"It sounds like a helicopter."

"You got to be kidding me." Clemens got out of the truck and searched the sky. He heard it, too. He looked over toward the air traffic control tower and saw four helicopters coming in from the south and landing. "Christ!"

Clemens tried contacting Esther on his wrist comm. "Esther, come in . . . Esther, can you read me?" Static followed. "We're too far out," he told James. "We need to get back."

They climbed into the truck and headed toward town on Kelsey Road. James flew the drone half a kilometer ahead of them, monitoring for any possible assailants. Clemens was armed merely with his bolt pistol, which was only effective at close range. There were no alternative routes back into town and he felt exposed on the main road. "Faster," he commanded and the truck accelerated.

"Hey dad, I think I see something," James said. James paired the feed from the drone's controller to the truck's windshield display. They saw two helicopters flying South toward the center of town. A red flare ignited in the sky and then another. "It's our guys. Are they signaling us?" James asked.

The helicopters turned toward the flares. "No. They're baiting those choppers. Gutsy move."

"Should we go help them?" James asked.

Clemens was torn. He felt a responsibility to lead his troop but his wife's safety took precedence. Plus, that laser cannon would be more than adequate to handle a couple of helicopters. He had faith in his team. "They have all the firearms they need. We'd only get in the way. We need to get back to your mom."

The drone had been focused on the activity up ahead so it didn't see what was approaching from behind. Clemens heard a loud smash as the back window shattered. They both crouched down as close to the floorboards as they could, with pebbles of glass raining upon them. A barrage of rounds pierced the rear and roof of the truck and finally the tires. James cried out.

"Are you hit? Did you get shot?" Clemens yelled but his

son was speechless with pain—his eyes squeezed tight like fists, his teeth bared. "Son!"

With the tires blown, the truck automatically enacted it's safety protocol by pulling over and coming to a stop. Clemens leaned over to examine his son but he was curled in on himself in a protective posture. Clemens tried to pull on his arm and he cried out even louder. "I'm sorry! Where are you hurt, son?" James slowly unraveled himself to reveal blood pooling into his shirt sleeve around his elbow. Clemens felt strangely relieved. He would survive whatever this was.

He looked behind him and two helicopters had landed on the road and six men were running toward them with guns. He might have been able to pick off one or two but he'd get mowed down by the rest. He looked James in the eye. "You're going to be okay, son. Don't resist them. Do you hear me? Do not resist!" James nodded.

"Step out of the vehicle," came a voice from a bullhorn. They were surrounded with guns pointed at them. "Hands where we can see them!"

Clemens opened his door and raised his hands. "My son is shot. He's unarmed. I have a gun on my right hip. Please be careful with my son!" The men pulled his arms behind his back, cuffed him, and removed his pistol. They opened the passenger door and regarded the blood. One of the men called for another to bring a stretcher. Tears pooled in Clemens' eyes. "It's going to be okay, son!"

They placed James on the stretcher and loaded him into one of the helicopters. They walked Clemens to the other. "Wait. I want to be with my son. Can I go with my son?"

"Shut up! Get in!"

"Please, he needs me. Plea—" Clemens felt a blow to his head and then it went dark.

CLEMENS AWOKE SUDDENLY as a bucket of frigid water splashed his face. He gasped and as soon as he could blink open his eyes, another bucketful hit him forcefully in the face. "Alright!" Clemens shouted. "Alriiight!" The men said nothing and left the room with empty buckets. Clemens sat in a metal chair with his arms tied behind the chair back, water dripping from his soaked body.

He couldn't tell where he was being held or how long he'd been there. He wondered if his son was nearby. Where did they take him? Was he getting medical attention or had they strapped him to a chair, too? Moments later a well-groomed man in a grey suit with long slicked-back dark hair stepped into the room. He didn't look anything like the thugs who had been after them.

"Good afternoon, Sergeant."

"Where is my son?"

"He is receiving medical treatment as we speak. I'm afraid his elbow was shattered in that unfortunate dust up. He'll live."

"Where?"

"They flew him into Thompson. It's the nearest hospital this far north."

"Where am I?"

"We're still in Churchill, but hopefully not for long. This place is . . . bleak. Once I get what I need, I'll gladly reunite you with your son and we'll be on our way."

"Who the fuck are you? What do you want?"

"Alright, enough with the pleasantries. My name is Victor Crowe. Maybe you've heard of me?"

Victor Crowe was the CEO of the largest pharmaceutical company in the world. He was credited for environmental philanthropy as well as bringing a sense of economic stability throughout North America by funding the CPC and other regimes after the fall of nations. When Clemens and his team sent in their evidence against the Canadian People's Guard for sex trafficking, Crowe was identified as a major kingpin.

"Yeah. I heard of you," Clemens said scornfully.

"It is possible, in this day and age, that information is not always the most reliable, is it not? Perhaps you and your team have been fed misinformation."

"What do you want?"

"I want you to live stream a recantation of your defamation attacks."

"They're not attacks. We had no interest in you until the red strings all happened to point to you. It's called police work."

"Ah yes, I almost forgot who I was speaking with. Sergeant Daryl Clemens, Winnipeg's son. Decorated Air Force Captain. Champion of justice. Warrior of truth. Forgive me. You and I do not operate from the same paradigm. Even if we may share certain goals, we have different methods for achieving them. You've been trained to jump through hoops, wait your turn, play by the rules. I don't have the time or the patience for that. The world needs men of action." He leaned in within inches of Clemens' face. "I know what you must think of me, Sergeant. One day you'll see that I was right all along. The world needs me. I'm the only one actually doing anything to save this goddamned planet."

"You're insane."

"There is a fine line between insanity and genius."

"Then you're deluded."

"I get things done. The CPG should have taken you out long before, but they let it go too far and I was forced to take matters into my own hands. Now, I'll make a deal with you. You're supposed to return in CPG custody to face whatever charges of treason they've made against you. I couldn't care less. But if you can cooperate with me, I'll make sure you and your little band of refugees are far from their reach. All I need you to do is go live across all major news outlets and read what I've written here." He laid a typed statement on Clemens' lap.

"I won't do it." He jerked his knee and let the paper float to the floor and into a puddle that quickly soaked the page and the ink began to run.

Victor smiled. "We have three of your officers in our custody and if you don't cooperate, I'm certain one of them will. Especially, that Corporal Boone, who I understand has a bounty on her head for killing two CPG officers." He shook his head. "Tsk, tsk, tsk. It's not looking good for her."

There would be no fair trial for Sylvia if she were to return with them. Clemens knew how their broken system of justice played out. Then again, what proof did he have that they even had Sylvia in their custody? He looked into Crowe's shifty eyes and called his bluff.

"I'd rather die than let you off the hook you piece of shit!" Clemens jerked and twisted his body in the chair, unable to free himself.

"Have it your way." Victor Crowe buttoned his jacket. "Once I get what I came for, I'll keep my end of the bargain. If I don't get that retraction, you won't like the consequences. Good day, Sergeant," he said and walked away.

Clemens spit in his direction, but Crowe had already left the room. He pulled hard on his bonds, and when they did not loosen, hung his head and sobbed. He'd led his crew right back into the hands of their enemies.

CHAPTER 32

A SECOND CHANCE: REBECCA

REBECCA HEARD a vehicle pull up outside the Lazy Bear. Miguel, Sylvia, and Dutch had just left and Clemens and James had not been in contact for several hours. She tried to reassure Hannah that the men who had arrived at the Lazy Bear were not here for her, but Hannah couldn't tell the difference between traffickers and CPG, who routinely enabled and facilitated trafficking operations. Two men got out of an airport shuttle and walked up onto the front porch of the Lazy Bear.

Marjorie clutched her shotgun. It was an old-timey gun and Rebecca doubted it still worked. "Go away!" Marjorie shouted as two men approached the door.

"We're looking for a Sylvia Boone. Does that name sound familiar?"

"No. This is a private residence. Now please leave."

"I'm afraid we're going to have to come inside and take a look around."

"I'm afraid I'm gonna have to blow your head off if you don't get off my porch!"

"That wouldn't be wise, ma'am." He motioned toward the vehicle and two more men got out. These two were armed.

Esther hurriedly ushered Rebecca and Hannah toward the back door. "There's a utility shed over to the left," she whispered, "out past those propane tanks. Get inside and wait there for me to come get you. Go now!"

Rebecca didn't understand what CPG would want with her or Hannah, except to ask about Sylvia or Clemens who both had warrants for their arrest. Regardless, she didn't feel like being interrogated. Rebecca took Hannah's hand and led her to the shed, looking in every direction to make sure they were not discovered. Inside there were several tools, many of them rusted. It smelled of old grease and moth balls.

"It stinks in here," Hannah said.

"I know. It's just for a little while." It was dark, but she didn't want to risk calling attention to themselves. The natural light from two small windows on either side of the door illuminated the area just enough to find a suitable hiding spot between a wooden work bench and a vertical metal storage locker. She unfolded a dusty tarp and they crouched underneath it.

Hannah was a shaking with nerves. She kept murmuring under her breath, *no, no, no, no*. Rebecca walked her through some breathing exercises she'd learned in yoga. They waited there listening to the sounds of each other's breath for several minutes. Rebecca heard the sound of two officers talking to one another outside. "Check that shed."

Shit! Rebecca could hear Hannah's breathing accelerate. "Shhh. It's okay. Be still," she whispered.

The door opened wide and one man stepped inside. The

plywood flooring creaked under his boot steps. Rebecca held Hannah tight under the tarp. She felt Hannah's rib cage expand quickly, then contract, then expand again and she sneezed.

The tarp was ripped away and Rebecca held Hannah, shivering, head between her knees. The officer pointed a flashlight in Rebecca's face. She instinctively turned away from the beam. "Look at me!" He pushed Hannah's head up and shined the light in her face.

"Don't touch her!" Rebecca shouted.

"It's not her," he said to the other officer. He turned to Rebecca and projected an image from a small device. It was Sylvia's wanted photo. "Have you seen this woman?"

Rebecca shook her head. Hannah followed suit.

The officer squinted. "You're lying. Why are you hiding?" His eyes darted back and forth between Rebecca and Hannah. "Right. Let's go." He pulled them to their feet and bound their hands behind their backs. Hannah started crying. Rebecca felt like doing the same but resolved to remain strong for Hannah. They escorted them around to the shuttle and shoved them in through a sliding door.

"Where are you taking us?" Rebecca asked one of the men seated in front. He didn't respond. She turned to the men sitting behind her. "Where are we going?"

"Shut up!" a man in the front seat said without looking at her.

Hannah quietly sobbed. Rebecca wanted to hold her but her hands were tired behind her back, so she leaned over and rested her head on Hannah's. At last, Rebecca could make out what was obviously an air control tower.

They pulled into an empty warehouse with airplane

parts and heavy machinery at the far end. They cuffed them each to a metal column and left through a side door without saying a word.

Out of the shadows stepped Victor Crowe. Rebecca was stupefied. "Victor?!" She worried he'd catch up to her sooner or later.

"At last," Victor said holding his hands out as if welcoming a guest. "It's been some time."

"What are you doing here?" She looked at Hannah and rolled her eyes as if to say *I'll tell you later.*

"Oh, just a little business. You know how it is."

"Uncuff us!"

"Of course, love. I will. But first, I have some questions." He placed his hands behind his back and began to pace.

"Victor, I'm really not in the mood!"

"You know, it wasn't very nice of you to leave without saying goodbye."

"Are you fucking kidding me right now? Is that what this is all about? I'm sorry, okay?" Rebecca's apology dripped with sarcasm.

"Were you really that unhappy, my love?"

"Do we have to do this right now?" She motioned toward Hannah with her head. Hannah shouldn't have to hear this.

"Yes!" Victor shouted.

A chill rose up her spine. She'd heard him raise his voice in the past and that usually meant someone's head. He'd never directed anger toward her. "Fine," she said calmly to ease his agitation. "That was like a million years ago. You were gone most of the time."

"Did I not give you everything you ever wanted? The

villa, the Ferrari, jewelry, travel, your very own security detail. You had it all."

"Except *you*. I wanted a relationship, Victor. It was fine, at first. But in the end, I was alone. You were always too busy. My life revolved around your schedule. Finally, I just had enough. I wanted my own life. I knew if I told you that then, you'd just talk me into staying somehow."

"Rebecca," he said in supplication. "Am I really that unreasonable?"

Rebecca scoffed and pulled up on her shackles.

"Fair enough," he said. "I suppose you have a point. I'm not an easy man to live with. I don't live an ordinary life."

"What are you doing here? Did you track me down?"

"Finding you here is just as much a surprise to me as it is to you, my love. I'm here for an entirely different purpose. How do you know Sergeant Clemens?"

"He's my boy . . . my *ex*-boyfriend's boss. I came with them to get out of Winnipeg after the water crisis."

"I see. And who is this boyfriend?" He inclined his head and looked down his nose—still pacing.

"*Ex*-boyfriend. His name's Miguel. Why?" Rebecca was growing tired of this whole interrogation but she knew Victor well enough to know that sometimes it's best to play along.

"It seems your new friends don't think too highly of me." Victor contorted his face into a pout. In the past, this face might have inspired sympathy, but now it was just annoying.

"So? Most people don't. No offense." *Why does he care what my friends think?* she thought.

"Do you think I'm a bad person, Rebecca?"

"Victor! You're so weird. No, of course not."

"Your friends seem to think I am involved in some seriously heinous activities."

She took a deep breath. *This should be good.* "Like what?"

"The sex trade?"

"That's ridiculous. *Why* would they think that?"

"Because I'm a man of means, love. Therefore, I always have a target on my back. The world is full of evil. Someone has to be blamed for it, right? People like us are always easy targets."

"Us? Victor, I'm not like you."

"But you were, and you could be again. What do you say we give it another go? Come back to Chicago with me. I've learned my lesson," he said placing both hands over his heart. "You can come with me when I have to travel. I'll never leave you alone again. Won't you give me a second chance, darling?"

Rebecca sneered. "Sorry, but that ship has sailed."

"Darling, is this really the life you want? Traipsing around the wilderness with wanted fugitives? Come on! This is an easy choice, my love."

Rebecca looked over at Hannah. "What are you going to do with Hannah? And the rest of them?"

"Everyone is safe. I haven't harmed any of your friends and I don't intend to," he said with a chuckle. "I simply need one of those cops to recant on their distasteful allegations against me. You know I could never hurt you, Rebecca."

"You swear to God, you had nothing to do with the sex trafficking?"

"Please! Rebecca, you know me. As soon as I have my

name cleared, I promise, I'll do everything in my power to find out who is behind this travesty. You have my word."

She believed him. To Rebecca, Victor was a handsome and eccentric workaholic billionaire with a below average libido. She assumed he was likely a white collar criminal at best, but never a diabolical maniac. He treated Rebecca like a pet. He lavished her with material effects. He wasn't the best boyfriend, but he wasn't a monster.

Rebecca had never truly been in love with Victor. She was attracted to his social status and enjoyed the opportunities that afforded her. She traveled with him to Guangzhou, Kuala Lumpur, Sydney, São Paulo, and Paris. And she enjoyed the company of dignitaries, socialites, and celebrities, but Victor was usually occupied in closed door meetings. The times they were alone together almost always got interrupted with an important phone call. If they ever had enough time together to make love, Victor never stayed with her through the night. Even if he didn't suddenly have to fly to Johannesburg, or Cairo, Victor always had some other obligation to attend to.

"Fine," Rebecca said. She looked at Hannah who was now sitting at the base of the metal column, watching this whole interchange in silence. "But Hannah gets to come with me. And you have to promise to let everyone else go—unharmed."

"Deal," he said. A wide grin swept across his face.

She would miss her companions, especially Miguel. But she had to be reasonable. They would be better off without her. She'd felt like a burden and now they didn't have to carry the extra weight. At the very least, she would be safe with

Victor. Hannah would be better off, too. She had no reservations about Hannah's safety under Victor's protection. After all, she never took him for a person capable of sex crimes. He was much too busy. How would he have time to get involved with that sort of thing?

MIGUEL SAT BEFORE A VIDEO CAMERA, face swollen. They carefully removed his bandages and did their best to clean off the blood. They combed his hair and dressed him in a clean button-up shirt. He squinted when they switched on the studio lighting. A man in headphones pinned a lapel mic onto his shirt. "Say something."

"Something." Miguel looked into a small monitor off to the side. They had applied a filter to augment his appearance on screen—as if he hadn't just been beaten senseless in order to extract a retraction.

The man in headphones gave Victor a thumbs up, then turned to Miguel. "Okay, Corporal Estes. Whenever you're ready."

Victor stood by the cameraman, hands clasped behind his back. Miguel looked up at the teleprompter. He felt sick at the thought of giving into their demands. He had to. They were going to kill his friends. *Let's get this over with,* he thought. The numbers flashed: 3, 2, 1. He read the following in an insipid, monotone manner.

"My name is Corporal Miguel Estes of the Canadian People's Guard, 9th precinct. Last week, reports surfaced in the media, implicating officials within the Canadian People's Guard and Victor Crowe, CEO of Crowe Pharmaceuticals, in a worldwide human trafficking operation. These reports were entirely fabricated and categorically false. Victor Crowe is a leader in global efforts to reverse climate change and bring life- sustaining medication to every corner of our planet. It is with great conviction that I renounce any claims made against him or the Canadian People's Guard from any member of our ranks. Please disregard these false allegations as pure misinformation, distributed solely for political and nefarious ends. Thank you for your time."

"We got it!" They switched off the lights and removed the lapel mic.

"So that's it then?" Miguel asked. "You'll let 'em go now?"

The men busied themselves loading up their equipment. Victor was talking discretely to one of his men.

"Hey!" Miguel shouted. "You said I could see my friends after I did the thing. Hey!!"

Victor left the room and the man he was talking to came over to Miguel. "This way, sir."

"Are you taking me to my guys?" Miguel asked.

The man did not answer. He ushered Miguel outside and into the bright sunlight. A helicopter sat on the tarmac. Its engine hummed and rose in frequency as its blades slowly began to rotate. "Get in!"

Miguel looked around for any signs of his crew. The men seized his arms and shoved him onto the helicopter with three other armed officers, plus the pilot. The scruff-faced guard sitting across from him stared intensely into Miguel's eyes as if begging him to make the wrong move or say the wrong thing. Miguel broke eye contact. Another guard, chewing gum with his whole face, flashed a ghoulish smile. The helicopter lurched off the ground.

"Where are we going?" Miguel shouted over the clamor at the guard sitting next to him. The guard nodded as if asked a yes or no question. They flew over open water further and further away from the shore. The Hudson Bay glistened like a jewelry case in the afternoon sunlight. The next twenty minutes felt like an eternity with all of Miguel's what if's and worse-case scenarios racing through his head. Would he be executed and tossed into the bay? Were his friends still alive? He could bear almost any punishment, as long as he knew ahead of time, what it might be. The uncertainty tortured him.

"We're here," the pilot called back.

Miguel looked out both sides of the fuselage. They were easily a kilometer from the shore to the south. "Where?!"

The scruff-faced guard seized Miguel by the back of his neck. "How good of a swimmer are you?"

Miguel twisted loose and elbowed the guard in the chin. Miguel felt a sharp punch from another guard, splitting his lip open again. He kicked at the guards as they descended upon him. Another fist landed just below his sternum, knocking the wind out of him. As he struggled to inhale, they shoved him out of the helicopter.

The waves received his body without so much as a splash. He plunged deep into the water as the cold arrested his limbs. His muscles contracted in the frigid water and he couldn't tell which way was up. He forced himself into an open posture and the water eventually lifted him upward.

Miguel reached the surface and gasped for air. He oriented himself toward a distant tree line like the ends of thin brush strokes in greens and browns. He swam. Muscles burning and winded, Miguel was determined to reach land. Arms reached one after the other in a meditative rhythm. After a while, he could no longer feel his legs kicking. He assumed they were, but he couldn't be certain. Exhaustion overtook him and Miguel began to slip beneath the surface of the water. He wasn't going to make it.

Just as Miguel had surrendered to a frozen death, he felt himself being pulled up by his collar. He gasped for air as he broke the surface and an arm that may have belonged to a giant, wrapped around the front of his chest. "I got you," Dutch said. Dutch swam backward with one arm while holding Miguel with the other. Clemens waded out and helped pull him onto the beach, where Miguel continued to throw up water on hands and knees.

"Where are we?" Miguel asked when he'd finally caught his breath. Beyond the rocky beach a dense forest loomed.

"I'm not sure," Clemens said. "But I think if we follow the coastline west, eventually we'll get back to Churchill. It could be a day's hike. Maybe two."

"Did you two get dumped in the ocean, too?"

Clemens smiled. "Yeah, but just right over there." He pointed out over the water. "You must have pissed someone off to get dropped that far out."

Miguel shrugged. "I take it Sylvia will be next. Maybe we should wait here?" Miguel suggested with his last shred of optimism.

Clemens shook his head solemnly. "The bounty," he muttered. "They'll want that bounty."

"But Crowe said he wouldn't turn her over to the Guard if he got his retraction," Miguel said.

"Well, I didn't give it to him, did you?" Clemens asked.

Miguel looked away. "He said he'd start killing you one by one until he got it. What choice did I have?"

"It's alright," Clemens said, patting his shoulder. "You can't believe anything that comes out of that psychopath's mouth. He'll say whatever he needs to say to get what he wants."

"I'm sorry," Miguel said. "At the time it seemed like the only option. How did they find you?"

"They spotted us coming in on the main road. James got shot. They took him to the hospital back in Thompson. We need to get back to Churchill and make sure the others are safe. Then we'll go to Thompson and get my son."

"What about Sylvia?" Miguel asked.

"My guess is she's going to be tried back in Winnipeg," Clemens said.

"You know damn well she won't get a fair trial," Dutch said. "If she even makes it that far."

"We're not going to let that happen, are we?" Miguel asked.

Clemens swallowed. He stared out over the Hudson Bay for several seconds and brushed his hand down over his mustache. He looked Miguel in the eye. "No. We're not going to let that happen."

THEY HIKED along the coast in wet clothing as the aurora borealis stretched its green and purple bands across the night sky. They debated how they might attempt to rescue Sylvia now that they no longer had any weapons and were wanted in Winnipeg. They would need access to the CPG data base to locate her whereabouts.

"I guess we'll have to use your login, Dutch," Clemens said.

"No. They scanned my retinas back there. They know I'm helping you. Pretty sure, I'm blacklisted, too."

"Ah, I'm sorry, Dutch," Clemens said. "I'm sorry I got you mixed up in all this."

"I made this choice all by myself," Dutch said. "I knew the risk I was taking. Besides, knowing what I know now, I don't think I could live with myself working for those corrupt assholes ever again."

"What about your mom?" Clemens asked.

"She'll be fine. I transferred my entire payout to her account before we left. She can get that procedure now.

Besides she had tons of friends and family in town. They'll take good care of her."

Exhaustion overtook them sometime after midnight. They hadn't eaten in several hours but it was too dark and they were too tired to forage for food in the forest. They found a cluster of trees that would have to serve as minimal shelter from the wind. None of them had the energy to start a fire. Sleep hit them hard and fast there on the forest floor.

CLEMENS AWOKE four hours later at sunrise. He stood, stretched, and walked a few paces away to relieve himself and allow his eyes to adjust to the morning light as it glimmered across the bay. As he scanned the coastline, sunlight reflected off an observatory in the distance—the Churchill Observatory. They were almost there.

They hiked for another hour until they could see a paved road up ahead. They walked along the trail until they reached a ranger's station. Dutch kicked in the door. The cozy one-room cabin had a loft for sleeping and a small kitchenette in one corner. They raided the cabinets for anything remotely edible.

"Anything?" Miguel asked. He was rummaging through a wooden desk at one end of the cabin.

"Nothing," Clemens said. "Wait!" Clemens pulled a box of cereal from behind a curtain under the sink. As he lifted the box, a mixture of stale cereal and rat droppings spilled from a chewed up corner of the box. He flinched at the odor and dropped the box on the floor.

"Hey Sarge," Dutch said. "Look at this." He pulled a key with a plastic key chain from a hook on the wall.

Miguel and Clemens followed Dutch outside and around the back of the ranger station, where they discovered an old golf cart.

"Beautiful," Clemens said. "Well, what are you waiting for? Start her up!"

Dutch placed the key into the ignition and the golf cart started up as if no time had passed since its last patrol. They piled into the old four seater and pulled onto the paved road, which led them to the main road into Churchill.

When they arrived at the Lazy Bear, Esther ran down the front porch steps and leapt into Clemens' arms. He held her tight and lifted her off her feet. "Oh God, I missed you."

"I thought you were gone for good," Esther whimpered. "What happened to you?"

"It's a long story." Clemens looked up and James was coming down the steps, one step at a time. His arm was in a cast up to his bicep, held supportively in a sling. He embraced his son as tears fell from his eyes. "Son! How did you . . ." He looked over James' shoulder as the front door opened and Terrence LeBlanc stepped out onto the porch with a wide grin sweeping across his familiar face. He offered a two-finger salute.

"Terrence? How?" Clemens looked back at Miguel and Dutch, who seemed just as surprised. Esther was beaming. "What are you doing here, Terrence?"

"Oh, I thought you could use a hand." He chuckled. Clemens held his son by his shoulders and looked him over once again. "How did you get back here?"

"LeBlanc picked me up from the hospital in Thompson," James said. "You should see his ride."

"What ride?" Clemens asked, looking around at the empty parking lot.

"I pulled some strings up at CSIS. It's just a loaner."

"What is?"

LeBlanc walked them around the side of the building where a gun metal gray aerial hovercraft with four horizontally positioned rotors built into the wings perched in an empty lot. "This is the BX-9. It was designed for urban policing, but only a few hundred made it into production. You see them in New York and Chicago. I think Toronto has a few. Anyway, I happened to get a hold of this guy back at the agency and we worked something out. It's fast. I mean, like hypersonic fast. It'll get you back to Winnipeg in a little less than an hour."

"How did you know about James?" Clemens asked.

"Well, I knew Thompson was the nearest hospital up here so I set up an alert in case any of you checked in. Sure enough, when James was admitted, I got the alert. I came as soon as I could, which didn't take too long in this baby."

Everyone examined the aerial hovercraft up close. None of them had seen this technology before in person. LeBlanc reviewed the main features—sonic, microwave, and other non-lethal weaponry, including rubber bullet gatlings and tear gas cannons for crowd control. It was a modern marvel and looked distinctly out of place in the bare parking lot of the Lazy Bear Lodge.

"Where's Rebecca?" Miguel asked, looking back toward the lodge, hoping to see her emerge at any moment.

Esther shook her head. "They took Rebecca and Hannah. Did they get to Sylvia?"

"We think so," Clemens said.

"So why do they still have Rebecca and Hannah?" Miguel asked. "I assume the Guard were using them to get to Sylvia."

"Crowe!" Clemens said. The realization that Crowe might have taken them as sex workers made him sick.

"Who?" LeBlanc asked.

"Victor Crowe."

"Crowe Pharmaceuticals Victor Crowe?" LeBlanc asked, taken aback.

"That's the one," Clemens confirmed. "He was implicated along with the Guard over this sex trafficking business. And now he has Rebecca and Hannah."

"Who's Hannah?" LeBlanc asked.

"She's a girl we rescued down in Grand Rapids. She was being trafficked. And now the king trafficker has her!"

"That does not sound good," said LeBlanc gloomily. His eyebrows raised suddenly along with an index finger. "But hey, if they're with him, we got all his info. We got a stack this high on him." He held an imaginary stack between his hands. "CSIS is all over that guy. He's got his hands in all kinds of enterprises so we keep a close watch. We know where all his properties and businesses are."

"That's a good start," Clemens said. They climbed into the hovercraft and sat at the control panel. LeBlanc typed on a keyboard and a two-dimensional map projected before them. Red dots spattered across the North American continent. LeBlanc entered additional information into the search and several dots disappeared. The remaining dots clustered in and around Chicago.

"His main residence is here," LeBlanc said pointing to a zoomed in region of the Chicago area. "But I doubt he has them there with his wife and family. I'm guessing here." He pointed at another dot and zoomed in using voice command. "This is where he brings dignitaries and hosts out of town visitors. It's protected with a smart perimeter so you can't just fly into his air space unannounced."

"Well, that's the best and only lead we've got," Clemens said. "What are we waiting for?"

"Can I fly?" Dutch asked.

"You think you can handle it?" LeBlanc asked.

"The question is, can it handle me?" Dutch boasted.

Clemens turned to his son. "James, I need you to stay here with your mother."

"Dad! Come on! I can still shoot with this hand. Plus, I'm almost eighteen and isn't that when you enlisted? Have some faith in me for once."

Clemens could see himself in his son's eyes and in the way he set his jaw in determination. He looked to his wife.

She nodded. "It's okay, Daryl. We'll be alright here. The danger's long gone. Take him." She placed her hand on her son's chest and looked up to make eye contact. He'd grown a good six inches taller than his mother. "You do exactly as your father tells you. Understood?"

"Thanks, mom." He looked to his father whose worried countenance shifted to one of pride. The right handlebar of his mustache lifted slightly.

"Fine," Clemens said. He placed a strong hand around the back of his son's neck and squeezed. "You're a braver man than I was at your age. Come on. Let's load up."

CHAPTER 35

EVEN IN SPACE THERE ARE STARS TO GAZE UPON: SYLVIA

SYLVIA'S HEAD POUNDED. Muffled voices seeped into her consciousness, followed by light. Shadows moved before her closed eyelids. Sounds became gradually more distinct. Murmurs. Footsteps. The urge to speak arose at the top of her shallow breath but receded like a crested wave. Her eyelids, garage doors secured with heavy chains and padlocks, disobeyed. Even her breath, she observed, was not within her command. She could feel the rise and fall of each breath, but she could not increase the pace of or deepen the inhales and exhales. She tried holding her breath without success. Each breath, a metronome click that she had not set in motion and was unable to alter.

Sylvia focused her full attention on the sensation of her right hand. *Move!* She lay like a stone monument, albeit a conscious one. A teardrop escaped from the outside corner of her eye. She followed it as it dripped across her temple and into her hairline. The direction of the teardrop's descent let her know that she was horizontal.

She tried to gather as many sensory inputs to discover

more about her circumstances. A cold sensation radiated from her left arm inside her elbow, moving upward toward her shoulder. An IV, perhaps? Cold air entered through her nostrils. Oxygen? She did not feel the restrictiveness of clothing, yet she sensed she was covered. She strained to make out the words from the murmuring just a few feet from where she laid.

"... every four hours ..."

"... when he gets back ..."

"... buyer in Vancouver ..."

"... It's his money! (Laughs) ..."

"... In you go."

Her body jostled. She felt herself sliding backward. The light coming through her eyelids suddenly extinguished. The acoustic openness of the room gave way to an enclosed tunnel-like surrounding. Her body jostled again as the platform she laid upon locked into place. Footsteps faded and she was left alone in a soundless, lightless void. She imagined she was floating in space. But even in space, there are stars to gaze upon. She was wide awake now, with no way to prove it.

Go to sleep. Go to sleep. Please, just go back to sleep!

CHAPTER 36

WE'RE NOT PRISONERS: REBECCA

REBECCA STEPPED DOWN from the helicopter and reached behind her taking Hannah's hand. She never thought she'd ever return to Chicago. A pasty-faced butler, wispy hair tossed by the thrashing wind of the helicopter blades, awaited their arrival on the green lawn. Hannah squeezed her hand. Rebecca attempted to reassure her with a smile and led her toward the house.

The 11,000 square foot modern villa perched upon a grassy plain, a precarious stack of white boxes on a thick green carpet. This was not Victor's official residence. Its main purpose was to house visiting guests, dignitaries, and other elites. When Rebecca lived there, she was happy to play hostess to world class VIPs. She had looked forward to the company when Victor was indisposed.

They stepped into the pristine foyer onto gleaming white marble floors. Picasso's *Guernica* hung in the main salon, taking up the entire wall, twenty-five feet across.

"That's creepy," Hannah said looking at the massive painting with a scowl.

"It's a Picasso," Rebecca said.

"What's a Picasso?"

"Not what. Who. He's a famous painter. I think he's dead now."

Rebecca ushered her up a floating staircase of solid white oak steps and stainless steel handrails and showed Hannah to her room.

A dark wood platform bed with white bedding dominated the minimalist space. Two matching nightstands flanked the bed and a teak reading chair sat unobtrusively under a rectangular box window. The closets were clandestinely built into a single wall. Rebecca placed her finger on a sensor and two, three-foot panels slid apart, revealing a naturally lit cedar-planked dressing room with full- length mirrors, shoe racks, shelves, and drawers centered around two black leather dressing chairs. Several changes of clothes in Hannah's size had been hung, designer tags still attached.

Another doorway led to an immaculate bathroom—gleaming white with natural wood accents. "This whole bathroom is mine?" Hannah asked.

"Yep. What do you think?"

"I've never seen anything like this? It's so posh."

"Get used to it. I feel disgusting. I'm going to shower and I'll meet you downstairs in a half hour, kay?"

Rebecca found her old room as she'd left it. Fresh white tulips, her favorite, adorned every corner of the room. A card placed at the foot of her bed read: *Welcome home. Love, Victor.* She sat on the bed and sighed. *Here we go again,* she thought. She showered and slipped into a floral sundress. Rebecca, hair still wet, walked barefoot onto the back deck where Hannah sat by the pool. She was still wearing the same dirty clothes from the day before.

"Do you want to swim?" Rebecca asked. "I think I have an extra swimsuit that might fit you."

Hannah held her knees and shook her head. Her apprehension was understandable, given what she'd been through.

"Hannah, look at me. We're fine. Victor promised nothing would happen to you, and you can stay with me as long as you want."

Hannah nodded, unconvinced. "Can I ask you something?"

"Anything."

"What do you even see in him?"

"Who, Victor? He can be charming, sometimes." Rebecca smiled. "He's handsome. Don't you think?"

"I guess, but," Hannah scowled, "he's like, twice your age."

Rebecca's smile faded. "The main thing is we're safe now. We don't have to be on the run anymore. We can just start over."

"What about the others? Will we ever get to see them again?" Hannah asked.

"Of course! We're not prisoners. We can leave whenever we want to."

Hannah sat in quiet reflection for a moment. "Why was he after them again?"

"I know. Sweetie, it's complicated. The CPG, the ones who were looking for Sylvia and them, are not Victor. He wouldn't hurt anyone, not on purpose anyway."

"But doesn't the Guard work for him?" Hannah scrunched her face, trying to comprehend.

"Yes and no. They're just like, guns for hire. Victor isn't one of them." Rebecca read confusion on Hannah's face. "We were fugitives, see? We weren't supposed to leave Winnipeg. I'm sure it's like that in Toronto, too, right?"

"Yeah."

"Okay, so they were after us from the beginning. When we found you, we were already on the run. But Victor is way more powerful than anyone in the Guard. And you're under his protection now."

Rebecca sincerely believed Victor Crowe was a decent man. At least, she didn't believe him to be the monster everyone was making him out to be. He'd never spoken with her about his business dealings. She didn't care much about them anyway. Victor had only ever been loving toward her, except of course, when he wasn't there. While she enjoyed the lavish lifestyle, it was the adventure she was after. Sitting in an immaculate mansion for days on end with only hired help with whom to converse was hardly the adventure she'd signed up for, which is why she was so happy to have Hannah there with her.

"I want to go back," Hannah said. "I need to know if everyone is okay."

"I know. We will," Rebecca said. "Let me talk to him. I'm sure he just wanted to get us out of there to keep us safe. I'll talk to him, okay?"

"So what are we supposed to do now?" Hannah asked. It must have been unsettling not knowing what was coming next. "I feel like a sitting duck out here."

"I wish you could just relax and enjoy this," Rebecca said with her arms out to display their palatial surroundings. "Isn't it beautiful?"

"Yeah, I guess."

"How about some gelato?" Rebecca said with a smile. She pulled Hannah by the hand into the gourmet kitchen.

Rebecca tried her best to cheer her up, but Hannah could not be appeased. Rebecca's thoughts returned to Miguel. Surely, Victor let him go as he said he had. He wasn't petty enough to retaliate against him out of jealousy. That was beneath him. Wasn't it?

SYLVIA DREAMED OF FLYING. She broke through the clouds and swooped toward the city below, barrel rolling down and along the surface of the river, she grazed the water with her fingertips. She felt a tug from around her neck and raised her head to glide upward again. She felt the pull toward the right and she veered right. Then to the left. She turned around and saw a male figure straddling her back holding reins that were tethered to her neck. She tried to fight him off, but he dominated her movement. He pulled up on the reigns and flew her toward the sun.

Her eyes squinted even before they fluttered partially open, florescent lights accosting her vision. The room was white, sterile, cold. Her muscles tensed and she pulled up on her arms, which were cuffed to a table. A carbon fiber collar squeezed her neck and delivered a low-level electric shock.

"Ow!" Sylvia cried..

"You'll get used to the collar," Victor said. "Try to relax. It'll loosen if you relax. The more you struggle, the tighter it gets."

"Where am I?" Sylvia asked.

"You're in Chicago. Not that it matters. Let me show you how this thing works." Sylvia strained again and pulled up on her restraints and received a more aggressive electric shock as the collar tightened around her neck.

"Relax! Relax. You're only hurting yourself. Look," Victor said, taking a demo collar from a shelf. "This is really cool. It's a bio-responsive compliance collar. I've been working on it for months. It's attached to your spinal cord and reacts to the tension in your muscle fibers. As you can see, if you tense your muscles, the collar contracts around your neck and issues an electromagnetic pulse right into your nervous system. Not too comfy, right? So the key is to stay calm. Just relax. Now I'm going to remove your restraints and I want you to practice relaxing." He spoke as if he were talking to a colleague rather than a victim of a diabolical torture device.

Victor typed a code into a keypad near her feet and the steal cuffs retracted back into the table. Sylvia leaped down and immediately fell to the floor convulsing and drooling onto the tile. The electric pulses ceased only after her body had fully succumbed.

"I do hope you're a quick study, for your own sake. Now get up!" When she did not immediately comply, Victor delivered another pulse from a wristband remote. This time she involuntarily urinated. "Get up!" Victor shouted. Sylvia scrambled to her feet. "Good. You're starting to get the hang of it."

"Please," Sylvia whimpered. "Please, don't do this. I'll do the retraction. Whatever you want."

"It's much too late for that, dear. I already got what I needed. That Miguel folded like a cheap suit."

"Why are you doing this? What is this thing for?" Sylvia felt the collar around to the back of her neck where the device inserted itself into her spinal cord.

"It's my latest compliance technology. I have to admit, you were right all along, Corporal. You got me! You! I couldn't believe it when you started digging up the bones. You are an impressive investigator. Not even the CIA nor the FBI were able to connect the dots. I thought I was being pretty smart. But I have to hand it to you, Corporal. You outsmarted me."

"But why? You're one of the wealthiest men on the planet. Why would you get involved in such a terrible industry? How do you benefit? I don't understand."

"Believe it or not, Corporal, not everything I do is always for my benefit alone. I don't care about money or wealth. I care about the survival of our planet. It's not just PR. Governments couldn't, or wouldn't, save the planet when they had the chance. I stepped in and just look what's been accomplished in the last decade. My corporate climate change policies were written into law throughout every regime on this continent the moment I stepped in. But it's not enough. We have to be more aggressive. Do you know what the number one contributor to climate change is?" Before she could answer, he blurted, "Humans. Nine billion of them. This planet cannot sustain the burden much longer. We have to reduce the planet's population by at least forty percent."

"What does this have to do with the sex trade?"

"I'm glad you asked. I've spearheaded a worldwide sterilization program. We've sterilized over twelve million women over the last five years, all of them essentially prisoners already. And it's working! Birth rates have been declining steadily year after year!" Victor beamed with hubris. "I have no interest in the sex trade. It's been around since the beginning of time. It is disgusting and I don't profit from it, believe me. But it does provide me with a significant enough population to work with. I don't abduct these women. They've already been forced into servitude. My only involvement is that they undergo a sterilization procedure before they are put into service. These workers were always getting pregnant and adding to an already overpopulated gene pool with children they didn't even want. If you think about it, I'm doing them a great service."

"You have no idea how twisted you sound, do you?" Sylvia said, but he ignored the question. "So what are the collars for?"

"Well, part of the deal I've made with the traffickers, is that I agreed to provide the pharmaceuticals to keep the workers compliant and docile. I miscalculated the cost of keeping millions of women doped up day in and day out, not to mention the impact of opioid laden waste seeping into the water supply over time. Some of these women are in service for ten, fifteen years, depending on when they start and they cost a fortune to medicate for so long. So, while the collars cost a bit more to manufacture, roughly the cost of a years worth of opioids, it's a one-time purchase. So you see, I have nothing to do with the trafficking industry itself. I'm simply utilizing it to bring about my vision for the salvation of the entire planet."

Sylvia was speechless. *He's insane.* She wondered, now that she was wearing one of these compliance collars, if she was meant to join the ranks of sex workers in service centers or was she to be one of Victor Crowe's personal slaves. She was at an age that most sex workers were aging out. He said he didn't abduct women, yet here she was.

"Now, let's get on with your training. We're going to skip over some of the preliminary tests and go straight to the big one. Are you ready? Good! Listen closely, Sylvia. I have a bolt pistol tucked into the back of my pants. I want you to walk over here and pull it out."

Sylvia paused just long enough for Victor to raise his wristband. Not wanting another electrocution, she stepped gingerly toward Victor. The wetness from the urine-soaked gown felt cold on her legs.

He stretched out his arms like Christ. "Go ahead," he said. "Take the gun."

Sylvia reached warily around his torso. She smelled his aftershave and shivered at the feeling of his warm breath on the nape of her neck. Sylvia made contact with the weapon and wrapped her hand around its grip.

"Good," he said. "Pull it out."

Sylvia questioned whether she'd be quick enough to blast him before he could issue electric shockwaves directly into her spine from his wristband remote. Of course, that's what he would expect her to try. *What was this sick game?* She carefully removed the pistol from his waistband and stood trembling before him.

"You're doing so well. Now . . ." He stepped to her, cupped her chin in his hand, and brushed his thumb across her mouth, gently peeling her bottom lip from her top. "Put the gun in your mouth," he said, almost whispering. It was apparent he was enjoying this.

Sylvia shook her head.

"Ah-ah-ah," he said raising his wristband remote.

Tears trickled down her cheeks as she pressed her eyelids shut. She did as he said. Her teeth rested on the barrel and she tasted metal.

"I'm going to count to three, and then you're going to pull that trigger. You got that?"

If he merely wanted her dead, he could have easily done it by now. Sylvia was less fearful of death than she was spending the last few minutes of her life with someone who derived pleasure from watching someone else take their own life. There was nowhere for her to run. Sylvia decided at that moment that this was it. It all ends now. Everything that she'd been evading had finally caught up and she shouldn't have been surprised.

"One," he said.

She did the best she could. Everyone has to go some time. Her father's smile flashed before her mind's eye. Where had he gone? Maybe she was about to find out. Maybe he'd been waiting for her all this time. She hoped he couldn't see her at this moment. She prayed, *please look away, daddy*.

"Two."

This is a gift, really, she told herself. She was tired of running. Her friends had been arrested so they couldn't save her. What kind of life could she reasonably hope for, constantly looking over her shoulder, never able to rest or be at peace? This was the only way she could ever truly be free. *I'm ready*, she thought. A peaceful warmth washed over her. She exhaled and promised herself she would not hesitate.

"Three."

Sylvia pulled the trigger.

"Congratulations," he said.

Her eyes blinked open.

"You passed. You're ready."

Sylvia released the gun and it clattered against the tile floor. Sylvia fell to her hands and knees and wept. She wept for the death that she'd been promised. How cruel to have taken that peaceful rest from her. Freedom would never be hers, not that it ever had been. She crawled back onto the table to where she'd formerly been bound. Restraints were no longer required.

Victor brushed the hair that clung to her face with tears. Quiet sobs bubbled up from her chest. "There, there. You'll do just fine. When you wake, you'll be in Vancouver. A very prominent man has offered an obscene amount for your company. As long as you remember your training here, you'll do just fine. It's been an adventure, Sylvia Boone. Sweet dreams."

He tapped a button on his wristband and her body suddenly lost all mobility once again. She remained fully awake, a prisoner in her own mind. The sobs continued with no outlet, no release. *I'm in hell*, she thought. She'd fallen in and out of consciousness over the last twenty-four hours, finding herself in this silent black box with only her thoughts to torture her.

Sylvia tried to plan her next moves. *Is this so-called 'prominent man,' another billionaire like Crowe? Is he just as much of a psychopath? Maybe he'll get bored with me after a while. Most men do,* she thought. In the meantime, she wouldn't have much control over what he might do with her inanimate body. She decided that was the only way anyone would ever have dominion over her ever again. And then she had a wonderfully mischievous idea. She would refuse to play the game as she had been trained. She resigned herself to suicide by voluntary electrocution. *Worst sex slave ever.* The thought would have made her grin if she had any muscular control over her face.

AFTER A HEAPING SERVING of blackberry gelato and an almond biscotti, Hannah was beginning to loosen up to her current situation. After some playful cajoling, Hannah agreed to borrow Rebecca's bikini and go for a swim. She emerged to the pool's surface after a perfect dive. She pushed her chestnut hair back and wiped water from her face. Hannah heard the approaching sounds of helicopter blades in the distance, which immediately put her on edge.

"What the . . ." Hannah lowered her head to the surface of the water. "Who's that?"

"It's Victor!" Rebecca said excitedly.

Victor disembarked from the helicopter and walked sure-footed across the lawn. Hannah suddenly felt self-conscious in her borrowed bikini. She got out of the pool and wrapped a towel around her shoulders. She stood on the deck, teeth chattering, as water pooled around her feet.

Victor stepped onto the deck in Italian leather shoes, chest hair sprouting from a charcoal cashmere V-neck. Rebecca, also wearing a designer bikini, did not seem particularly concerned about her appearance. She was laying on a pool-side recliner and sipping a cocktail. Victor leaned over the back of the chair and kissed her cheek. He stood and turned toward Hannah.

"Hannah," he said extending his hand for her to shake. As she reached out, her towel slipped from her shoulders and fell in a pile around her ankles. Victor lifted her small hand to his lips and kissed it. "Charmed," he said with a grin. Hannah smiled awkwardly and quickly recovered the fallen towel. She wrapped it around her shoulders again, this time clutching it tightly around her neck with both hands.

"How's the staff treating you?" Victor asked. "I trust they're taking good care of you?"

"Yes, thank you," Hannah said with a shaky voice. Her teeth chattered from the chill of the cool evening air against her goose-bumped wet skin.

"I'm sorry I didn't introduce myself earlier. And I apologize for the inconvenience I've caused you and your pals. I'm afraid I've made a terrible first impression. I hope that in time you will see that I am not such a brut."

"He's a puppy dog," Rebecca said, smiling playfully with the cocktail straw between her teeth.

"Now," Victor said, turning to Hannah. "I understand you want to be reunited with your friends. I totally understand and I don't want to inconvenience you any further. I can assure you everyone is safe back in Churchill. The Guard have returned to their posts in Winnipeg and they will not be a problem for you or your friends any longer. I can promise you that. I have a short trip to Vancouver and when I return, I will take you back to Churchill myself. How does that sound?"

Hannah nodded. Something in the way he spoke didn't sit right with her. He had a slight accent that she couldn't quite place. That, and the condescending grin he wore, gave him a contrived sense of sophistication she didn't trust.

"When will you be back?" Rebecca asked.

"Couple of days. In the meantime, please make yourself at home. Relax. Paulo is a certified master chef. He'll make you anything you like!"

"Do you have to leave right now?" Rebecca whined.

"I'm so sorry I can't stay. I promise when I get back we can catch up. And Hannah, it was a pleasure meeting you. Don't worry about a thing. I'll make sure you are reacquainted with your pals. That's a promise." He leaned over the chaise and kissed Rebecca on her shoulder. He smiled and waved with both hands before jogging back toward his helicopter.

"See?" Rebecca said to Hannah. "He's not so bad. You get used to him coming and going like that. You okay?"

"Yeah," Hannah barely said. She didn't want to get used to him.

Rebecca smiled. "I know who you really want to see," she teased in a sing-song voice.

"Stop it!" Hannah said, blushing.

"You *looove* that boy!"

Hannah couldn't suppress the smile that swept across her youthful face. "Shut up!" Hannah said, her smile breaking into a giggle. Rebecca pulled Hannah by the arms, shrieking, backward into the pool.

COMPARED TO WINNIPEG, Chicago was a smoldering wasteland. Wrecked cars, debris, and dead bodies filled city streets. Several of its most iconic architectural wonders had been reduced to rubble. While Winnipeg had been overrun with authoritarian thugs, Chicago appeared to have no order at all—a Darwinian free-for-all. Chicago was run by its own private police force, but from what they could tell from a distance, they seemed to have had no presence at all.

Victor Crowe's villa was located outside the northwestern edge of the city and surrounded by a smart perimeter. Laser-guided smart missiles anticipated any unauthorized breach of air space within twenty miles of the property. They wouldn't be able to simply land on the front lawn and knock on the door. Besides, other than the non-lethal weaponry aboard the BX-9, they were unarmed.

They researched every possible detail related to that property, from service personnel to delivery couriers. They put the BX-9 down in a former wheat field on a deserted farm about forty miles north of Victor's palacial villa.

"Pull up a live feed of the property," Clemens said. "We need to log every movement in and out of the main gates."

Service personnel were shuttled in and out to other locations inside the city limits. This evening, it was Paulo the chef who was being driven from the clandestine mansion to a restaurant parking lot in Lincoln Park, his own as it turns out. The next morning at 7:30 a.m., two women in grey uniforms were shuttled onto the property, likely housekeeping staff. Later that morning at 11:15 a.m. a landscaping truck was allowed through the gates. Three landscapers worked the grounds until 3:30 p.m. and left the way they came.

They tracked the landscapers back into town. The driver dropped the other two men off in a sketchy part of town with bars on the windows and then to his own middle class neighborhood. The sign on the side of the truck read *Chewy's Landscaping* and listed the phone number.

"That's our in," Clemens said. LeBlanc hacked into Chewy's work schedule and bookkeeping records from a commonly used online business management portal and found a list of current and former contractors. Chewy's Landscaping serviced the more exclusive neighborhoods in town. These days, only the super rich could afford landscaping services. Chewy was scheduled to work at Victor's villa again the very next day.

"Let me go," James said.

"Sorry, son. I'm pretty sure you need two functioning arms to get hired as a landscaper."

"I'll do it," Miguel said.

"Getting hired onto Chewy's roster is one thing," Clemens said. "Getting assigned tomorrow's Crowe job is another."

"The same two guys are scheduled to work tomorrow," Miguel said. "We need a way to put these two out of commission."

"I've got an idea," Dutch said. "We pulled a prank on this kid in high school once. It was really mean and I'm not proud of it, but I think it could work."

"Well, what is it?" Miguel asked. "What's the prank?"

"So we order a pizza and then we dust it with MaxLax and deliver it to their house. They'll say they didn't order any pizza and we just say, 'well, we can't take it back so you can just keep it.' Then they'll eat it because, you know, free pizza. Within an hour it'll be deuces wild and they'll have to call in."

Miguel and Clemens looked at one another. Either this was the stupidest idea Miguel had ever heard, or . . .

"Works for me," Clemens said. "Let's do it."

"Who's gonna deliver the pizza?" James asked. Everyone stared at him until what seemed obvious to everyone else finally clicked. "Right. I guess that would be me."

The plan went off without a hitch. LeBlanc tapped into Chewy's line to intercept the call that came through an hour later. They waited five minutes before Miguel called Chewy.

"Chewy's Landscaping," Chewy answered with a Mexican accent.

"Hi my name is . . ." Miguel started. He looked around the property from the cockpit of the BX-9 and his eyes landed on a metal sign bearing the LA Dodger's logo attached to the side of the barn. " . . . Dodger . . . Roger Dodger." Miguel slapped his palm against his forehead.

"Your name is Roger Dodger?" Chewy asked.

"Yes."

"Oh . . . kay. How can I help you Roger Dodger?"

"I'm looking for a job. I have a ton of experience in landscaping. And I can start right away," Miguel said.

"Well, you're in luck, Roger. Two of my guys just came down with something. I'll take you on a trial basis. If you work out, we can talk about pay. You good with that?"

"Yes, sir!"

"I got a job tomorrow morning. I'll pick you up. What's your address?"

"Uhhh . . ." Miguel quickly scanned a map of the surrounding area and pulled up a random address along the main route between Chewy's house and Victor's property.

"Good. That's on the way. I'll be there at 7:00 a.m. sharp," Chewy said. "Be ready."

"Thank you, sir. You won't be disappointed."

THE NEXT MORNING Chewy arrived to pick Miguel up at the agreed upon location. Miguel's face still hadn't healed from the beating he'd received back in Churchill. Chewy looked him over as he climbed into the work truck. "What the hell happened to you?"

"You should see the other guy," Miguel said jokingly and then diverted the conversation. "So whose house are we going to? Must be pretty rich."

"Yeah, he is," Chewy said. "But I can't tell you his name. I signed an NDA. That's how rich he is."

When they pulled up to the iron gates leading to the villa, Miguel whistled. "You weren't kidding," Miguel said, surveying the property.

Two armed men stood outside the gatehouse. One of them looked inside the truck. "Hey Chew. Who's this?"

"New guy," Chewy said.

"I'm gonna need your ID," the guard said to Miguel.

"Oh, right." Miguel patted his pockets. "You know what? I left it at home."

"Sorry, can't let you in without ID," the guard said. "You know the rules, Chew."

"Ah man, I forgot, bro," Chewy said. "My other guys got sick last minute. We're almost done anyway. Probably only be here a couple hours tops. Otherwise, I can't come back for two weeks."

The guard looked around. "Alright, Chewy, just this once." He looked at Miguel, "What's your name, pal?"

"Roger."

"Roger what?"

Miguel sighed. "Dodger."

"Roger Dodger?"

"Yeah."

The guard laughed. He turned to his partner. "Hey! This guy's name is Roger Dodger!" Everyone had a good laugh, including Chewy—everyone except Roger Dodger.

"Two hours, Chew. You got two hours." He slapped the hood of Chewy's truck and opened the gate. Chewy pulled around to the back of the house.

"Alright, your job is pretty easy, okay? I need you to finish mulching the flower beds along the west wing of the house and around the tennis courts. I'm going to be finishing up this new irrigation system over on the other side. When you finish, come over and help me with the install so we can get out of here on time. Got it?"

"Got it." Miguel slung a bag of mulch from the truck bed over his shoulder. He peered into the first-floor windows as he walked past, hoping to catch a glimpse of Rebecca. Would she be freely roaming around the house or would she be tied up in the basement? The thought gave him a dreadful sense of urgency. He came across the back entrance by the pool where he could see into the gourmet kitchen. He peered through the glass door and when he saw no one, tried to open it. Locked. He walked through the back gate around the side of the house and came across another set of windows.

Hannah was sitting sideways in a wingback chair in pajamas eating a bowl of cereal. Miguel tapped on the window and she nearly spilled the whole bowl on herself. She jumped up and ran to the window, eyes like sunshine. Miguel placed his index finger over his lips and waved her over to a side entrance.

"Oh my God!" Hannah said when she opened the door. "What are you doing here? Is James with you?"

"Yes! I mean not here. It's just me. Is Rebecca there with you?" Miguel asked.

"She sleeps in, like way too late. Come inside."

"I can't. I'm supposed to be a landscaper."

"What?" she asked with a giggle.

"It's a cover, so I could get onto the property."

"Oh. Why do you need a cover?"

"Because this place is locked up like Fort Knox. Are you hurt?"

"No. Why?"

"He's not making you, you know?"

"Who Victor? Eww! No, of course not. No, he's just

letting me stay here with Rebecca. I guess they're back together or whatever."

"What?! *Back* together? With Victor Crowe?"

"I know. He's like, so old, right? I don't get it."

"Wait. Sorry, this isn't making sense." But even as he said it, the pieces began to come together. Rebecca had mentioned living in Chicago, traveling abroad, and she had name dropped a dozen celebrities she'd met over the years, but never mentioned the name Victor Crowe.

"I guess they use to be a thing before she moved to Canada and since you guys weren't together anymore, she thought she'd give him a second chance."

"So what are you doing here?"

"Rebecca wanted me to come with her. She thought I'd be safer here." Her eyes suddenly widened. "Hey! You guys could all live here! There's like seven bedrooms. It's bananas."

"No. Hannah. He's not safe. You and Rebecca have to get out of here! Can you please tell her I'm here?"

"Yeah, okay." Hannah nodded and ran upstairs.

Miguel stepped back several feet and tried to see if Chewy was anywhere nearby. He opened a bag of mulch and haphazardly tossed its contents around on the ground. A few moments later Rebecca bounded outside wearing a silk kimono. She wrapped her arms around his neck, lifting her feet behind her.

"You're dating Victor Crowe?" Miguel asked.

"It's a long story. What are you doing here?"

"I'm here to get you and Hannah."

"Hannah said you were doing yard work?" She looked

around at the fresh mulch he'd laid. "Why are you doing Victor's yard work?

"I had to get a job as a landscaper to get onto the property."

"Ooh. That was smart."

"Rebecca, listen, I think you should leave. I know this might sound like jealousy or whatever. I mean, a little maybe. But I really don't think Victor Crowe is a safe person for you and Hannah to be around."

"I love it when you get all protective." She smiled seductively.

"Rebecca, he had me thrown into the ocean and threatened to kill the others. This guy is sick."

"That doesn't sound like Victor." Her forehead wrinkled.

"He took Sylvia!"

"What? Are you sure it was Victor and not Guard? She did have a bounty on her head."

Hannah stood in the open doorway, fully dressed now. "I thought you said we could leave whenever we wanted."

"Hannah, yes, but—" Rebecca started.

"But nothing. I'm not staying here. I want to go back. I knew there was something weird about Victor. I never trusted him."

"This may be our only shot," Miguel said. "You can both hide in the back of the truck. No one can see you, got it?"

"I'm not so sure about this," Rebecca said.

"I didn't think I'd have to convince you," Miguel said. "Do you actually love him?"

"No! Love isn't everything, Miguel. I'm tired of being on the run. The only reason I was a part of that whole thing was because we were together and I thought we could make it work. Well, now we're not, so there's really no reason for me to go back. Victor may have his faults, but he would never hurt me. Trust me. I'm safe here and so is Hannah."

"He had you kidnapped from the Lodge!"

"No. That was the Guard. They were looking for Sylvia. Victor didn't know it was me until he came in to question us."

"He's a predator, Rebecca! He's probably trafficking Sylvia right now!"

"You don't know that, Miguel. That just doesn't sound like the Victor I know."

"He's lying to you!"

"I'm going with Miguel." Hannah pushed passed Rebecca.

"Excuse me!" Rebecca scolded.

Hannah spun back around. "I don't get you, Rebecca. Why do you want to be with Victor? He's a total creep. I thought you were Sylvia's friend. How can you just look the other way?"

"A) I was never Sylvia's friend. She doesn't even like me. Pretty sure she hates me. And B) We don't know any of that is true. That trafficking stuff just sounds . . . crazy."

"Oh, does it? Does it sound crazy?!" Tears welled in Hannah's eyes.

"Hannah, no, that's not what I . . . I meant, it's crazy that he would be involved in anything like that. Look, I get it if you want to leave. Fine. Go. I'm going miss having you around, that's all."

"You're only going to miss me because you don't have anyone else to talk to. Your weird, old, creepy boyfriend is never even here!"

"Roger!" Chewy called from the back of the house. "Get over here!"

Miguel shook his head in disappointment and walked away toward Chewy, who looked entirely displeased.

"Yeah, boss?" Miguel said.

"What are you doing? We're not supposed to talk to the residents!" Chewy hissed.

"I'm sorry, sir. I didn't know. She was asking me when we'd be done, that's all."

"We're not going to get done on time if you don't get back to work! Come on, you should be done with this side by now. Hurry and finish this and then take the truck down to the tennis courts so you don't have to make too many trips." Chewy tossed him the key fob. "I'm already down one guy. Get the lead out!"

"Yes, sir." Miguel turned back and Rebecca was gone. He didn't know what else he could say. She'd made her choice. He finished up the beds on the side of the house and drove the truck down to the tennis courts as he'd been instructed. He haphazardly distributed mulch along the fencing of the tennis courts, calculating the distance to the front gates and how much speed he'd have to gain in order to break through them.

"Hey," Hannah said with a backpack flung over one shoulder. "Are we really doing this?"

He stood up dusting mulch from his knees. "Rebecca's not coming?" Miguel asked even though he knew the answer. Hannah shook her head. "Did anyone see you come down here?"

"No."

"Okay. Climb in the back. Get under that tarp. Whatever you do stay hidden until I come for you. Got it?"

"Got it." She climbed into the truck bed and pulled the tarp over her body. She stuck her head out. "Hey, are you sure James is okay?"

"He's a little banged up, but I'm sure he'll feel a lot better when he sees you."

Hannah smiled.

SYLVIA AWOKE in a state of immobility at the sound of landing gear making contact with the tarmac. She didn't remember boarding a plane. She must be in Vancouver now, where Victor Crowe would be selling her to some cretin billionaire. She had no idea who. Sylvia struggled mightily to open her eyes, but to no avail. She listened closely as jet engines wound down to a light hum. When the plane had finally come to a stop, she heard movement inside the cabin and the high pitched sound of hydraulics.

Sylvia felt her body rock back and forth as she was carried out of the plane's cabin and down the boarding stairs. She imagined herself to be inside a coffin, being carried by pall bearers in too big of a hurry. She heard the sound of a cargo door opening. Male voices negotiated her transfer into another vehicle, presumably a van, or a hurst. Short jerks jostled her container into place as the familiar sound of ratchet tie downs secured her into place. She heard them closing the cargo doors. Another door opened and closed.

The engine started and she could feel the motion of the vehicle as it drove away.

"I don't know if you can hear me or not," Victor said from outside her container. His voice would forever be branded in her brain. "We'll be parting ways soon. Your new owner's name is Daemon Lovelace. He owns the world's largest biotech company in the world. You should feel very lucky. If you play your cards right, you may never see the inside of a service center. Such terrible places. You'll probably live a very comfortable life here. It could have been so much worse for you. I hope you realize that."

I should feel lucky? Sylvia thought. *Is he fucking kidding me?* She could not comprehend the depths of Crowe's lunacy. She could only hope that this Lovelace character was not a complete sociopath.

When they arrived at their destination, Sylvia was transported indoors, presumably the home of Daemon Lovelace. He and Crowe exchanged pleasantries and began discussing various business dealings and market trends. Sylvia couldn't follow the thread, which was cordial, yet somewhat stilted. At no point during the transaction did either of these giants of commerce mention or even hint at, what utility Sylvia might serve.

"So, let's get down to business," Lovelace said. "Show me how this thing works."

"Would you like to see a demonstration?" Victor asked.

"Certainly."

Sylvia prepared herself for the moment her faculties would return. But instead, Victor called in one of his men.

"Sir?"

"Put this on," Victor said casually.

"Excuse me, sir?" the man asked, his voice trembling.

"Did I stutter?"

"No, sir."

A few moments passed and then Sylvia heard the pained groans of a man and then a thud, which must have been the man falling to the floor.

Victor went on to demonstrate various settings on the remote device, including the one that Sylvia was now experiencing—conscious immobility.

"Very impressive," Lovelace said.

It became evident to Sylvia after some time, they were not negotiating over her at all. Lovelace was buying collars. Lovelace was perfectly capable of obtaining his own sex slaves if he wanted them. Sylvia was nothing more than a bonus offer to sweeten the deal. A commemorative beer mug one might take home from a baseball game. A logo-printed tube of lip balm at the bottom of a swag bag.

The men exchanged genial farewells and Victor took his leave. Lovelace remained in the office with Sylvia. She could sense him hovering over her lifeless body. She listened carefully and braced for his unwanted touch. His heavy breath and throat clearing made her queasy.

She heard the familiar beeps from his new wristband. And just like that, she could move again. She quickly sat up and scooted backward away from Lovelace, pulling her knees to her chest. "Don't touch me!"

"Take it easy. I'm not going to hurt you. But if you want this thing off, I'm going to need you to be very still."

"You want to take the collar *off*?" Sylvia asked. She looked down to see she had been dressed in a black graphene bodysuit with Crowe Industries, Inc. printed across the breast, both understated and pretentious at the same time. She was barefoot. The container she'd been transported in was exactly as she imagined it to be—an oxygenated casket, more or less. Only it had a rounded, glass lid that retracted into one side of the casket. She must have looked like a toy action figure, sealed in its packaging.

"What's your name?" Lovelace asked.

"Sylvia. Boone."

"Sylvia, listen to me." He took the remote device off his wrist and handed it to Sylvia, which provided her a modicum of relief. "I don't know your history with Crowe, but I can imagine you've been through quite a lot. There are very few men that I fear in this world. Victor Crowe is one of them. He's insane, truly. Delusions of grandeur. He thinks he's some kind of savior. That's why violence comes so easily to him. He justifies every wicked act as a means to some greater end."

"Why are you doing business with him?" Sylvia asked.

Lovelace smiled. "I'm not. I just got him to hand over his latest and most destructive technology since the biochemical weapons he designed during the tech wars."

"What do you want with these collars?"

"I want the technology. The way it interfaces with the nervous system. I'm working on a neural interfacing artificial intelligence. Imagine a spacial computing device that gets implanted onto the skull so you don't have to carry it around. Holospecs rely on voice command and retinal movement for input. Plus, you have to carry them around and they get lost and have to be replaced far too often. This new technology would operate directly from your thoughts. We haven't quite mastered the neural connectivity. Until now that is."

Removing Sylvia's collar was simpler than either of them expected it to be. Disconnection instructions were available through the settings menu on the wristband. With a tap of a button, the circuitry released its tendrils from her spinal cord and retracted back into the device. Not a single drop of blood escaped the site of entry. Lovelace marveled at its exquisite design.

Sylvia glided her hand across the back of her neck. She was free once again. She vowed right then and there that not only was she going to stay free, but she was dedicating her life to bringing down Victor Crowe. Sylvia stood before him, more grateful than she could ever remember. A tear trickled down her cheek. "Thank you."

"For what?"

"For helping me. For being kind."

"I'm no saint just because I'm not a complete savage. You shouldn't have to thank someone for not being the worst kind of human. Besides, I want Crowe to fail just as much as you do."

"Well, I am grateful."

"Let's get you out of that ridiculous outfit." Lovelace called his butler and had him bring a change of clothes. "They're my daughter's. You look to be about her size. I'll leave you to get dressed and then meet me in the lounge, just down this hall, when you're done."

She was surprised the clothing, even the boots, were a perfect fit. She walked down the hall, admiring the art on display along the walls. Lovelace was seated at a bar and sipping a bourbon on the rocks.

"Good! They fit," he said. "Do you want a drink?"

"No, thank you."

"I'm sure you're eager to get home."

"Not home exactly. I'm wanted in Winnipeg."

"Wanted, eh? Do tell." Lovelace leaned forward.

"I killed a CPG officer when they shot my dad. Not to mention, I was the lead investigator that implicated Crowe in the sex trade. He finally caught up to me, but I won't let that happen again."

"I hope you're right," Lovelace said taking a sip of his drink. "Well, for all he knows, you're with me now. I doubt he's coming back for you."

"Which is why now is the best time to shut him down."

Lovelace almost choked on his drink and he spit an ice cube back into his glass. "Shut him down? How?"

"I don't know exactly, but I need to get back with my friends, the ones who escaped with me, former CPG."

"I take it he got to them, too."

"Yeah, but just to get a retraction, which he got. So I'm hoping he's let them all go by now. We were in Churchill when we got captured."

"Churchill? Where's that?"

"Manitoba. The northernmost point along the Hudson."

"Jesus. He must have really wanted that retraction. So what do you plan to do once you reunite with your friends?

Sylvia rubbed the back of her neck were the collar had pierced her. "We have to stop his whole operation. He can't manufacture these collars. I know what it's like to be incapacitated and still be fully awake. At least with the drugs, these women are out of it. They don't know what's happening to them and they don't usually remember it. I know that's not great either, but to have to experience rape over and over fully conscious?" She shook her head. "I can't even imagine."

"I never even thought of that. I figured it couldn't get any worse as it is."

"I can't let this happen," Sylvia said, shaking her head. "I have to stop it."

"What kind of transportation do you and your friends have access to?"

"We have a rover. It's great for the tundra but slow as shit on the open road."

Lovelace squinted his eyes. "I have an idea. Do you know how to fly a drone?"

"Yes. It's part of our training."

"Follow me."

Lovelace called to have a car brought around and then led her outside into the bright sunlight. A sleek black car waited in the driveway.

"Where are we going?" Sylvia asked.

"To my hangar."

She climbed into his car and he sat across from her.

"Nice car," Sylvia said, gliding her hand over the hand-stitched leather seats. Leather had not been used as a material in car interiors since the meat industry collapsed several decades ago. "Is this real leather?"

"If you think this is nice, you should see the BX-10," he said.

"What's a BX-10?"

Lovelace pulled up a video on his windshield's holo-screen that demonstrated the drone's main features. The car drove directly onto the tarmac where the BX-10 was being prepped. The sun reflected off its polished black surface.

"She's fully charged, sir," called the mechanic when they got out of the car.

"I've never seen anything like this," Sylvia said.

"It's the fastest non-military aircraft in existence. They only made a few hundred of these. I have three." He pushed a button on a key fob, which brought the boarding stairs down on one side. He handed her the key fob. "Take it."

"Seriously?" Sylvia was beside herself. She followed him inside the aircraft. "You're coming with me, right? You know, to make sure I don't crash it?" Sylvia asked.

Lovelace chuckled. "I have two more. If you've flown a drone, you can fly this. All the controls are pretty intuitive. Plus, I have to stay here. Business."

She shook her head. "It's so expensive. What's it worth, like ten mil?"

"Eighteen and a half million, actually."

"Eeesh," Sylvia said pulling her lips downward to indicate her apprehension.

"I'd pay ten times that to see Victor Crowe defeated," Lovelace said.

"Right. When do you need it back?" She sat in the pilot's chair.

"How about you hang onto it until you take out Victor Crowe?" The left side of his mouth raised into a half grin.

Sylvia gave him a hard look to verify his sincerity. He wasn't kidding. She turned back to the console, running her fingers along the control panel. "I'll take good care of it, I promise."

"I know you will. Listen, I've got to get going. I have another meeting to get to. My personal contact is in the com system. Keep me posted." He began climbing back down the boarding stairs.

"Wait," Sylvia said, getting up from the pilot's chair. "Thank you."

Lovelace gave her a two-finger salute, then climbed down the boarding stairs and walked back to his car.

Sylvia, still baffled at the day's turn of events, watched him drive away. She oriented herself to the controls. She switched on the computer and a female voice welcomed her aboard. A sophisticated holoscreen illuminated across the windshield and she quickly located a three dimensional communications icon. She reached out and touched it.

"Who would you like to call?" the computer responded.

"Call Lazy Bear Lodge, Churchill, Manitoba." The system dialed the listed number.

After a few rings Marjorie appeared on the windshield's holoscreen, amazingly clearer than any holographic projection she'd ever seen.

"Marjorie!"

"Sylvia? Oh my God! It's Sylvia!" Marjorie called over her shoulder and Esther rushed into the frame.

"It *is* you! Where are you? Are you safe?" Esther asked.

"I'm in Vancouver. Is Clemens or Miguel there?"

"Oh my God! Sylvia! We've been so worried." Esther cried.

"Is everyone alright?" Sylvia asked.

"Well, they took Rebecca and Hannah. The guys left for Chicago yesterday to go find all of you." "In the rover?"

"No, LeBlanc came with this crazy spaceship-looking thing. BX-something or other."

"You don't say." Sylvia grinned. What were the odds? "Can you share their contact info?"

"Of course. I have their coordinates, too, if you need those."

"Yes, please!"

She strapped herself into the pilot seat, set the engines to hover, and the BX-10 gently lifted off the ground and hovered around ten meters off the ground. She typed in the coordinates, which gave the exact location of LeBlanc's BX-9 just outside Chicago, and the drone oriented itself to the east and darted into the pale blue sky as nimbly as a hummingbird.

REBECCA DIDN'T KNOW what to believe. She knew Miguel had her best interests at heart and she deeply appreciated his concern, but he didn't know Victor the way she did. The sex trade accusation sounded utterly ridiculous. There simply had to be another explanation. Still, she wondered, what was this evidence against Victor? What did they find? If not trafficking, Victor must have been guilty of something. But what?

She looked out the window and saw Hannah bounding across the lawn toward the tennis courts, a backpack slung over one shoulder. Rebecca shook her head. She knew this was a bad idea. Hannah was going to get herself, and Miguel, in big trouble. She heard the caller notification from the holoscreen in the kitchen. It was Victor.

"Hey, Victor!" She tried to sound upbeat to hide her concern. "What's up?"

"I'm on my way to you now. I just wanted to check in and see how things were going. How is Hannah settling in?"

"Oh, Hannah? She's . . . she—"

"Is everything alright?" Victor asked.

"She's trying to run away," Rebecca blurted. "I tried to talk her out of it but she won't listen!"

"That's not safe, Rebecca. She can't just walk into the city unsupervised. She'll get taken."

"I know! Can you promise her you'll take her wherever she needs to go once you get here?"

"Of course. Put her on."

"Well . . . she kinda already left," Rebecca said.

Victor sighed. "I'll take care of this. Patch me through to the gatehouse, please."

Rebecca patched him through but instead of hanging up, she muted herself and listened in.

"Sir?" answered one of the guards.

"One of my guests, a girl, she's trying to leave the grounds. I need you to be on high alert. Who else is on the grounds today?"

"The landscaping crew. They checked in at . . . 7:34 a.m."

"And who exactly checked in."

"Chewy and some new guy."

"New guy? Well, what's his name?"

There was a pause. "He said his name was . . . Roger Dodger, sir."

"That's not a real name, you idiot! Did you do a background check?"

"No, sir. Very sorry, sir."

"Detain him! Do *not* let them off the grounds or it's your ass! Do you hear me?!"

"Yes, sir!"

"Oh, and I want them alive! I want the pleasure of slaughtering that pig myself."

"Yes, sir!"

The call ended and Rebecca was struck with horror. She couldn't believe her ears. She had never heard Victor say anything the least bit violent. But he did say it. He said he was going to kill Miguel! She accessed the security cams on the holoscreen and selected the guardhouse. Two armed guards hopped into an ATV and headed toward the tennis courts.

She ran to the window to see Miguel climbing into the cab of Chewy's truck. Miguel drove directly toward the approaching ATV. One of the men yelled for Miguel to stop through a bullhorn. At the last second, Miguel swerved right as the ATV swerved left and the truck drove up the front side of the ATV like a ramp and flipped onto its side.

"What the hell!" Chewy yelled as he raced toward the overturned truck. "My truck!"

The guards, protected by the ATV's steel cage, emerged unharmed and detained all three, lining them up on their knees.

Rebecca ran barefoot across the lawn toward the overturned vehicle. "Wait! Wait! This isn't necessary," Rebecca called as she approached the men.

"Stand back, Miss. We have orders to detain these folks."

"Seriously? Where are they going to go?" Rebecca gestured to the overturned truck.

"Miss, we have this under control. Please, go back inside."

"You can't order me around! This is my house and these are my guests. Untie them at once!"

"I'm sorry, Miss. We have orders."

"And I have these!" Rebecca unbelted her kimono and pulled it open. The guards fell into a momentary trance at the sight of Rebecca's spectacular form. Like a reflex from her cheerleading days, Rebecca took the opportunity to high kick one of the guard's pistols from his hand and it went flying into the air. The gun fell onto the grass and Rebecca scrambled on her hands and knees to recover it. Rebecca got to the gun first and shot the guard, once in the arm, and a second time in his chest.

As the second guard too aim at her, Miguel launched from a kneeling position and head butted him in the stomach, knocking him to the ground. They wrestled on the lawn and Miguel struggled to keep the guard's pistol pointed away from him. Rebecca had her weapon aimed in their general direction, but was unable to get a clear shot as they wrestled back and forth. Miguel beat the guard's arm onto the ground a number of times. When the guard released his grip of the gun, Miguel recovered it and shot him in the head.

"On second thought, we should probably leave," Rebecca said.

"That's what I've been saying," Miguel muttered.

"You guys are fuckin' crazy, man!" Chewy shouted.

Rebecca ignored him and turned to Hannah. She placed both hands on her shoulders. "Hannah, I'm so sorry. You were right. I was being selfish. Please forgive me?"

"Does this mean you're done with Victor?" Hannah asked.

"Done." Rebecca turned and looked at Miguel.

"What about my truck?" Chewy shouted.

"Chewy, I don't think this is going to work out," Miguel said, tossing him the key fob. "I quit."

"I knew Roger Dodger wasn't a real name!" Chewy yelled back. He threw his hat onto the lawn and then picked it up again before walking down to his truck, cursing under his breath the whole way.

Miguel, Rebecca, and Hannah climbed into the ATV and headed toward the gates. Rebecca reached over and held his hand as they turned onto the main road leading back to town. "I love you," she said. "Always have. Always will."

"Eww! Get a room!" Hannah teased from the back seat.

Miguel's smile faded quickly from his face when he spotted a line of black SUVs heading their way. "This can't be good!" Two SUVs formed a blockade in the middle of the two-lane road. Two more vehicles came up behind them occupying both lanes. "Hold on!" Miguel yelled as he turned off the road and into an open field.

Rebecca turned around to see all four SUVs following them into the field. They pulled up on either side of the ATV, guns drawn. Two more SUVs approached from the rear. Up ahead a helicopter descended and touched down directly ahead of them. Boxed in and out of options, Miguel brought the ATV to a stop.

Several men jumped from their vehicles with their guns drawn. They ripped Miguel from the ATV. They were especially combative with Miguel, punching him in the stomach and forcing him to his knees. Two men held Hannah by her arms as she kicked and tried to jerk her arms away. Instead of yanking Rebecca from the ATV, one guard offered her his hand to help her out. They must have been given strict orders regarding her handling. She slapped his extended hand away and got out on her own.

Victor emerged from the helicopter, buttoning his jacket,

and casually strolled toward Rebecca who now had two guards standing behind her. Without saying a word, Victor pulled the sides of her red kimono together at her naval. He tied the belt of the silk robe securely while looking intently into her eyes. His black pupils, accentuated by light blue circles, reminded her of a beautiful and feral animal. Lips thin and perfectly horizontal. Black wavy hair pushed back from his pale face.

"Vic. Please," Rebecca pleaded.

He looked over at Miguel, on his knees, hands tied behind his back. "Is this man trying to steal you away from me?" Rebecca remained silent. "Doesn't he know that you are my whole world and that I cannot bear to lose you again? Doesn't he know that you belong to me?"

Victor sauntered over to Miguel. "Oh yes, of course. I remember you. You're the guy who cleared my name. I never got a chance to thank you in person. How fortuitous! Miguel, is it? I understand you and my Rebecca had a bit of a fling. A summer romance, I presume? I certainly don't blame you. I should probably thank you for keeping her under your watchful eye while she was away. But rest assured, my Rebecca is home now. She will be safe with me. No need to check in on her anymore. Do you understand?"

Miguel did not respond. He kept his eyes on the ground, as if it were his last act of defiance.

Victor cupped his hand behind his ear. "I'm sorry, I didn't hear you?" He gestured to one of his men, who brought the butt of his rifle down onto the bridge of Miguel's nose and he cried out.

"No!" Rebecca shouted. "Please, leave him alone. Just let him go, Victor."

"You know," he said, wagging his index finger. "If I didn't know any better, I'd think you still had feelings for this young man. No? I mean, just look at him. Strong. Handsome. A real *macho* man!" He turned to Miguel once again and crouched down to eye level. "Are you a *macho* man, Miguel?" Victor motioned to one of his men who kicked Miguel in his ribs and he slumped to the ground.

"Stop!" Rebecca screamed. "That's enough!"

"Is it enough, my love? I'm not so sure. I mean, look how far he's come to take you from me. I'm not sure it is enough. Only one way to be sure this cannot possibly happen again."

"Victor, you made your point," Rebecca said. "He gets it. Don't do this."

His eyes narrowed. He turned his attention to Hannah. "Hannah! Dear, dear Hannah," Victor ambled over to where she was being held. Hannah refused to look him in the eye. "You've had a nice little vacation, haven't you? I offered you my protection. I let you stay in my villa and eat my food. And this is how you repay me? So ungrateful. Especially, given where you've been. I think it's time you get back to work, dear. You'll have plenty of time to think about how good you had it once you're back in the service centers."

"No!" Rebecca shouted. "No, you can't send her back there. Do *not* send her back there!" She started to move toward Hannah, but the two guards standing behind her seized her arms. "Let me go!"

Victor gestured with a nod of his head and the guards holding Hannah shoved her into the back of an SUV.

"Let me go!" Rebecca shouted. "I can't believe I defended you," Rebecca said to Victor. "So it's true? What they said?"

"It's business, love. Best you not get involved. Oh, I

almost forgot." Victor summoned one of his men who brought over a black velvet box. "I wanted to give you this." He opened the case to reveal a multi-stranded platinum necklace. A breathtaking five-carat emerald adorned the center. "Here, let me." He placed the necklace around her neck. "It looks beautiful on you." He clasped the choker at the back of her neck.

Rebecca cried out when she felt a sharp prick at the nape of her neck. A fine needle pierced her skin and extended micro-tendrils that wrapped themselves into and around her spinal cord. "What was that?" Rebecca asked.

"Let's call it your last chance," he said and then addressed the guards, "Let her go." They released Rebecca's arms. "Get into the helicopter."

"No! Not until—" Victor issued a low-level electrical pulse into her spine and she fell to her hands and knees.

Miguel cried out and a guard zapped him with a taser wand.

"The answer we're looking for is, 'Yes, dear.' Now, let's try that again. Get on the fucking helicopter!" Spittle escaped his lips as he yelled. His eyes were wild and menacing.

Rebecca had never seen Victor in such a deranged state. She wasn't sure what he had put around her neck, but the fear of receiving another shock humbled her into submission. She climbed onto the helicopter. Victor followed and took his seat next to her. She took one look back at Miguel, who was yelling something, but she couldn't hear him over the helicopter rotors. One of the guards electrocuted him with a taser wand until he fell to his side again. Rebecca buried her head in her hands and sobbed.

CHAPTER 42

SORRY WE SHOT YOU: CLEMENS

BACK AT THE FARM, Clemens and Dutch watched the live satellite feed from inside the BX-9, as Victor's goons beat Miguel mercilessly. Dutch held both hands atop his bald head. Clemens slammed his fists on the console. It was a long shot. Not only did it fail, it made the situation so much worse.

"Well, that's it," Clemens said. "That was our Hail Mary."

"There has to be some other way," LeBlanc said pacing back and forth with crossed arms. "Keep thinking." Clemens had three satellite feeds open. One of them stayed with the SUV, which was transporting Hannah back into Chicago. The second followed Crowe's helicopter, which was heading east. A third feed remained with Miguel on the ground in that field, surrounded by armed guards. Miguel's situation was most urgent since Victor no longer had any use for him. It was also the least plausible situation for the team to carry out any rescue operation, given their inability to breach the smart perimeter.

"I say we follow Hannah," James said.

"They'll probably take her to some kind of holding facility, like the place where we found her, before anything bad happens to her. They're going to *kill* Miguel," Clemens said.

Outside the muffled buzz of drone rotors grew closer. An alert flashed on the holoscreen: *Approaching Aircraft.* Dutch touched the screen to zoom in on the incoming craft. "It's another BX-9!"

"Who the hell is that?" Clemens shouted. Clemens had never seen a BX-9 in his life and now he had seen two on the same day. "You think it's Chicago police? Way out here?" They were well outside the city limits. Not that the police would have been limited by jurisdiction.

"I don't know," LeBlanc said. "Computer, identify approaching aircraft."

The computer replied: *BX-10, urban policing unit, model number—*

"Identify owner," LeBlanc interrupted.

The computer replied: *This BX-10 is registered to Kalipso Enterprises, Inc.*

"Kalipso?" Clemens pondered out loud. "That's a biotech company isn't it?"

"I think you're right," LeBlanc said. "But what are they doing here?"

The craft landed gently in the field next to the BX-9. It looked exactly the same except for the black paint job. They watched from the front windows as the boarding stairs extended toward the ground and Sylvia stepped down.

"It's Sylvia!" Dutch cried. They rushed out to greet her in the barren field and wrapped their arms around her from all sides.

"Where'd you get a BX-9?" LeBlanc asked.

"It's a BX-10," Sylvia said raising her eyebrows. "It belongs to Daemon Lovelace. It's a long story. Where's Hannah?" Sylvia asked.

"Victor's men have her. They're transporting her somewhere in Chicago. We're tracking her location."

"And Miguel?"

"They've got him at one of Crowe's properties about forty miles from here," Clemens said. "It doesn't look good."

"Well, what are we waiting for?" Sylvia said.

"He has a defense system around his property. We can't get anywhere near his airspace or we'd get shot out of the sky."

"Not if they can't see you," Sylvia said.

"Go on," LeBlanc said.

"The BX-10 has stealth mode."

"What's stealth mode?" Clemens asked.

"It's an invisibility shield."

Clemens shot a wide-eyed look at LeBlanc. "Did you know this thing had a freakin' invisibility shield?!"

"I think I would have known about that," LeBlanc retorted in defense.

"No, I read about this," Dutch said. "That feature wasn't ready when the BX-9 first came out. Only later models had it and it came standard on all BX-10's."

"Okay, well, now we're getting somewhere," Clemens said.

"What about Rebecca?" Sylvia asked.

"Victor has her," Clemens said. "We think he's controlling her with some kind of electroshock device around her neck."

"I'm familiar," she said. "He's making these compliance collars to control abductees. We have to shut him down."

"We will, but Miguel doesn't have much time. If you can bypass Crowe's defense system, we should go now."

"What about Hannah?" James asked.

"Go find her! Clemens, come with me to get Miguel."

Clemens followed Sylvia into the BX-10 and strapped himself into the co-pilot seat. As Sylvia manned the system's navigation system, Clemens gave the computer a voice commend to enter stealth mode. The computer replied: *Stealth mode enabled.* The aircraft blended into its surroundings like liquid glass. Sylvia entered the coordinates for Miguel's precise location and when she hit enter on the control panel, the automatic pilot took over and flung them to their destination.

It took less than eight minutes for them to arrive at the field near Victor's property. Three SUVs surrounded the ATV Miguel had been ripped from. Seven or eight guards stood in a semi-circle around Miguel, who was kneeling a bit unsteadily on the grass. The onboard weaponry was specifically designed for crowd control, which meant that whatever assault they were to bring upon these men would affect Miguel just as severely.

"How accurate are these rubber bullets?" Sylvia asked.

"Not very," Clemens replied. "We could try to aim high, but there's no guarantee Miguel won't suffer collateral damage."

One of Victor's goons received a message into his earpiece. He nodded to the other men who stepped back. He pulled his sidearm from his holster and placed it at the back of Miguel's skull.

"Now!" Clemens shouted.

Sylvia fired the rubber bullet gatlings directly at the gunman and surrounding men, who crumpled to the ground, writhing and disoriented. A few of them seemed to be knocked out cold. Miguel was also hit and he fell over sideways.

"I got him," Clemens said. He released a grappling hook and zoomed in close to maneuver it through the zip ties binding Miguel's hands. Once the connection was secure, Clemens retracted the cable back toward the aircraft, lifting Miguel off the ground like a massive fish hoisted from the ocean.

One of the men scrambled to his feet and spun around, a look of confusion on his face, as if trying to ascertain from where the assault was coming. He spotted Miguel ascending into the air, both hands together as if he had miraculously summoned the power of flight. He groped for his sidearm and took aim, but by the time he could get off a shot, Miguel was safely inside the hull.

Sylvia entered new coordinates into the navigation system. Miguel regained consciousness as Clemens tended to his wounds.

"Victor has Rebecca," Miguel managed to eke out.

"That's where we're headed," Clemens reassured him. "You might need to sit this one out."

"You trying to bench me, coach?" He tried to smile, but his lip was too swollen to comply.

Clemens chuckled. "No. Of course not."

"Sorry, we shot you," Sylvia said from the pilot seat. Miguel hadn't seen her yet. "How's the head?"

"Sylvia? Is that you?" A look of relief sparkled in

Miguel's one operable eye. He tried to get up but winced in pain.

"Careful," Clemens said. "Just take it easy."

"Victor has Rebecca," Miguel repeated himself.

"Don't worry. We're tracking his location. You'll see her soon enough. Try to get some rest. We've still got work to do."

CHAPTER 43

AN AMBITIOUS UNDERTAKING: SYLVIA

THE BX-10 steadily gained on Victor's helicopter, which they had been tracking all along. Sylvia remained far enough away to maintain a low profile. Miguel had fallen asleep somewhere over Lake Michigan. She reached back and ran her fingers over the slightly raised insertion point behind her neck. Motivated by righteous vengeance, Sylvia aimed to take down Victor Crowe's entire operation. She wanted to see him suffer. She wanted him to know that it she was the one who brought him down.

Sylvia had spent the last eighteen months in Winnipeg trying to do it the right way, legally. It was painfully clear that the right way wasn't going to cut it anymore. She had plenty of information about the Guard's operations locally, but Victor's level of involvement was higher than she or anyone else had ever aimed. Maybe Crowe wasn't leading the trafficking operations on the ground, but his contributions enabled and incentivized human rights violations worldwide.

"What's your plan, Syl?" Clemens asked.

"I don't know," Sylvia said, biting the edge of her thumb.

"Looks like he's headed to Motown," Clemens said. His fingers danced along the computer keyboard. "I'm guessing Victor has a plant there. Must be where he's manufacturing these shock collars."

"We have to destroy the plant," Sylvia said. "How do we do that?"

"If we know where to aim, we could fry their entire computer system with a concentrated microwave beam," Clemens said. "That would at least disrupt production for a while. At least until he finds another factory and retools."

"Okay, okay, that's a start," she said hopefully.

"I think I have the location," Clemens said entering the coordinates into the control panel. "Soma Bionics. They make robotic human replacement parts and other bionic hardware." He pulled up a holographic schematic of the building. "This is the main floor. Most likely that's where the factory computers are housed. If we aim that beam directly at any part of the network, it would be like cooking a pair of holospecs in a microwave oven, sparks and all."

"Sounds like a plan," Sylvia said, satisfied. "Let's go sabotage a factory."

"And then what?" Clemens asked.

"And then I spend the rest of my life making sure Victor Crowe doesn't get a second chance."

Clemens examined her for a moment with searching eyes. "What did he do to you, Syl?" Clemens inquired with a fatherly compassion.

Sylvia crossed her arms. A tear formed in the corner of her eye and she quickly wiped it away. She waited for the lump in her throat to dissipate. "He showed me a part of myself I never knew existed, or at least, I never wanted to know."

"What part is that?"

She shook her head. "It doesn't matter. What matters is, I know what I have to do. I finally know what I'm meant for."

"You found your purpose," Clemens said.

Sylvia gave the slightest nod. "It all started back in Winnipeg. I'd always known trafficking was rampant, but when we discovered our own men were involved, I knew I had to do something. And that something ended up getting my dad killed. He was just trying to protect me." The lump returned to her throat and she forced it back down. "If I run away and hide, they win. It means my dad died for nothing." She shook her head. "I can't live with that. I won't rest until every last one of those women and children are free."

Clemens held her gaze. "It's an ambitious undertaking. But I can't think of a better person to lead the charge."

"This is *our* mission. We started this months ago."

"I know we did. Listen, I know ranks don't mean anything anymore, but I'm promoting you anyway. Captain."

Sylvia searched his eyes for sincerity. A smile slowly crawled across her face. "Captain?"

"Captain," he said and gave a singular nod. "Let's fry that motherfucker."

CHAPTER 44

BUCKET: HANNAH

HANNAH HAD BEEN HERE BEFORE. King's Cross Anglican Church had been in ruins for decades. The roof had caved in years ago and graffiti covered the walls inside and out. Traffickers used sites like these as waiting stations for trafficked women and children before delivering them to service centers or trading them with other players in the ring. God hadn't been here in ages.

She recognized a familiar musty smell, dank and old. The room was mostly dark. A shaft of light created a rectangular box against the far wall. She distinctly remembered that rectangular box. It was a year ago that she learned to disappear into that sliver of light, her only escape from the monotony of her captive existence.

She wasn't alone. Her eyes hadn't adjusted enough to make out any bodies, but she could hear them breathing. She felt the familiar sensation of her body floating, unable to delineate where her body made contact with the stained mattress beneath her. She felt no pain, like her body existed far inside a protective cloud. Hannah fought the urge to go back to sleep. She tried to stand up, but her legs failed to support her.

Hannah reached to her right and her hand rested on a warm surface, prickly as she moved her fingers over the contoured mass. Skin. A leg? Judging by the length of its stubble, this woman must have been a newer captive. If she had been a veteran, her leg hair would have been longer, softer. This woman had shaved in the last three or four days. She squeezed the leg. She patted it. "Hey," Hannah managed to whisper. She cleared her throat and tried again with minimal vocal strength. "Hey."

The prickly prisoner moaned.

"Hey," Hannah said again. "Wake up." She shook her leg gently. "Wake up."

The prisoner moaned again, "Nnuursh . . . muh."

"Hey! Come on. Wake up."

"She ain't gonna wake up," another voice said from across the room.

"Who are you?" Hannah asked. She couldn't quite see the person speaking.

"Nora. You?

"Hannah. How long have you been in here?"

"'Bout a week. This yo first time?"

"No. But it's going to be my last."

Nora laughed. "Oh, you think so? How old are you, baby?"

"Seventeen."

"Honey, I hate to break it to you, but you got a lot of years left up in here. You young. You white. And you pretty."

"I have people out there. They'll come for me."

"Okay baby. You keep telling yourself that."

Hannah sat pensively for a moment. Nora wasn't wrong. The odds were against her. She recalled the faces of her rescuers with fondness and hope. She also remembered that it was her who got their attention in the first place. Hannah was the one who decided to smash her head against that window over and over. She didn't care if she gave herself a concussion. She was determined to find a way out and she did her part.

"You know, you're right," Hannah said. "I can't wait around to be rescued. I have to do this on my own."

Nora laughed again. "I'm sorry, baby. I ain't laughin' at you. You seem like a real nice kid."

Hannah tried standing again, this time making it onto her feet. She braced herself against the wall. Her eyes had adjusted to the darkness. She could see the moaning woman lying on a mattress beside her, wearing nothing but a tank top and panties, waistband twisted and insufficiently covering her posterior. She could see Nora sitting against the wall, her legs stretched out in front of her in a V.

Hannah used the wall for support and made her way over to the two concrete steps leading up to the steel door. She remembered from before that this door was accessed with a security card attached to a retractable lanyard on the guard's utility belt.

"When was the last time they were in here?" Hannah asked.

"Not since you got here. 'Bout three hours ago. Why?"

"So they'll be back again in an hour for another dose."

"You *do* know the drill."

"I've been here before. In this room actually. Where's the bucket?"

"Over there, in the corner." Nora pointed to a dark corner of the room.

Hannah used her feet to locate the five-gallon bucket and heard the slosh of human waste when she kicked it. The smell of shit and piss wafted up into her sinuses. She gagged. Hannah found the handle and tried to lift the bucket, but it was too heavy.

"Can you help me? Nora?"

"Whatchu mean, help you?"

"Help me carry this over to the steps."

"Uh-uh, you on ya own, honey. I don't even touch that thing when I have to use it."

"Please? I have a plan."

"Oh, you have a plan?"

"Okay listen. First, we cover the steps with poop and when the guard opens the door he'll slip on it and fall down the steps. And then we take his gun and his access card and get the hell out of here."

Nora laughed again and clapped her hands. "Girl, you crazy! I like you, though. I do!"

"Please? We have to try. I'm telling you. I have people and they're coming. They're CPG—well, former."

"The fuck is a CPG?"

"They're like police in Canada."

"Is that suppose to reassure me? Who the fuck you think took me from my home when I was twelve years old? The police, that's who."

"Trust me. These people are good. They rescued me, twice. They're trying to put a stop to all of this."

"Why you back here den?"

"We got separated and I got caught. It's a long story, but they're coming for me. I know it."

"How they gonna find you up in here?"

"That's why I have to get out."

"Oh Lord, have mercy!"

"So will you help me?"

"That ain't no plan! What if he don't fall?"

"Come on! Don't be negative! We have to try!" Hannah felt a knot forming in her throat and started to cry. "I have to at least try."

"Ah shit," Nora said. "Don't do that. Don't cry. Alright, alright. Come on now. What the hell? Fine. I'll help you, but this sho ain't gonna work."

Reluctantly, Nora helped her carry the splattering bucket to the steps. They tipped the bucket over and poured its putrid contents onto the steps.

"Ooh. Oooh, Lord! This stank!" Nora had exceeded her disgust tolerance. "Okay, what we do now?" Nora asked holding her shirt over her nose.

"We wait," Hannah said.

The sleeping woman moaned again, this time more loudly.

"They got this bitch fucked up," Nora said, shaking her head. "Whachu tryna say, baby?" Nora asked the woman sweetly and helped her into a sitting position.

Hannah sat next to the drugged woman, helping to brace her from the other side. "I'm Hannah and this is Nora. What's your name?"

"Anita." She scrunched up her face. "What's that smell?"

"Oh, that's our shit!" Nora said looking directly at Hannah. "Tell her about your plan."

"We're getting out of here," Hannah said. "And you're coming with us. Can you stand up?"

Anita could barely sit upright without help, much less stand. "How? How are we getting out?" Anita asked. "There's guards all over."

"We're going to take out the next guard that comes in here. We're going to take his gun and his access card and we're busting out!" Hannah explained with great zeal.

Anita glared at Hannah with a raised eyebrow. She turned to Nora. "Is this bitch crazy?"

"Girl, that's what I said. But under the circumstances, crazy is all we got," Nora said.

Hannah nodded in agreement. Nora gets it.

"Why is there shit everywhere?" Anita asked pulling her shirt up over her nose.

"Oh, that's part of this white girl's plan to take out the guard," Nora said. "Tell her."

"He's going to slip on it," Hannah explained with full confidence.

Anita scoffed. "Damn, you are crazy. I don't want nothin' to do with your poopy plans. I'm in enough trouble as it is."

At that moment, the door buzzed and opened. The tubby guard slipped on the shit-covered stoop, but caught his balance. "What the fuck?! Oh fuck! That's fucking disgusting! Which one of you bitches shit on the floor? That's what the bucket is for, goddammit!"

"Oh, I'm sorry," Nora said. "I thought it was for this!" Nora swung the empty bucket against the guard's face with all her might and he fell backwards against the wall. As he staggered to regain his balance, his foot slipped on the fecal soup and he fell directly onto his tailbone. Nora whacked him again on the side of his head.

Adrenaline overtook her and Hannah jumped on top of the guard like a wild puma. "Grab his gun!" Hannah yelled.

Nora wrestled the bolt gun from its holster and blasted him before he could get to his knees. Hannah removed the guard's access card and a taser from his utility belt.

"Anita, now's our chance!" Hannah yelled. "Are you in?"

"Fuck it! Help me up," Anita said.

She and Nora helped the still-woozy captive to her feet, placing her arms around their necks. Anita had not fully regained use of her legs and they would buckle and slip from under her every two or three steps.

They ascended a narrow stairwell and another guard busted through the door at the top of the stairs. Nora shot him and he fell toward them. They clung to the railing on either side as he tumbled past them. When they reached the ground floor, it was empty. Screaming could be heard in the distance.

They made their way toward a half-lit exit sign. The screaming grew louder and two guards ran into the hallway ahead of them from another direction, followed by a dense fog. The men ran out the exit door screaming and covering their faces. "What the f—" Nora coughed mid-sentence. Hannah's eyes began to burn and she choked. Within seconds all three were coughing uncontrollably, eyes watering, as they painstakingly made their way toward the exit.

Hannah heard something else amid the shouting. It was muffled and frantic, but she could have sworn she heard her name. A dense fog filled the hall. She continued to feel her way toward the exit, still a ways away, with her eyes shut tight. More gunshots rang out from inside the building. "Hannah!" She heard again, this time closer, still muffled, but she couldn't open her eyes. She held Anita up with one arm and held the taser out in front of her with the other. She felt a hand on her shoulder. "Hannah, it's me Jaaaaa—" She jabbed the taser into James' ribs before realizing who he was.

"James!" Hannah called out between coughs. She forced herself to open her watery eyes and pulled the gas mask from his face. "Oh no!" she cried. "I'm so sorry!"

James forced a smile. He placed the gas mask over her face and covered his with his shirt as they stumbled toward the exit. Once outside the building, all four fell to the ground coughing and wheezing.

Outside, men ran in all directions. What could only be described as a spaceship descended onto the church lawn, firing rubber bullets into the crowd.

"Come on!" James yelled. "That's our ride!"

Nora looked suspiciously at the hovering aircraft, its passengers waving them over.

"It's okay," Hannah yelled over the shouting and smiled widely. "I told you. I have people!"

They must have dropped tear gas into a gaping hole in the church roof. Many of the guards dispersed into nearby storefronts and abandoned homes. The remaining dug into strategic alcoves and around blind corners as they fired shots at the aircraft.

James and the women crouched at one of the back exits, tucked into a partially covered exterior corridor.

"Come on!" James shouted and helped Anita to her feet. As soon as they emerged from the alcove, they too, were under fire. One slug found its way into James' kevlar vest and he fell to his knees. Hannah pulled him back into the relative safety of the alcove.

An armored military vehicle approached the church from the rear. It was twice the size of the arctic rover and could have held up to twenty soldiers. The front of the vehicle opened like a mouth, lowering its jaw bridge to the ground as armored soldiers piled out. Rubber bullets ricocheted from their helmets and shields as they approached the building.

The spaceship positioned itself between them and the approaching soldiers. James received a message from a wrist com. It was Dutch. "Cover your ears. Engaging sonic blast in 5-4-3—"

James turned to the women, cupping his hands over his ears, and shouted, "Cover your ears!"

Even with her hands pressed firmly against the side of her head, Hannah heard what sounded like a car horn turned up to eleven. The soldiers fell to the ground holding their ears and writhing in pain like bugs who had been stepped on but not killed.

Once the sonic attack had ended, James and the women ran toward the hovercraft. LeBlanc jumped out and helped them safely on board. "Is everyone okay?" LeBlanc asked.

"James got shot," Hannah said. LeBlanc helped him remove the kevlar vest to assess the damage. His ribcage was red and bruised.

"I'm fine," James said. "Are you okay?" he asked Hannah.

Hannah kissed his cheek. "I am now."

As they flew safely away from the site, LeBlanc handed out water bottles to the newly rescued women. "What are your names?" he asked the newcomers.

"Nora."

"Anita."

"I'm LeBlanc and this is Dutch."

Dutch turned and nodded.

"Do you have a place to go?" LeBlanc asked.

"My grandma's," Anita said. "She lives in Arlington Heights."

"On it," Dutch said and entered the Chicago suburban destination into the navigation console.

"And you, Nora? Where can we take you?"

"I ain't been home in fifteen years. Ain't nothin' back in Toledo for me. Where ya'll headed."

"Nowhere safe, I'm afraid," LeBlanc said.

"Safe? I don't even know what the hell that means," Nora said. "Ya'll some kind of vigilantes or somethin'?"

"Oh, I don't know about that," LeBlanc said. "But I don't hate the sound of it."

REBECCA COULDN'T BELIEVE Victor had turned out to be exactly as Miguel described—worse. She knew he could be ruthless in his business dealings, but she never thought he could be as cruel and inhumane as he was proving himself to be. She couldn't even look at him. They flew over a large industrial complex in central Detroit, where his factory was located. Victor insisted on being present at Soma Bionics to witness the very first batch of compliance bands to roll off the assembly line. He was almost giddy to see his newest invention come to life.

"Victor, please. This isn't necessary," Rebecca said as she tugged at the elegant necklace steadily tightening around her neck. "It's choking me!"

"Relax!" Victor said. "You're choking yourself. Relax and it will loosen."

"You don't expect me to wear this thing forever," she said. She didn't yet believe that could have possibly been the case. While she was astounded at his brutality, a side of him she'd never before seen, she still couldn't believe he would direct such cruelty toward her. He'd always treated her like a princess. He never even tried to argue with her, much less physically control her.

"You must think I'm some kind of fool," he said. "I know you still have feelings for that cop. I know that given the chance, you'd run away with him again. I can't allow that to happen. Not again."

"How do you think this is going to work, Victor? How can I learn to love you freely, if I'm not free myself?"

"I'm sure you'll find a way. Besides, the alternative would be much less satisfactory, I can assure you."

"So am I your girlfriend, or your prisoner?"

He gazed intently into her youthful eyes. "Yes," he said plainly.

Victor presented her with a green strapless gown, shoes, and earrings to match her new platinum compliance band. "I want to showcase the possibilities for customization and you are the perfect model."

Rebecca snatched the items from him with huff and dressed hurriedly without saying a word. She had no choice but to acquiesce, but the scowl on her face conveyed contempt and disgust.

Victor received an incoming message from one of his men back at the property.

"Sir, he got away."

"What?!" Victor's eyes widened in disbelief. "How?"

Silence followed.

"How?!" Victor demanded.

"He flew away, sir."

"Goddammit, you'd better start making sense this fucking

instant!" The veins on his neck looked as thought they might burst.

"We were ambushed . . . by someone, or something. Then he just flew into the air like . . . like Superman . . . and disappeared."

Victor paused a moment. "What's your name?"

"Gary, sir."

"Put someone else on."

"Yes, sir," another deeper man's voice said.

"Kill Gary!" Victor shouted at the top of his lungs.

Victor's helicopter landed on the roof of the plant. Victor held out his hand, but Rebecca refused to take it. She looked ravishing in the green dress, the sunlight reflecting off her exquisite jewelry. The melancholy constitution of her face was a mismatch against her otherwise dazzling appearance.

Victor straightened his tie and opened the roof access door to a concrete staircase that led down to the assembly floor. The plant foreman and another operations mechanic awaited their arrival in lab coats and hard hats. A photographer was present to document the occasion, although it was not to be released to the public. This was a private celebration. A brief tour of the assembly line ended at an overlook where the control panel displayed large green and red buttons.

"This is it," the foreman said. "Whenever you're ready, sir." The photographer snapped several photos. Rebecca was not smiling in any of them. The foreman gave him a nod and Victor pressed the green button. A loud buzz sounded and the assembly line jumped into action. Another photo of Victor shaking hands with the foreman.

The whole production was completely automated in a

highly advanced robotic assembly line. The version that was currently being fabricated was the kind Sylvia had worn. Black carbon fiber construction, roughly a half-inch wide, quite sleek looking even without frills or precious gems like Rebecca's. Victor's eyes twinkled at the process.

Rebecca saw a red notification illuminated on the console. Victor was too preoccupied with the assembly line to notice. A single spark and then a flurry of sparks jumped up from the control panel. Smoke and the smell of burnt metal arose from a computer console. A popping sound caught Victor's attention. He jumped back and waved his hand back and forth to fan away the smoke. The backlit keyboards and switches flickered off and on, and then off. A loud buzz sounded and the entire production line halted.

"What the fuck! What just happened?" Victor shouted.

"I don't know, sir," the foreman said. "I'm getting word that the entire building went offline. I am so sorry, sir. We're going to fix this, trust me."

Victor slammed his fist onto the console and then quickly pulled it back. "Goddammit!" He cried as he massaged his burnt hand. The metal surface was glowing red now. He turned to the foreman. "I have orders to fill! If these aren't distributed on time you can kiss your contract goodbye. Fix it!!" Victor commanded.

As he ranted and flailed his arms about, Rebecca noticed smoke rising from his wrist remote, the one that controlled her compliance band. Victor continued berating the foreman and kicked over a recycling bin. Sparks jumped from his wrist. At first, due to his foment, he didn't even notice. Rebecca slowly stepped backward away from the fireworks that began to spray from his wristband. Suddenly, his wrist and hand ballooned up like a hot dog, tearing his jacket sleeve and popping the fried wristband from his arm.

Victor cried out in pain. His eyes bulged at the sight of his arm exploding right before his eyes without any plausible explanation. He held his arm far away from him as though he were rejecting it as part of his body. He slumped to the floor and looked to Rebecca as if she might have had any way to remedy his monstrous limb.

The necklace slipped from around her neck and fell to the floor with a clank. Rebecca removed her heels and ran down the steps leading up to the overlook and across the factory floor.

"Wait!" Victor cried as he scrambled to his feet, holding his bloated appendage. "Stop her!" Victor shouted to anyone who would listen, but no one did anything to stop Rebecca from reaching the exit.

Rebecca looked back as she opened the metal door. Victor screamed unintelligibly, pushing past shocked factory workers as he chased after her into the stairwell.

"Where do you think you're going?" Victor shouted up the flight of stairs.

When she opened the roof access door, she saw Miguel standing in the hull of a drone hovering a few feet above the roof. Miguel extended his hand toward her. "Come on!"

"Get back here!" Victor howled from a flight below her. He climbed up the stairs cradling his hot dog arm. Spittle suspended from his lips when he spoke and his hair hung loose in his face. "Rebecaaa!"

She cinched up her dress and ran toward the drone. She turned and threw a shoe toward Victor, which missed by a long shot. The second one managed to strike him right between the eyes. His face contorted in maniacal fury. Rebecca tripped over a protruding roof vent and fell, tearing her dress along its side seam.

"Grab my hand!" Miguel called from the steps.

Rebecca scrambled to her feet and Victor clutched her by the arm. She turned to him and sunk her knee into his groin and he released his grip as he doubled over and fell to his knees. She reached the aircraft and took Miguel's hand. He pulled her up onto the boarding stairs and they ascended, leaving Victor defeated and alone on the factory roof.

SIX MONTHS LATER, Sylvia sat at the edge of a long pier gazing into the peaceful and frigid waters of the Churchill River Estuary. It was January and a glistening blanket of snow covered every surface, keeping everything frozen in place—frozen in time. She kept returning to this very spot the last three weeks, hoping to see a beluga whale. Although there were fewer and fewer each year, she'd been informed that if she was going to see one before they became extinct, this was supposedly the ideal spot.

She heard footsteps crunching the snow behind her, but she didn't turn around. A grin reached across her face.

"Heya Cap. I thought I'd find you here. May I join you?" LeBlanc asked, approaching the edge of the pier with a thermos in hand.

"Be my guest. *Director*," she replied, emphasizing his new title. LeBlanc had reinstated his tenure with the Canadian Security Intelligence Service as Director of Human Trafficking Prevention, a department that hadn't been staffed since Canada's fall. She swept snow from the wooden deck to her right, giving him a relatively dry place to sit.

"Brought you some hot tea." He handed her the thermos. He blew into his hands and rubbed them together before sitting down.

She unscrewed the cap and steam escaped into the cool air. She poured herself a cup and let the warm contents thaw her fingers.

"Any luck?" Leblanc asked, scanning the still surface of the water.

"Not yet. Have you ever seen one?"

"A beluga? Oh yeah! Strange looking things. They kind of freak me out, actually."

Sylvia laughed. "Really? Why?"

"I don't know. It's those beady eyes. I just can't with those beady black eyes!"

She laughed. It was a sound she was getting used to making. The more she made it, the easier it got. She was holding her father's dog tags that hung from her neck. He was the last person she really laughed with. He was the last person who truly believed in her—told her she could do anything, be anything. Now, with her father gone, she was surrounded by people like LeBlanc and Clemens who constantly affirmed this belief. And she was grateful.

"How long are you here for this time?" Sylvia asked. He'd been flying back and forth from Ottawa since his new appointment with CSIS.

"That's what I wanted to tell you. They approved my request to relocate to Churchill."

"Really? That's great! So are you going to be staying with us at the Lazy Bear?"

"Marjorie's already setting up my room. Yeah, they thought I was crazy wanting to move up here to the middle of nowhere."

"It's not so bad," Sylvia said. "It's quiet."

"You got that right."

Sylvia held the cup with both hands and took a sip. "I can't believe they just handed over a blank check," Sylvia said. She was referring to the resources that came with LeBlanc's new appointment with CSIS.

"Well, I wouldn't call it a blank check. But we have more than enough to cover anything we need for surveillance and intel support. I can't believe how fast the HLF is spreading."

The Human Liberation Front, which was privately funded by none other than Daemon Lovelace, who supplied them with an arsenal of high-tech weaponry, carried out a number of rescue operations all across Canada. The CPG regarded the Human Liberation Front as an unlawful insurgent militia who posed a direct threat to their authority over the region. To the public, on the other hand, they were regarded as a heroic force for good. They were gaining new recruits every week—soldiers and lay informants alike.

"I know. We just authorized a new outpost in Calgary this week," Sylvia said. "It's the podcast. It's really pulling supporters out of the woodwork."

Sylvia and her crew released a podcast series to the public with each episode calling for any information about regional trafficking operations. The podcast, "Bad Traffic," became widely popular among the public and accounted for hundreds of tips leading to several successful raids. Each episode detailed a real rescue operation with audio from the front lines, interviews with victims, and fierce interrogations with perpetrators. Critics called it "Thrilling," "Suspenseful" and "Ruthless."

"It was a brilliant idea, I gotta say," LeBlanc said. "How many downloads are we at now?"

"I lost count. The last episode is already at ten thousand and it keeps climbing."

"Have you read the comments? The people are fed up and they're not afraid to speak out. It's putting the CPG in a real bad light."

"I hear they can't get new recruits," Sylvia said.

"People don't want to be associated with trafficking. I don't blame 'em."

In their last raid, they apprehended a CPG board member. He begged them to turn him in. But Sylvia knew better. She knew he'd get nothing more than a slap on the wrist if they delivered him back to the CPG. It didn't do any good to go through legal channels. Instead, they implanted a tracking device into his neck. They posted his tracking location to the HLF's website, where anyone could see it live, along with his photo and other identifying information. If the CPG wouldn't administer justice, the public would. Two days later his tracking pin stopped moving.

Sylvia heard mirthful squealing and laughter in the distance. Hannah and James were throwing snowballs at each other. They'd been inseparable ever since Chicago.

"Time out!" James shouted. "Time!" When she stopped, he whipped another snowball he'd been hiding behind his back. She shrieked and tackled him in the snow.

"Can't say we didn't see this coming," LeBlanc said and chuckled.

"It's non-stop with those two. Kinda cute, actually."

Hannah and James finally approached the pier, half running, half bumping into one another, faces reddened from the cold. "Sylvia!" Hannah called, still panting. "Hey!"

"Hey!" Sylvia replied, trying to match Hannah's youthful enthusiasm.

"You're not going to believe this!" Hannah said. "You know Megan Stone?" Megan Stone was Canada's most watched journalist and had a television show out of Montreal.

"The talk show host?"

Hannah nodded enthusiastically. "They called and asked if you'd be interested in going on the show!"

"The Megan Stone Show? Me?" Interviews and spotlights were never Sylvia's forte.

"Yeah," James said. "They're booking out their summer line up and want you for their human rights series. Isn't that crazy?"

"Yeah. I don't know," Sylvia said with reservation.

"It could be really good exposure for the podcast," Hannah added.

"That's true," LeBlanc said. "The more exposure the better."

"And they asked for me specifically?" Sylvia asked.

"Well, yeah," Hannah said. "You're kind of a big deal."

"You are the face of this outfit," LeBlanc said. "You inspire people."

How? Sylvia thought. This did not compute. Sure the work might be inspiring. She could see that, especially for those whose lives had been affected by trafficking. But Sylvia was not particularly charismatic or expressive. Even on the podcast, her contribution was only what could be heard through her mic in the midst of battle. Sometimes they used clips from their strategy sessions, which showcased her no-nonsense leadership style, her decisiveness. But she didn't do commentary or confessional style cutaway interviews post-raid.

"You have to!" Hannah said. "You'll be great."

"I'll think about it," Sylvia said.

"Dutch and Miguel are meeting us at the soccer field. You guys wanna play?" James asked.

"I'll watch," LeBlanc said. "My knees can't handle much more than that."

"Syl?" Hannah asked with those beguiling eyes.

"Alright, but you better bring your A game." She smirked.

"Come on!" James said and pulled Hannah away by the arm.

Sylvia shook her head, smiling. She imagined this must be what it was like to have siblings. She was grateful for her new family. Sylvia stood and helped LeBlanc to his feet. She looked out onto the water once again giving the belugas one more chance to make a last-minute appearance. *Maybe tomorrow,* she thought. She nodded. *Tomorrow.*

SYLVIA BOONE HAD AGREED to a live interview with Megan Stone on the anniversary of her liberation from Victor Crowe. She spent most of her life hiding, fading into the background, staying out of the spotlight. Today, millions tuned in to hear her speak live for the first time in public.

HLF fighters surrounded the city block, along with the network's own security forces as an extra precaution against terrorist attacks. The CPG had relinquished its control over Montreal, which was now under the same regime as New York, Philadelphia, and Boston. It was just as authoritarian, but without the blot of being associated with human trafficking. The network flew the original troop in from Churchill. When they arrived, two producers led them down to the backstage area, which had been lavished with catered food, flowers, and gifts from adoring fans.

"This is nuts," Sylvia said looking at the sumptuous spread.

"No," Dutch said with a straight face, holding out a bowl of mixed nuts from the food table. "This is nuts."

Sylvia shook her head with a grin. She had decided after all these months together, that Dutch, of all people, was probably her most favorite person in the whole world.

A holoscreen in the green room projected a live feed of the auditorium as eager audience members took their seats. There was an energetic buzz in the air.

"They love you, Syl," Miguel said.

She stood nervously holding her arm. "Are you sure we can't all go out there? I mean, this isn't just about me."

Clemens smiled. "You'll be fine, Syl. Just say what's in your heart. Everyone out there is on your side."

"And so are we," Esther said.

Sylvia nodded, clutching her father's dog tags.

A producer with a headset and clipboard entered the room. "We're on in five. Ready?"

"No," Sylvia blurted.

The producer laughed at what he must have thought was a joke. It wasn't. "It's a sold out crowd tonight! You'll do great!" And then he left again.

"Great," Sylvia said sarcastically to herself. She kept wondering why they couldn't have just done a video feed. Why go through all the trouble to fly everyone out for this?

A make-up artist knocked and entered the green room. She patted Sylvia's face with a powder puff. "You have beautiful skin," she said. "I'd kill for those cheekbones." Sylvia ignored the compliment and looked everywhere but into the girl's eyes. The girl paused. She'd hardly applied any makeup at all. Tears welled in her eyes and then she said, "I promised myself I wouldn't cry." She waved her hands at her face and tried to collect herself. "I just want to say thank you." She looked at the others gathered on couches and grazing at the food table. "Thanks to all of you, my little sister is safe at home again." Tears flowed. "I am so grateful to you." She hugged Sylvia, who stood there stiff as a board and glanced at the others who seemed to delight in her discomfort.

"Um . . . I'm glad to hear she's safe," Sylvia said awkwardly. She wished she had something more impactful to say, but she wasn't sure what that might have been in the moment. She was caught off guard.

The girl released her and smiled. She nodded to everyone, wiping her tears, and backed out of the room.

"You better get used to that," Esther said with a chuckle. "You're a beacon of hope for millions of people, Syl. You're making a big difference in people's lives. Not just the victims. Everyone is looking to you for inspiration. For hope."

"It's all of us," Sylvia said. "We all are."

"Yes, but you're a symbol. And you're the reason we're all here fighting beside you."

Clemens interjected, "When we left Winnipeg, we were running for our lives. Safety was our main goal. And when we failed at that, we returned to our original aim and started seeking justice again. It was you who steered us back in the right direction. That's why they look to you, Syl, just like we do."

"I don't even know what to say to that," Sylvia said.

The producer knocked and entered the green room. "It's time."

The lights came up in the studio and the show's theme music blared through the sound system. Two hundred audience members stood and cheered. Megan Stone walked confidently onto the stage waving with both hands at the adoring crowd. She wore a bright yellow belted dress and high heels.

Her captivating smile beamed across the auditorium. Two white leather chairs centered by a bold blue area rug occupied the middle of the stage.

"Good Evening! Hello!" The crowd continued cheering. "Thank you! Thank you so much! Thank you!" She stood at the center of the stage and waited for the crowd to simmer down. "We have a very special guest today." The crowd erupted in cheers again. She nodded in accord with their enthusiasm. "Yes! Yes, we have a very special guest as part of our human rights series this month. She's a freedom fighter with the Human Liberation Front, and co-hosts the wildly popular podcast, "Bad Traffic." Please welcome to the stage . . . Sylvia Boone!" The crowd erupted once again and took to their feet. A sixteen-year-old girl on the front row was in tears. She held a sign that read: *You Saved Me!*

Sylvia stepped out from backstage and walked straight to Megan and shook her hand, too nervous to look out into the clamoring audience. Megan held Sylvia's hand and turned again to the cheering crowd, forcing Sylvia to pivot into the bright lights. She tucked her hair behind her ear and looked out upon the audience. She was overwhelmed by the show of support. She placed her hands together in front of her lips and bowed her head.

"We love you, Sylvia!" a rowdy audience member shouted. Megan gestured for Sylvia to take her seat. The house lights dimmed and the crowd became silent.

"Thank you so much for being here," Megan said.

"Thank you for having me," Sylvia said.

"We didn't think we'd get you here. I don't think we've ever had so much security!" Megan said. "We don't usually frisk our audience at the doors!" The audience laughed.

"Sylvia, you're a freedom fighter for the Human Liberation Front. I think we all know what that is, but can you give us a rundown on just what it is the HLF does?"

"Well, using intel from CSIS and the wider public, we locate human trafficking operations and rescue as many captives as we can find. Then we turn the perpetrators over to the public."

"Now there is some controversy over your tactics," Megan said.

Sylvia nodded.

Megan went on. "Most would support your overall cause, but some would consider the implementation of certain strategies to be unlawful."

"I would agree," Sylvia said. The audience applauded.

"You don't deny that."

"No. Originally, we were officers with the Canadian People's Guard in Winnipeg . . ."

"Winnepeeeeg!!" an audience member shouted.

"I think we have some Winnipeggers in the audience," Megan said. The crowd laughed. "I'm sorry, they're a little rowdy tonight. Please, go ahead."

"So we followed the law back there," Sylvia continued. "We did everything by the book. But when our investigations implicated members within our own ranks, they shut us down. They threatened our lives."

"So you identified officers and officials inside the Canadian People's Guard who were enabling these activities," Megan added.

"Yes. So how do you follow the law when the law itself is corrupt?" Sylvia asked. The crowd applauded, shaking their heads with collective disgust on their faces.

"So you've decided to take the law into your own hands?" Megan pressed.

"Damn straight!" The crowd jumped to their feet in raucous applause. Sylvia was startled by their response.

"You certainly have a lot of fans out there. Many people really support what you're doing. Let's take a look at these images."

The house lights dimmed and a video appeared on a giant holoscreen behind them, accompanied by high-intensity music. The first image was street art with the stencil ELO and a silhouetted profile of Sylvia's face, her hair characteristically falling forward. Another image showed a bumper sticker with the same elements in a different layout. Another of a protest outside a Winnipeg CPG station holding signs. One said, I Stand With Sylvia. Another said, Human Rights Now! Another sign with a stenciled fist and the letters ELO. The final image, a close-up of a protestor in mid-chant with the letters ELO tattooed on his neck. The music faded and the lights came up again.

"What goes through your mind when you see all of this?" Megan asked.

Sylvia was sitting with her hand covering her mouth. "I'm blown away. It gives me so much hope. It really does."

"ELO, what does that stand for?" Megan prompted.

"It stands for Every Last One."

The crowd cheered and began to chant, "Every last one! Every last one! Every last one!"

When they settled down again, Megan continued. "And you really mean that, I take it. You've made this your life's mission to save every last one of these victims."

"Absolutely," Sylvia said.

"You've sort of become the face of this movement, haven't you? You're a celebrity! How do you feel about that?" Megan asked with an encouraging smile.

Sylvia blushed. "It's a little embarrassing, I guess. This . . ." Sylvia pointed at the lights and the cameras. "This is all new for me. I agreed to come here because I know so many people are behind us and they need to know that . . ." Sylvia turned directly toward the audience. " . . . we hear you. And we need you. You've provided us with tips that have led to the liberation of so many women and children. So I came here to say, don't stop! Keep fighting! Until every last one has been freed!" The crowd rose to their feet in applause, chanting: Every Last One! They, too, were part of the movement.

After they'd settled back down, Megan leaned in. "Today is the anniversary of your own liberation, from the hands of Crowe Pharmaceuticals CEO, Victor Crowe."

Sylvia nodded and the audience booed in solidarity.

Megan went on. "He's been named among the top players in this worldwide sex trafficking enterprise. I understand you've had a very personal and traumatic encounter with this man. That must have been such a harrowing experience."

"It isn't my favorite memory," Sylvia replied. The audience offered supportive chuckles and compassionate smiles.

"What would you say to Victor Crowe if he were watching right now?"

Sylvia looked directly into the nearest camera. "Run."

I had a blast researching the various locations that appear in this book. The Lazy Bear Lodge, for example, really was built with hand tools from reclaimed wood from forest fires by a man named Wally in 1995. There really are no roads to Churchill. The railroad, Churchill's only dry land connection to the rest of Canada, is currently operational.

Gaffers Restaurant and Lounge is a popular Lockport establishment serving steak and seafood dishes. The Becker Mini Mart that gets looted in the first chapter exists today as a Canadian convenient store chain.

Esso, a trading name for ExxonMobil, are all over Canada. They currently supply petrol and have not yet begun their conversion to EV charging stations.

Reindeer Island has been an ecological reserve since 1976. The lore about its association with Santa Claus is not entirely fabricated. Gull Harbour exists today exactly as Clemens remembered it from his childhood vacations.

Great care was taken in my depiction of Canada's First Nation People, the Cree in particular. I wanted to suggest that the indigenous tribes, which existed long before governments pushed them out of urban centers, continue to flourish even after our governments have disintegrated.

I hope you enjoyed reading *Every Last One* as much as I enjoyed writing it. Please take a moment to leave an honest review on Amazon. Even a simple star rating goes a long way to increasing the visibility of this little indie book. Thank you for supporting this indie author and indie publishing in general. You rock!

Tourist Trapped

Wild Rumpus Press

2023

ACKNOWLEDGMENTS

This book has been through so many different iterations since its initial conception back in 2020. I've had a number of beta readers throughout this period that have helped steer *Every Last One* to where it is today.

Jason Jenkins and Michael Carrasco were among the first to ever lay eyes upon its nascent form. Thanks to Amanda Herber, Jessica Goeken, and Stefanie Barnfather for their invaluable feedback.

Thanks to Shaun Baines for developmental editing. He did such a thorough job and was relentless in his eye for unnecessary exposition.

Rebecca Ira created this amazing cover and I couldn't be happier with how it turned out. I am extremely grateful for her endless patience. I can't be easy to work with.

Finally, I couldn't have done any of this without the support of my family, who generously shared me with Sylvia and the rest of the *ELO* gang.

ABOUT THE AUTHOR

J. B. Velasquez has always been an avid reader and lover of witty, satirical, and thoughtful fiction. His writing reflects upon his own inquiries and observations about life through the lens of interesting and deeply flawed characters.

J. B., a psychotherapist of twenty years, lives in Tucson, Arizona with his beautiful wife and two kids who refuse to stop growing--no matter how much he tells them to cut it out.

For blogs, short stories, and author updates, subscribe to the Readers List at jbvelasquez.com.

x.com/JBVelasquez75

instagram.com/author_jbvelasquez

facebook.com/authorjbvelasquez

threads.net/@author_jbvelasquez

www.ingramcontent.com/pod-product-compliance
Lightning Source LLC
Chambersburg PA
CBHW021211310726
48971CB00006B/1521